STEPPING THROUGH THE
STARGATE

Edited by P. N. Elrod and Roxanne Conrad

STEPPING THROUGH THE
STARGATE

Science, Archaeology and the Military in Stargate SG-1

BENBELLA BOOKS
Dallas, Texas

BenBella Books Edition October 2004

BenBella Books
6440 N. Central Expressway
Suite 617
Dallas, TX 75206

Send feedback to feedback@benbellabooks.com
www.benbellabooks.com

Printed in the United States of America
10 9 8 7 6 5 4 3 2 1

Library of Congress Cataloging-in-Publication Data

Stepping through the stargate : science, archaeology and the military in Stargate SG-1 / edited by P.N. Elrod and Roxanne L. Conrad.
  p. cm.
 Includes bibliographical references.
 ISBN 1-932100-32-6
 1. Stargate SG-1 (Television program) I. Elrod, P. N. (Patricia Neal) II. Conrad, Roxanne.

 PN1992.77.S738S74 2004
 791.45'72--dc22

                    2004012939

Cover design by Todd Michael Bushman
Interior designed and composed by Paragon PrePress, Inc.

Distributed by Independent Publishers Group
To order call (800) 888-4741
www.ipgbook.com

Contents

RAMBLING FROM
THE EDITORS

THERE ARE TWO STORIES about how this book came about. In the interest of fairness, both will be presented, and you can judge for yourself.

ROXANNE'S (LARGELY FICTIONAL) VERSION

"Hey," Roxanne Conrad says to P.N. Elrod on the phone one day, about two years ago. "Are you watching this show that's on the Sci-Fi Channel now, *Stargate SG-1*? The one that was on Showtime?"

"Never have," says P.N. (aka Pat).

"It's pretty good."

"Yeah? Well, it's not like I've got time for . . . ."

"That Jack's pretty cute. You'd like him. I'm all about that Daniel guy, but still . . . ."

"That's great, but I've got these deadlines and . . . ."

"It's Richard Dean Anderson."

There is a brief, significant pause on the phone, and the sound of a remote being picked up. "What channel was that again?"

And so it begins. At least in the fictional land of Roxanne.

Well, however it happened, two years later, two otherwise sensible professional writers still have the bug. We have the BDUs. We have the patches. We have the DVDs (I even ordered them from Britain, as the American releases weren't coming fast enough, dammit). We learned the words to the theme song, and sing it on command. We'll talk *Stargate* at the drop of a boonie hat.

Personally, I never imagined we'd get the opportunity to put together our dream project . . . finding others who share our fascination, and putting their words in print. BenBella Books has given us the chance to make this a reality, and I've been amazed at the people we found lurking out there, willing to contribute a line or two to the book, and quite a few (you'd recognize their names) who've just given us encouragement and cheered from the sidelines.

Between these covers you'll find NASA astronomers and physicists, Air Force officers, highly honored philosophers, special effects wizards, actors, screenwriters, medical doctors and best-selling tale-tellers. In short, it's a humbling group with which to be associated, and I'm amazed that we managed to somehow take this project from a wistful idea at a convention all the way to the Embarkation Room . . . and beyond.

PAT'S (LARGELY NONFICTIONAL) VERSION

That's "Gate room," not "Embarkation room," Rox. Jeez, get it right, will ya??? Huh, what? I get to tell my side now? Yasureyoubetcha! Gather close, campers. . . .

No, Rox, sorry, you've got it ALL wrong on how this started. I never had Showtime and only saw the series when it aired on a local channel—if they bothered to air it. You're the one who's got more reception hardware in your TV room than NASA and kept track of things—I've been trying to cut back on my viewing! But you wouldn't take no for an answer, would ya?

I distinctly recall you and another bud writing back and forth about *Stargate SG-1* on a board while I was just kibitzing, enjoying the interplay. You guys were so a-flutter about the charms of Daniel, and I couldn't understand why you two never seemed to notice that O'Neill and Teal'c were also scorch-worthy hotties.

So I put my two cents worth in on the oversight, and in a strangely brief span of time got thoroughly caught up in your shared insanity, but by then I didn't care. I was having way too much fun.

That's the truth, gentle readers, of how our paths to the Gate converged. But the wholesale addiction DOES include our going to a military surplus store and acquiring combat boots and olive drab BDUs, locating official SGC patches to put on them, sprinkling our conversations with phrases like "Sweet!", "Got your six" and "Ya think?", and ultimately my making camouflage slipcovers for my couch, car seats, work desk . . . *IS ALL ROX'S FAULT!* IT WILL ALWAYS *BE* ROX'S FAULT!!!!

THAT'S how it began, and I still have the e-mails to prove it.

How this book began stemmed from our publisher watching our costumed antics at a convention and getting curious as to why this one show turned two cheerfully warped but otherwise totally professional writers with seriously solid track records in the publishing industry into crazed, giggling lunatics.

The turning point was a panel we three were doing on publishing, trying to explain how book deals are made. We were cutting up and laughing at the time, and as an example of the madness I turned to Glenn Yeffeth—who IS BenBella Books—and said, "Hey, ya wanna do a non-fiction collection on the *Stargate* series like you did for *Matrix* and *Buffy*?" He was laughing, but nodded enthusiastically and replied, "Yeah, we can do that!" Then I turned to the audience: "Did you catch it? We just made a book deal!"

Sort of. I wasn't going to hold Glenn to it, not really. But I did go by the BenBella table to see if he might just perhaps consider doing this collection after all. Much to my breathless shock, he confirmed he was quite serious about making it happen, and we'd talk about it later.

I don't remember much of the rest of the con, though I know Rox and I—there was no question that this would be a team effort—discussed five thousand "what if" details on the drive home.

Still wearing our BDUs and combat boots.

Glenn watched our progress through the process, offering encouragement, suggestions, applause and occasionally falling in with our madness. When I once answered the phone with "Stargate Operations, Major Elrod's office," he fired right back with "This is Stargate Command, General Yeffeth calling." I dang-near snarfed my coffee. What a guy!

Now the "what ifs" have become a reality far better than anything my imagination could have provided, thanks to Roxanne, Glenn and the contributions of these other outstanding fans of a wonderful, wonderful show. I'm delighted and honored to be a part of it, but most of all grateful to the people who made *Stargate SG-1* such a terrific series in the first place. Thank you, all, and please keep it coming.

And now . . . I'm ready to step through the 'gate. . . .

Please join us.

P.N. Elrod & Roxanne Conrad
Stargate SG-1.2 (revised)

Bill Fawcett

HIGHLY TOP SECRET

U. S. Air Force
HIGHLY TOP SECRET
Eyes only
Not for distribution beyond Stargate Command.
Copy 3 of 7 _____
Initial here upon receipt
Preliminary Analysis
Alien Technology
Item SGA 8903496 GHL Mark 0001
Usage Name:
This weapon has been referred to as the "Staff Weapon."

The purpose of this report is to determine the alien artifact's value for future research and development. This weapon is nearly two meters in length, but weighs no more than if it was made entirely of fiberglass. It has only one moving mechanism, a covering that opens before the weapon can be fired. This delay in going from ready to firing status can be considered a significant defect that could be exploited.

An apparently larger version of the MK0001 has been recorded as being used by a number of System Lords, but SG-1 appears to have, to date, unfortunately destroyed all examples. A suggestion that they preserve the next example was met with less than enthusiasm by all members of the team.

PROVENANCE

This device was one of the first objects retrieved for analysis by an SG team. Technically it was not obtained, but rather brought by an alien (code name: Bald Eagle) who accompanied the team returning for a mission. This alien had defected from the service of one of the System Lords. (For details see the accompanying report titled "The Bald Eagle has Landed.")

Understanding of the item requires some awareness of the nature and background of Bald Eagle. When encountered, Bald Eagle was acting in a paramilitary position for one of the System Lords. GHL MK0001 was the primary weapon employed by the unit he commanded. The unit's role appears to have been multi-functional, involving both inter-System Lord combat and enforcement activities. Since this analysis began it has been determined that almost all forces of all System Lords are similarly equipped with the GHL MK0001.

CLOSE COMBAT APPLICATIONS

The GHL MK0001 is generally referred to as a "staff weapon." Its sturdy construction allows it to be used in a melee or hand-to-hand combat mode, or as a ranged weapon. Detailed re-creation of the fighting techniques determined that its effective use in a close combat situation would require extensive training such as is found in disciples of the oriental martial arts. This leads to the conclusions that either (1) the individuals employing the GHL MK0001 receive years of training (2) some sort of advanced training technique is used or (3) the weapon is automated in a manner not understood. Bald Eagle has described his training as beginning in youth, making (1) the likeliest possibility . . . though the consistently surly and withdrawn attitude manifested by Bald Eagle when questioned makes all such conclusions subject to outside analysis.

The weapon itself compares unfavorably to the use of a bayonet, as used on issue weapons for close combat, since the weapon cannot be fired when used as a striking weapon. This is especially true when taking into account that a bayonet can be employed effectively with a few weeks of training rather than years. It is speculated that the advanced level of System Lord technology has rendered most close combat obsolete and the training referred to in reverent tones by Bald Eagle is primarily anachronistic, ritualized behavior. Such behavior would serve as a bonding factor for the hereditary para-military class in which Bald Eagle claims to be a major figure. It must be remembered that most individuals that defect in any war tend to grossly exaggerate or seriously understate their importance to the opposition; his claimed status needs verification.

RANGED COMBAT APPLICATIONS

The range of the GHL MK0001 staff weapon appears to be severely limited. The weapon in all forms can fire only with line of sight. This is further complicated by the requirement that the weapon be fired instinctively, indicated by the fact that it possesses neither sights nor a range finder. No reason for this lack has been ascertained by questioning Bald Eagle, whose reactions suggest some sort of brainwashing or cultural bias against assisted sighting on the weapon. Extensive study of the effectiveness of the weapon also shows an unusual bias that causes the weapon to almost always miss members of SG-1, with the exception of missions occurring during "sweeps week." Further, recurring characters also normally share this unexplainable immunity. It proves almost invariably fatal, however, when fired at those still loyal to the System Lords and unfamiliar member of high numbered SG teams, even when fired by SG team members with little training on the weapon.

The reasons this benefits the System Lords whose forces employ these staff weapons are discussed below. In the hands of a human who is trained to use normal weaponry the GHL MK0001 has an effective range of no more than ten meters. Compared to the general issue M16 infantry weapons system, the staff weapon suffers from a number of disadvantages as determined below.

Rate Of Fire

The GHL MK0001 is single shot weapon. This is a disadvantage that is partially compensated for by the rapid rate at which the weapon can be fired and by the push-button firing mechanism which allows for a firing action that is more similar to clicking a computer mouse than pulling a trigger. This is caused by the lack of moving parts, which is apparent in all internal components of the GHL MK0001. Such an arrangement regarding the firing button leaves a concern for accidental firing when the weapon is used in close combat (see above), but no incident of this type has been recorded.

Round Fired

The GHL MK0001 fires neither a solid bullet nor a beam of light. The actual propellant emerging from the end of the GHL MK0001 appears to be some form of superheated plasma. This material has many unusual properties that cannot be explained within the scope of this analysis. It is not only able to kill most targets with a single hit, but is also able to differentiate between a credited SG member and other, more expendable characters, only wounding said credited members even when fired at the closest range.

Power Supply

The Staff Weapon GHL MK0001 seems to have an unlimited power supply. This innovation conflicts with the primitive firing and sighting mechanisms. Dismantling damaged examples of this weapon recovered by other SG teams and intact examples obtained in an undetermined way has determined that there appears to be no internal power-generating source. Since much of the mechanism built into both the staff and head continue to defy metallurgical analysis, the lack of power source cannot be stated definitively. Among the possibilities currently being investigated is that the power source is some form of broadcast energy, though this hypothesis is suggested against by the successful use of such a weapon on the Earth, where no broadcast can be detected. Still it is likely that the power is obtained from the weapon's environment, the planet's magnetic field or solar energy being worthy of investigation. A final possibility is that trace elements of naquadah in the casing are sufficient to power the weapon. Since Bald Eagle has apparently used this original GHL MK0001 thousands of times without stopping to reload, there is no record of the maximum, if any, number of times the staff weapon can be fired.

Limited Range

The range of the bolt fired by the GHL MK0001 staff weapon is limited by its very nature. The plasma bolt is neither aerodynamic nor able to maintain its integrity in an atmosphere for any distance. It also appears to move unnaturally slowly, allowing it to be visible when fired. As such there is speculation that the original staff devices were created for combat in a vacuum, where the range would be infinitely increased. Additionally, the effective range of the GHL MK0001 staff weapon is limited by the sighting method and awkward length. This range is far inferior to all but the shortest barreled submachine guns . . . which does not explain why most SG teams are now equipped with exactly that variety of short-ranged weapon. (This combination of equipment does lead to visually and audibly powerful fire fights.) This committee suggests extensive equipping of SG teams with the 50mm sniper rifle and similar weaponry to take advantage of the weapon's near two-mile range, over twenty times that of the staff weapon.

CONCLUSIONS

There is a definite superiority in thes unlimited ammunition supply of the GHL MK0001. This makes the weapon superior for use by isolated garrisons and on extended missions in hostile territories. It also allows for almost constant firing, resulting in a large number of explosions during any combat, as the moisture in any object expands violently when flash-heated by the plasma ball fired by the GHL MK0001. Duplicating this feature, however, would require an understanding of the technology behind the weapon, which we do not possess.

The staff weapon has been in use in its present form for at least three (and possibly five) millennia. It has also remained apparently unchanged, at least in appearance and function, for this span of time. During the same period human weaponry grew from bronze swords to our present lethal array. The reason for this totally static weapons development is not understood. While the System Lords have been in constant competition and always in search of an edge over the other, there seems to have been no development at all in the primary weapon used by their ground forces.

The pervasive nature of the GHL MK0001 staff opens the door to speculation as to why virtually all of the military forces of all the System Lords are equipped with identical weapons. Several theories are available for investigation, but Bald Eagle was unable to clarify, stating that such considerations were not part of or perhaps were below the station of a warrior.

The first possibility is that the technology for these weapons is universally agreed to in some unknown treaty. This then changes the nature of the System Lord warfare into more of a duel or game, a conclusion that may be consistent with their desire for and apparent obsession with immortality or near-immortality.

Another possibility is that automated factories obtained in the conquest of a now-vanished race produce the weapons, and they are distributed from this neutral source by some agreed upon formula, but this is a behavior more civilized and stylized than that which their treatment of subject races would imply. Still, this, along with the longevity of the individual weapons, would explain the ubiquitous presence of the weapons and their unchanging nature.

A third theory is that to avoid mutual destruction, limits in military technology have been agreed upon and are enforced by the majority of the System Lords or some other unknown agency.

One strongly supported theory is economic in nature. This theory posits that the System Lords operate on very limited budgets. They could be likened to a production company with limited money for special effects: they are using what is on hand if it does the job. The staff weapons are there already and long lasting. Since the weapon never needs ammunition, there is no incentive to replace it. Or perhaps the GHL MK0001 is simply relatively inexpensive to produce. Since the purpose of the System Lord's warfare, at least until threatened by outside forces, is personal aggrandizement, there is no incentive to spend money on weapons that could otherwise be spent on more mundane and satisfying self-indulgences, such as palaces and eye makeup . . . money may be kept from the military and spent on domestic programs. The idea that the spending priorities of the Democratic Party and the System Lords has any resemblance beyond that of possibly sending troops into combat with aged weapon systems should not be too readily inferred.

A final theory, which is supported by the defection of Bald Eagle, is that the System Lords distrust their own forces sufficiently to limit their soldiers' weaponry to that which the System Lords personally can easily overcome. The frightening corollary of this is that the System Lords then may have access to weapons far superior to the GHL MK0001, to which they can resort should our forces actually be perceived as a viable threat. (The secondary conclusion is that we have not yet achieved that status, since such weapons have not yet been employed.)

FINAL ANALYSIS

The GHL MK0001 staff weapon is neither an efficient nor combat ready system. It is inferior in four of five categories of combat effectiveness, and while a novelty, employing technologies that are not yet understood, spending the resources and time to duplicate the weapon is not warranted.

Bill has been a professor, teacher, corporate executive and college dean. He is one of the founders of Mayfair Games, a board and role play gaming company. As a book packager, a person who prepares series of books from concept to production for major publishers, his company Bill Fawcett & Associates has packaged over 250 titles for virtually every major publisher.

Bill began his own novel writing with a juvenile series, Sword-quest, for Ace SF in the early 80s. The Fleet series he created with David Drake has become a classic of military science fiction. He has collaborated on several novels, including the Authorized Mycroft Holmes novels, Making Contact, *a UFO contact handbook, and* It Seemed Like a Good Idea. *As an anthologist Bill has edited or co-edited over fifty anthologies. When not writing, Bill designs computer games. He is the editor of several books about the SEALs, including* Hunters and Shooters *and* The Teams, *two oral histories of the SEALs in Vietnam.*

David Gerrold

STARGATE TREK

WHEN YOU TALK about science fiction on television, there's *Star Trek*—and then there's everything else.

And that's unfortunate, because a lot of the "everything else" is pretty damn good—oftentimes even better than *Star Trek*.

Case in point: *Stargate SG-1*.

Trek's essential formula is this: the multi-species crew of a faster-than-light starship travel from planet to planet, seeking out new life and new civilizations, sometimes so they can defeat the sinister alien threat of the Borg.

Stargate's essential formula is this: a multi-species team of commandos use a faster-than-light wormhole through space to travel from world to world, seeking out new life and new civilizations, sometimes so they can defeat the sinister alien threat of the Goa'uld.

Or let me say it another way. *Star Trek* is about "the civilization of the week." *Stargate* is about "the civilization of the week." See the difference?

Not clear yet? *Star Trek* had Spock to explain those strange new worlds. (And later on, Worf.) *Stargate* has Teal'c to explain those strange new worlds.

Okay, so the two shows are identical—

—but then, so are *Star Trek: The Next Generation*, *Voyager*, *Enterprise*, *Andromeda*, *Farscape*, *Seaquest*, *Sliders*, *Firefly*, *Battlestar Galactica* . . . . (Did I leave anybody out?) Those shows are also cloned from the same vat of television DNA.

Let's take it point by point.

1.   Both shows have a home base.

The starship *Enterprise* is the home base for *Star Trek*'s heroes. This is the starting point, the safe harbor, the standing sets that give us a sense of familiarity and comfort.

The Cheyenne Mountain Stargate complex is the home base for the SG-1 mission team; their place of familiarity and comfort.

Both settings provide access to the external story, and both do so through the device of teleportation—*Trek* uses the transporter beam to get its people down to the surface of a world; *Stargate* uses the Stargate, of course.

Strictly from a production point of view, teleportation is the easiest (least expensive) way to move characters around a universe. Early in the planning of the original *Star Trek* series, Gene Roddenberry and staff realized that it would be prohibitively expensive to show the *Enterprise* landing on each new planet. It would also use up valuable story time. So Gene postulated the transporter beam to get the heroes down to the planet with a minimum of fuss and budget. In that regard, the transporter beam makes the spaceship redundant.

Plus, teleportation is always a great visual effect. The twelve-episode 1939 serial of Buck Rogers, starring Buster Crabbe, proved that. *Star Trek* used a $600-dissolve, overlaid with flickering golden sequins; *Stargate* uses a computer-generated liquid space effect.

It's also worth noting here that during the planning stages of *Star Trek: The Next Generation*, Gene Roddenberry briefly entertained the idea of eliminating the *Enterprise* altogether and just having the crew use a long-distance transporter beam to travel about the galaxy. This idea was scotched quickly when it was pointed out that for many viewers the *Enterprise* itself was the star of the show. You won't find this information in any of the "official" histories of *ST:TNG*, but I was there, I was in the room, okay?

2. **Both heroes are macho enough for Joe Sixpack at home, but smart enough to know their limits; they hold back while they assess the situation.**

    The hero of *Star Trek* is Capt. James T. Kirk, mid-thirties/early forties, strong-willed, independent, prone to disobeying orders if necessary and not without a visible sense of irony.
    The hero of *Stargate* is Col. Jack O'Neill, mid-thirties/early forties, strong-willed, independent, prone to disobeying orders if necessary and not without a visible sense of irony.
    Okay, that's not entirely fair. James T. Kirk couldn't keep his pants on. He bedded every alien princess between here and the Orion Nebula, and a couple on the far side as well. Colonel O'Neill doesn't seem to run into all that many princesses, but it doesn't seem likely that he will ever cut as many notches into his sword as Kirk apparently did.
    Other than that, the two could almost be interchangeable. Kirk doesn't seem to have any permanent emotional attachments; O'Neill buried a son before the series began, and that chapter of his life is now closed.

3. **Both *Star Trek* and *Stargate* have "tame aliens."**

    Star Trek had Spock. *Star Trek: The Next Generation* had Worf. Later iterations introduced a variety of other alien crewmembers. *Stargate* has Teal'c.
    In the case of all three characters—Spock, Worf and Teal'c— the alien is a person of extremely high repute on his home world, intelligent, strong and possessed of unique abilities, which are often essential to the success of the mission.
    All three characters frequently serve as "Murray the Explainer," providing necessary exposition about the alien cultures the team has encountered—except when, for story purposes, "it's life, Jim, but not as we know it." Then, the answer is, "I dunno. I've never seen anything like this before."
    None of these fellows display much emotion. They are stoic and dispassionate—able to fight, but holding back until necessary.

Obviously, they're all graduates of the Charles Bronson school of acting.

The "tame alien" can also be used to provide moments of deadpan comedy, based on interstellar culture clash. You can build a whole scene around, "Why do you humans push your faces together like that?" ("It's fun—don't you understand fun?" "Fun? Me stupid alien. Me not know this word 'fun.'")

4. **The female members of the team are always beautiful. They all have marvelous chests and cheekbones. And incidentally, they're brilliant.**

Star Trek (the original series) had the beautiful and brilliant Lieutenant Uhura. *Star Trek: The Next Generation* had the beautiful and brilliant Dr. Beverly Crusher.

Stargate has the beautiful and brilliant Maj. Samantha Carter. And the beautiful and brilliant Dr. Janet Fraiser.

In the science fiction universe, all women are young, beautiful, brilliant and not available to any man in the world except the hero.

The hero, of course, always keeps a respectful distance, because . . . well, because the tension of an unrequited love affair is more compelling than dealing with that messy business of actually ending up in bed with someone for the first time, trying to figure out what goes where, when, in what order, and if there's anything in the fridge for after.

And also because a love story would pull the entire series off base so badly that the show would stop being about the adventure and start being about the relationship. That's fine on *Melrose Place* or *Sex and the City*. It's out of place on the bridge of the *Enterprise* or in the Cheyenne Mountain complex.

In an alternate universe, however, O'Neill and Carter are engaged. Well . . . *were* engaged. That alternate Earth got destroyed by an alternate Teal'c. And once upon a time, Kirk actually kissed Uhura—although he had to be forced by god-like aliens to do so.

Ergo, the hint of nascent sexuality is always present, but never expressed.

5. Additional members of the team are irrelevant, redundant and replaceable—and at least one of them is a geek.

Star Trek showed that we could have an adventure without Sulu or Chekov or Scotty. Likewise, *Stargate* can have an adventure without Dr. Daniel Jackson or Dr. Janet Fraiser. These guys are all handsome and brilliant, of course—but they're sidekicks. They're second bananas. They're someone who can walk off screen with a tricorder to go scan that interesting rock formation and get blasted by a sinister alien force, recovering just in time for the last commercial.

Scotty is a techno-geek, the chief engineer who can cross-fabulate a quantum-defibrillator in four minutes flat, just in time to keep the dilithium resonance from distimilizing the doshes. Dr. Daniel Jackson is an anthropologist/linguist/archaeologist/all-purpose expert. Not having an engine room to putter around in, Dr. Jackson and Major Carter split whatever other geek-duties might crop up during a mission.

This isn't to say that the sidekicks don't occasionally get stories of their own, but in the last act, it's always Kirk/O'Neill who comes in to solve the *big* problem. Well, he's the star, you see . . . .

6. Authority can be disregarded. This is how the hero proves he's the hero.

Every time Kirk (or later on, Picard) mentioned the Prime Directive, it was because he was going to disregard it. There was never an episode where the captain of the *Enterprise* said, "Hmm. Getting involved here would violate the Prime Directive. Mr. Sulu, set a course for home."

Likewise, O'Neill has a track record of disregarding the orders of Gen. George Hammond, even arguing outright against them in front of the other team members. Not exactly good military demeanor, but this is a team that has been through a lot together and . . . well, it's allowed because:

7. *The team is family.* And everybody else isn't.

None of these folks have any other close personal relationships. Their primary loyalty is to the other members of the team. Their commitment to the team outweighs all other loyalties.

A typical episode of *Stargate* can often involve violating all orders and all safety precautions so that Carter or Jackson or Teal'c can be rescued. And once in a while, O'Neill. A typical episode of *Star Trek* can involve Kirk or Spock or Scotty risking the starship's safety to rescue Spock or Scotty or Kirk. And once in a while, McCoy.

8. **Nobody ever gets court-martialed for disobeying orders or going off the reservation.**

Or, if they do, the court always rules that their actions were justified. Being right confers immunity.

9. **Alien planets are homogenous.**

They're either a jungle planet, an ice planet or a desert planet—all the way from the poles to the equator, with no variation in terrain, flora or fauna.

On *Star Trek*, alien worlds always look like southern California. On *Stargate SG-1*, alien worlds always look like British Columbia.

10. **Aliens are always human.**

Humans with arched eyebrows and pointy ears, humans with crinkly noses, humans with darker skin and smooshed-up foreheads, humans with Dumbo-ears, humans with blue-skin and white wigs and little blue antennae, humans with funny insignia stamped into their foreheads . . . .

On *Star Trek*, most of these human-aliens are capable of breeding with real humans, of course. Otherwise, it's hard to find alien princesses who want to sleep with Kirk. *Stargate SG-1* has, for the most part, avoided this particularly messy question.

11. **Alien people all speak English. Stiltedly.**

Only our heroes use contractions. Aliens don't understand the apostrophe. Except in names. Like Teal'c and T'pau.

12. The shows are almost always about "the civilization of the week." We go somewhere, we meet some interesting people, we spend half the show trying to figure out the scale of this particular predicament and the other half trying to fix it.

Okay, that one's not quite fair—that's also the format for all those other shows I mentioned. In fact, it's the basic television formula. The first half-hour is about discovering the problem, the second half is about resolving it.

But in science fiction the predicament is almost always a gimmick of some kind: Kirk or O'Neill has been replaced by a robot so convincing that it isn't until the robot's arm is cut open that we discover it isn't the real person. Kirk or Jackson stumbles into an alternate reality, a mirror world, where things are *different*. An entity invades the *Enterprise* computers—or the Cheyenne Mountain complex computers. An entity takes over the body of Kirk or Carter. And so on.

But almost every week we are visiting a strange new world, seeking out new life and . . . etc. And every week, we are encountering a different alien environment. And with rare exception, these alien environments are always populated by human-aliens. *See above.*

Okay, you get the point.

Were I suitably motivated—I'm not—I could probably list another three-dozen equivalencies between the two television series. But perhaps on the Internet some obsessive-compulsive fan has already done an episode-by-episode comparison, pointing out where *Star Trek* has already boldly gone before *Stargate SG-1* got there.

The point is not that the two shows are mining the same shaft, but that despite the fundamental similarities of structure, they're still very *different* shows.

Here are a few of the differences:

1. *Star Trek* takes itself too seriously.

This goes back to Gene Roddenberry's 1986 assertion, "We're the Yankees." Everything on *Trek* is so important that characters are never allowed to remove the official Starfleet broomsticks up their asses. Even the occasional jokes are delivered as if they're *important*. Everything is portentous. Everything is a speech.

By contrast, *Stargate SG-1* has a sly sense of self-mockery. Col. Jack O'Neill is well aware of his own quirks and idiosyncrasies. He's equally aware of his teammates' personalities, and he doesn't hesitate to speak—and when he does, his remarks are grounded in the kind of casual familiarity that good friends express every day.

This same sense of irony extends to other characters as well. General Hammond, commenting on the similarities between O'Neill and a robot duplicate, observes that both the original and the copy have the same disregard for orders. Dr. Fraiser, urging Major Carter to take a rest, lists a few of the injuries she's suffered in the previous season, including having her consciousness transferred into a computer and back again. "That's got to take a toll." *These people are real.* And they're likable.

2. ***Star Trek* only has to solve a problem once.**

And it's resolved forever, we never have to go back. *Star Trek: The Next Generation* usually solved its problems in the last five minutes by recalibrating the counter-phased deconfabulator to allow for wargulated matriculation.

By contrast, no problem on *Stargate SG-1* is ever really finished. More than once, the team has had to return to situations they thought had been resolved. In one particularly startling episode, the team discovers twenty minutes into the episode that they've been turned into androids—their conscious minds have been transferred into robot bodies. Twenty minutes later, they discover that's *not* the case; they are in fact *copies* of the originals, but with the same feelings and memories. The tragedy here is that they can't ever go home. By the end of the episode, the viewer is left feeling more empathy for the android copies than for the originals.

In a subsequent episode, the SG-1 team arrives at one planet, gets captured by the local Goa'uld "god" and sentenced to execution. When Jackson is beheaded, we discover he's actually a robot. And so are the others. These are the robots from the previous episode, out on unauthorized missions of their own. The real team has to come in and help resolve the problem; but in the course of it, one by one, the robots die. Once again, the viewer is left with enormous sympathy for their sacrifice.

Star Trek often held its aliens and robots at arm's length, generating very little sympathy for anyone involved in the story. Okay, Spock never told his mother he loved her. But he was driving under the influence at the time . . . .

3. **Star Trek's technology is fabulous.**

And completely beyond any rational understanding. It's all magic beams and glowing lights. It's energy fields and energy beams and life energy and creatures of pure energy. Energy is such a convenient word. "I'm detecting a strange energy emanating from the creature/planet/device/alien starship/wormhole/nebula, Captain." What's strange about energy? It's either photons or electrons or gravitons. It's either modulated, coherent or random. If it's detectable, it's also measurable—it can be analyzed. What's the big deal? Every time Spock says, "It's life, Jim, but not as we know it," he's demonstrating that he didn't do his homework. A little old-fashioned sense-of-wonder is in order here. Remember Jeff Goldblum's awestruck observation? "Life will find a way."

Stargate SG-1's engineering is understandable, almost mundane; most of the technology in its stories is off-the-shelf, and most of its science is rooted in what we know is possible, not in what somebody makes up because he thinks it sounds good. (Yeah, you know who you are; stop trying to hide behind that dilithium crystal, the jig is up.)

Okay, to be fair, Stargate is based in the near future, sometime like next week; so it's not unlikely for our heroes to be running recognizable machinery. Star Trek has to extrapolate. But other movies and shows have extrapolated without falling into the ridiculous. The audience will suspend disbelief; they won't suspend common sense.

Right, you get the point. Star Trek is in love with itself.

In its subsequent iterations, it has become more than insular, more than incestuous; it has become a cannibal, feeding on its own past. Then, like some bemused jackal looking up from the meal it has made of its ancestors, it wonders why it's alone. Where has the adoring audience disappeared?

Meanwhile, over at the Cheyenne Mountain complex, *Stargate SG-1* is doing something else.

Yes, there's a common formula, "civilization of the week," but if a producer understands the formula—and that much of it is derived from the limits and the needs of the medium itself—then he also understands the inherent trap. This is the point at which the talented and skilled producers create the possibility of transcending the trap.

This is true of most great TV shows—what can you do that challenges the formula? What can you do that startles the viewer? What can you do that is the opposite of what's expected? What story can you tell that the viewers will still be talking about tomorrow morning? Or next week? Or a year from now?

To really challenge a show means to do episodes that disrupt what you've already established.

There's no formula for challenging the formula; however it's done, it's always a big dangerous step outside the box. It's a leap out of the comfort zone. You have to disturb yourself, your characters, and ultimately risk transforming the essential nature of the show. The cautious and conservative producers will recoil from the challenge; the brave ones relish it: "How far can we go today?"

You can tell which is which, just by watching their shows.

That's the real success of *Stargate SG-1*—not that it is another inheritor of a well-established formula, but that it has transcended that inheritance and established a unique and very likable identity.

David Gerrold is an imaginary companion. Please do not encourage him. He'll just go off and write another book.

Catherine Asaro & Dr. John K. Cannizzo

THROUGH THE APPLE

I N THE *STARGATE SG-1* EPISODE "A Matter of Time," Carter explains to Colonel O'Neill how they travel through time and space: "We burrow our way through the apple like a worm, crossing from one side of the galaxy to the other instead of going around the outside." The "wormhole" they use is a tunnel that connects two different places and times in the universe. The Stargate transfers matter—such as people—to a new place. It provides a great story mechanism for the travelers to cover immense distances in both space and time.

Could we really make such a gateway to the stars?

JUST AROUND THE BEND

We live in a universe with three spatial dimensions (up, down and across, essentially) and one temporal dimension. Taken together, these four dimensions define something called *spacetime*. Generally, we think of interstellar space as a great void or a starry sky, but it is actually a great four-dimensional surface that can curve into all sorts of intriguing geometries.

Imagine a tarp pulled taut and flat. Now suppose we put a bowling ball in the center of the tarp. It "sags" under the weight of the ball. If we set a marble on the tarp, it will roll in towards the center. The bowling ball represents a star, planet or other celestial body, perhaps Earth. The curvature of the tarp—of spacetime—is what we know as gravity. In the words of John Wheeler, "Matter tells space how to curve, space tells matter how to move."[1] The marble could be, say, a spaceship pulled toward the planet by gravity.

Spacetime can curve in many ways. It might go around like an apple or sphere, giving it positive curvature. Or we might warp it into a saddle shape, which has negative curvature. Or it could fold back on itself like a sandwich. If we were to punch a hole through the apple, saddle or sandwich—the wormhole of the Stargate—we could jump from one place to another. The "length" of the tunnel doesn't necessarily have to equal the distance between its two ends in space, so we might reach our destination much faster using the tunnel than if we went through normal spacetime. The tunnel may even be moving through space.[2] Depending on how spacetime curves and how fast the wormhole moves, we might even go forward or backward in time.

The question is, is it possible to warp space and create such a tunnel?

HOLES IN THE APPLE

The idea of spacetime tunnels goes back to a paper by Albert Einstein and Nathan Rosen, published in *Physical Review* in 1935.[3] They showed that—in principle—we could connect two distant regions with such a shortcut. They intended to use the tunnels as a means to account for elementary particles such as protons and electrons, but their idea didn't work. It wasn't until years later, in 1962, that John Wheeler revisited their theory.[4] He was the one who first called the Einstein-Rosen tunnel a "wormhole."

In our description of the tarp and bowling ball, the ball represents a body massive enough to create a significant curve in spacetime. Consider a star. When it is hot, nuclear reactions inside the star make it burn brightly. They hold the star up, preventing its gravity from making it collapse in on itself. Such a star is large and fluffy. As it cools, gravity causes it to shrink, becoming denser. Imagine our bowling ball decreasing in size but keeping the same mass, so the tarp sags over a smaller area. If the ball becomes small enough, eventually it pulls the tarp down until the top pinches closed over the ball. It creates a pocket. Any marble that rolled into the pocket could no longer get out. Not even *light* could escape.

We have now created a "black" hole.

Wheeler and his co-workers showed that in theory it is possible to connect two black holes with a tunnel. However, practical considerations would severely restrict anything we could do with that tunnel. For one thing, it would open and close *fast*, too quickly for us to traverse it. Physically, we would say that the tunnel pinches off into a singularity. Not even a beam of light would be fast enough to reach the other side in time. As a Stargate, such a tunnel would be a disaster and probably wipe out our stalwart team of travelers.

Even if we did keep the tunnel open long enough for the team to reach the other end, they would find themselves trapped by the black hole there. Every black hole has an *event horizon*, an invisible surface roughly spherical in shape with the black hole at its center. Nothing within that sphere can escape. It is like the marble on the tarp that rolled into the pocket: it can't get out again. We have reached the point of no return. Anything that goes past the event horizon of a black hole—including an SG team—is trapped. It does our travelers little good if they can go into the gate but never come out again.

It would also be hard to isolate and hold a black hole in a laboratory. Imagine having the mass of a star concentrated in your basement. Nor is that the end of our difficulties. In 1974, Stephen Hawking discovered that black holes emit huge amounts of brutally energetic radiation.[5] The power output of a black hole varies inversely as the square of its mass: the smaller the mass, the greater the energy. A small black hole could emit as much energy—every second—as an exploding hydrogen bomb.

And there's more! The forces within the event horizon are so great they would crush any travelers before they even reached the worm-hole. We might circumvent that particular problem by transforming the information needed to reconstruct the team into a series of light flashes. We can transmit this signal into the black hole; after all, no matter how great the tidal forces, they can't crush pulses of light. However, using such pulses wouldn't solve our other problems, each a showstopper in itself.

So how do we keep the Stargate travelers alive?

FROTHY PHYSICS

In 1988, Michael Morris and Kip Thorne rekindled interest in using such tunnels with their paper "Wormholes in spacetime and their use for interstellar travel: A tool for teaching general relativity".[6] After summarizing the objections to the tunnels, also called "Schwarzschild wormholes," they propose ways to circumvent the problems and create artificial wormholes tailored to interstellar travel. Their wish list of desired properties for the tunnels includes many items needed for a Stargate. The wormhole would have to lack an event horizon. Any tidal forces associated with it would have to be small enough that they don't crush the Stargate team. The tunnel must remain stable long enough for travelers to reach the other side. However, they also must be able to go through it in a reasonable amount of time; if it takes years to traverse the gate, it isn't practical for transportation.

At first glance, Morris and Thorne's requirements seem impossible to meet. To get rid of the event horizon and crushing gravity, we would have to use something other than black holes, which were essential to previous theories. We also have two thorny engineering problems: creating an artificial wormhole in the lab, and keeping it stable.

Morris and Thorne come up with an innovative solution: using *quantum foam.*

All matter in the universe consists of atoms, which contain protons, neutrons and electrons. Such particles are far smaller than anything visible to the unaided eye. If we go to scales even smaller than the diameter of a proton, the very nature of spacetime changes. It becomes frothy.[7] To understand why, we'll need to enter the strange and fascinating realm of quantum mechanics.

Quantum physics is the theory of how matter behaves on a small scale. It deals with molecules, atoms and subatomic particles. The theory revolves around a concept that itself sounds like the stuff of science fiction: solid matter behaves like waves. To develop a feel for what that means, imagine a sea wall with two vertical slits in it. When a wave washes against the wall, part of it flows through one slit and part through the other. Now suppose you throw balls at the slits. A ball either goes through one or the other, but not both simultaneously. It fits our intuition that a wave should go through both slits and ball through only one. But suppose our "wall" is the size of a molecule and the balls are electrons. If we throw an electron at the wall, we intuitively expect it to go through one slit. But it doesn't happen that way. Instead, it acts like a wave, going through both simultaneously. Yet we know from other experiments that an electron is a particle, a tiny bit of matter. Incredibly, it shows qualities of both particles and waves. In quantum mechanics, we call this *wave-particle duality*.

Quantum mechanics is one of the best-developed theories of physics, verified by many experiments. Yet it claims that solid matter behaves like waves, which contradicts the way we experience the world. If you enter a room through a door in a wall with two doorways, you don't simultaneously go through both doors. The reason you don't act like a wave is because the wavelength for macroscopic objects like you is so tiny that it is impossible to distinguish. The wave nature of matter becomes noticeable only on an atomic scale, where the wavelengths of particles are roughly the size of the particles themselves. This is the quantum realm.

In the quantum realm, the wave nature of a particle makes it impossible to simultaneously specify its exact position and momentum. Such particles don't behave like billiard balls bouncing off one another; rather, they are smeared out distributions of waves. This introduces a fundamental uncertainty into measurements of quantities such as position and momentum, a tenet known as the "Heisenberg Uncertainty Principle." If we go to scales less than the diameter of the protons and neutrons that make up an atomic nucleus, the theory predicts the uncertainty will make space and time frothy—a quantum foam.

Within the foam, the uncertainty becomes so pronounced that all manner of exotic things can pop into existence and disappear again. This not only includes every subatomic particle imaginable, but also any point-like entity containing energy, such as a black hole or wormhole. We might conceivably capture a wormhole during these quantum fluctuations. To use it as a Stargate, though, we would somehow have to hold, enlarge and stabilize the tunnel.

Morris and Thorne offer no details on how we might achieve this feat, other than stating: "One could *imagine* an exceedingly advanced civilization pulling a wormhole out of this submicroscopic, quantum mechanical spacetime foam and enlarging it and moving its openings around the universe until it has assumed the size, shape and location required for some specific interstellar project."[8] They concede that restrictions may exist, as yet undiscovered, to prevent such a process.

However, given the rapid development of our sciences and technology, we can just as easily imagine that such an advanced civilization would find a means to deal with, or circumvent, such restrictions.

THORNY ENGINEERING

Let's assume we can create a wormhole. Now we have an engineering problem—we have to stabilize the throat, or opening. We might do this by placing a material with a large cohesive force, or "radial tension," around the opening. Tension is the force that maintains the shape of a soap bubble and allows steel cables to support the weight of a suspension bridge. The surface tension of water is strong enough for some species of lizards to run across its surface. The tension in the material required to stabilize the wormhole throat would be huge. A Stargate portal, about ten feet in diameter, would require a tension millions of times greater than what exists at the center of a neutron star—the densest known matter in the Universe. Our future civilization will indeed need advanced technology to develop such a material.

Nor is that the only engineering challenge. For the wormhole to remain stable, theorists predict the tension in its stabilizing medium must exceed the rest-mass energy of the material itself.[9] The term rest-mass refers to the mass of the object when it isn't moving relative to the person measuring it. So what does it mean to require a tension greater than the rest-mass energy? To answer that question, we consider one of the most famous relations in physics—Einstein's mass-energy equation. If E is the energy of an object, M is its mass and c is the speed of light, then:

$$E = Mc^2$$

According to Einstein—and the many experiments that have verified his work—matter and energy are interchangeable.

The speed of light is a huge number, nearly seven hundred million miles per hour. As a result, we can convert a small mass into a large amount of energy. Matter-to-energy conversion is an integral part of our universe. Nuclear reactions occurring deep inside stars turn mass into energy, and thereby generate the light we see and the heat we feel. Our own sun converts four million tons of hydrogen into energy every second.

The tension of a material is the force per area it exerts. We can express force per area as energy per volume, so we can also talk about tension in terms of energy. Einstein's equation then allows us to associate the tension of a material with its mass M, using $E = Mc^2$. Specifically, the tension cannot exceed the magnitude of the energy density associated with its mass. Recall, however, that to stabilize the wormhole, we must reinforce it with a material that has a tension *greater* than the energy density determined by its rest-mass. At first glance then, it seems impossible to stabilize the tunnel. A solution to this dilemma exists, however; the material that shores up our wormhole must have an energy density less than zero. In that case, the tension would be small but positive, making its magnitude less than Mc^2 but its value larger. If E is negative, M must be less than zero. In other words, the stuff we use to reinforce the wormhole must have negative mass-energy.

Theorists have dubbed this intriguing material *exotic matter*.

CASIMIR AND HAWKING

The concept of negative mass is another idea that goes against our physical intuition. How would it affect the gravity of an astronomical body? Normally gravity is an attractive force: if an apple falls off a tree, gravity draws it toward the ground—which is why it konks us on the head. The gravity due to negative mass would work in the reverse; the apple would fly upward. Negative mass would create a repulsive rather than attractive force. For the wormhole, the repulsive force of the material at its throat would push it open, preventing the tunnel from collapsing. This is one of the most intriguing solutions developed by Morris and Thorne, that the wormhole would hold itself open with the repulsion of its own gravity.

At first glance, it seems impossible for the energy density of a material to be less than zero. However, the uncertainty principle of quantum mechanics comes to our rescue. During the time it takes to measure the energy density, the measurement may have an uncertainty large enough that it could be either positive or negative.

We can point to examples of negative mass-energy. Among the most famous is the Casimir force between two uncharged parallel plates. H. B. G. Casimir hypothesized the effect in 1948[10] and researchers at Los Alamos National Lab measured it in the 1990s[11]. The presence of the plates alters the *vacuum fluctuations*. Such fluctuations occur all the time in empty space; pairs of particles spontaneously pop into existence and then annihilate each other. This includes photons. If we introduce uncharged plates, close together, it disturbs the fluctuations. Certain separations of the plates correspond to a resonant wavelength of the photons. What this means is that the waves tend to cancel between the plates, so that slightly fewer photons exist between rather than outside of them. As a result, photons hitting the plates from the outside exert more pressure than those on the inside, pushing the plates slightly together. The force varies inversely; the farther apart the plates, the weaker the effect. On large scales such as our macroscopic world, it is too small even to measure. However, on tiny scales it becomes appreciable. For micro-machinery with moving parts separated by less than a micron, for instance, the Casimir force causes stickiness due to the attractive forces it creates between components.

Now consider this: if fewer photons exist between the plates than outside, the energy density should be less on the inside of the system. However, the plates are set up in empty space, which has zero energy density. So the energy density between the plates must be negative—which means we have a negative mass-energy.

Another interaction that involves negative energy is the "Hawking radiation" of black holes. Recall that the event horizon of a black hole marks the point of no return; once a particle falls into the volume of space defined by that horizon, it can never come out. Vacuum fluctuations go on everywhere in space, including just outside event horizons. Virtual pairs of particles continually create and annihilate, and every so often one falls into the black hole while its partner escapes. The free particle carries away energy, and therefore mass, so in that sense the particle falling into the black hole represents a flux of negative mass-energy.

These two cases suggest it is possible to create the exotic matter needed to stabilize a Stargate. Both examples involve physical systems where positive and negative energy co-exist, with a geometric boundary that breaks the symmetry between the two, either the plates or the event horizon. That boundary isolates the effects of the negative energy in a tangible way. To produce exotic matter for the Stargate, we would need to apply this strategy: that is, create a system where negative and positive energy co-exist, and where we can isolate the negative energy for our use.

Two physicists, Lawrence Ford and Thomas Roman, extended the ideas presented by Morris and Thorne.[12] In particular, they worked out details of the physical properties of exotic matter. The same uncertainty considerations that restrict the simultaneous measurement of position and momentum, and that make spacetime frothy, limit how much exotic matter can exist. They call these limitations "quantum inequalities."

Ford and Roman also show that exotic matter would probably exist in thin sheets, which we would roll into cylinders to line the wormhole.[13] If our Stargate portal had a diameter of ten feet, it would require a thickness of exotic matter one million times smaller than the diameter of a proton. Despite the incredibly thin sheet, the amount of energy required to create that material would equal the total emitted in one year by ten billion stars. It would take a small galaxy! The scale of effort required is far beyond that of any civilization we could currently develop. For the Stargate to be feasible, we need to find a means of creating exotic matter using a more manageable amount of energy. The requirements are stringent, but given the fast pace of scientific and technological advances in just the past century alone, it isn't inconceivable we will someday either develop such a procedure or find a way to circumvent its greatest difficulties.

A MISSIVE FROM THE FUTURE

Physics, as we currently know it, greatly limits the possibilities of wormhole travel. However, as our theories develop, we will better understand the science and technology required for tunnel creation and stabilization. Someday our descendants may overcome these challenges and create Stargate portals that cross exciting vistas of time and space.

Who knows—perhaps they will come to visit us. If that day does arrive, we might fulfill a prophecy foretold by the comic strip *Pogo*, with a slight twist: "We have met the future, and they are us."

REFERENCES

1. Misner, C. W., Thorne, K. S., & Wheeler, J. A. (1973) *Gravitation.* (Freeman, San Francisco)

2. One of the best summaries of wormhole properties, with excellent pictorial representations, appears in *The Illustrated A Brief History of Time.* Updated and Expanded Version, Hawking, S. (1996) pp. 201-211.

3. Einstein, A., & Rosen, N. (1935) "The Particle Problem in the General Theory of Relativity" in *Physical Review*, vol. 48, p. 73.

4. Wheeler, J. A. (1962) *Geometrodynamics* (Academic, New York)

5. Hawking, S. W. (1974) "Black Hole Explosions?" in *Nature*, vol. 248, p. 30.

6. Morris, M. S., & Thorne, K. S. (1988) "Wormholes in spacetime and their use for interstellar travel: A tool for teaching general relativity" in *American Journal of Physics*, vol. 56, p. 395.

7. Wheeler, J. A. (1957) "On the nature of quantum geometro-dynamics" in *Annals of Physics*, vol. 2, p. 604.

8. See reference number five.

9. See reference number five.

10. Casimir, H. B. G., & Polder, D. (1948) "The influence of retardation on the London-van der Waals forces" in *Physical Review*, vol. 73, p. 360.

11. Lamoreaux, S. K. (1999) "Calculation of the Casimir force between imperfectly conducting plates" in *Physical Review A*, vol. 59, p. 3149.

12. Ford, L. H., & Roman, T. A. (2000) "Negative Energy, Wormholes, and Warp Drive" in *Scientific American*, January issue, p. 46.

13. Ford, L. H., & Roman, T. A. (1996) "Quantum Field Theory Constrains Traversable Wormhole Geometries" in *Physical Review D*, vol. 53, p. 5496.

Dr. John K. Cannizzo grew up in Deming, NM. He graduated from the University of New Mexico with a double major in astrophysics and mathematics (BS, 1979). He pursued graduate studies at the University of Texas at Austin in theoretical astrophysics (MA, 1981; Ph.D., 1984). He was a post-doctoral researcher at Harvard University and an Alexander von Humboldt Fellow at the Max Planck Institute for Astrophysics. John is currently a research professor through the University of Maryland, Baltimore County, working at the Goddard Space Flight Center on various projects in computational astrophysics.

Catherine Asaro is author of fourteen novels as well as short fiction (published and upcoming), and is acclaimed for her multiple-award winning Skolian Empire series, which combines adventure, hard science, romance, fast-paced action and themes that challenge the status quo. Her stand-alone novel, The Quantam Rose, *won the 2001 Nebula Award. Her October 2003 novel,* Skyfall, *was just honored with the Romantic Times Book Club award for "Best Science Fiction Novel". Asaro's novella "Moonglow", in* Charmed Destinies *(November 2003) was followed by her fantasy novel,* The Charmed Sphere *(February 2004), part of the Luna Books launch. Also published in February, 2004, was* Irresistable Forces, *a six-author anthology for NAL, edited by Asaro, and including stories by Lois McMaster Bujold and Catherine, among other award-winning, best-selling authors.* Sunrise Alley, *her next novel, is due out in August, 2004, and* Triad, *the latest in the Skolian Empire Series, will be published in December, 2004. Asaro has a Ph.D. in chemical physics from Harvard.*

Melanie Fletcher

YASUREYOUBETCHA: SF-SPEAK THAT DOESN'T MAKE YOU WINCE

DANIEL: That's why we're here—to seek out the Tok'ra.
JACK (dubious): Assuming, of course, you *are* the Tok'ra.
TOK'RA: And if we're not?
JACK: Well, I guess we all start shooting, there's blood, death, hard feelings—it'd suck.

WHEN I FIRST HEARD that someone was turning the movie *Stargate* into a TV series, my first impression was, "Eh."

Don't get me wrong—I liked *Stargate* (and James Spader can be washed and brought to my tent any day). But the thought of yet another science fiction television show featuring quasi-military adventurers going forth to boldly split infinitives and meet up with a Funky Alien Race of the Week—yeah, been there, done that, whatever. If I really wanted to watch that sort of thing, I could turn on *Star Trek: DS9* (before it turned into *Star Trek: Macho Straight Guys Blowing Stuff Up* and made me wonder what the heck was going through the producers' tiny little minds—but I digress). And I never saw a lot of *MacGyver*, so the fact that Richard Dean Anderson was starring in the new series wasn't much of a selling point.

But I'm a science fiction writer, which means I feel obligated to support television shows in my genre by giving the first couple of eps a look-see. If they stink, they stink, but at least I know I gave the show a shot. So it was with a sense of duty that I sat down and watched the first episode of *Stargate SG-1*. An hour later, I turned to the husband and demanded, "Is this the permanent slot, or are they moving it sometime else? Because I *need* to see this next week."

Wonder of wonders, *Stargate SG-1* turned out to be one of those jewel-like rarities in television SF—a show that didn't make your ears bleed with technobabble, stilted speeches or big honking infodumps. In fact, the show's ability to combine intelligent, dramatic plots with equally intelligent dialogue was more akin to *The West Wing* than genre shows such as *Seaquest DSV*, where the plots were good but the dialogue was cringe-inducing (admittedly that was the first season; in the second season, the dialogue worked and the plots made you want to gouge your eyes out).

> HAMMOND: Now what?
> O'NEILL: Now we wait. If Daniel's still around he'll know what the message means.
> SAMUELS: So what if the aliens get it?
> O'NEILL: Well, they could be blowing their noses right now.
> SAMUELS: They could be planning an attack.
> O'NEILL: Oh, come on, Samuels. Let me be the cynic around here, ok?

So what makes the dialogue on *Stargate SG-1* work so well? For starters, *SG-1* has a production team that understands the secret of writing good SF—it should be about people, not machines that go *ping*. The writers, bless their hearts, aren't willing to shortchange their characters in favor of flashy technology; as a result, the episodes are multi-layered explorations of humanity interacting with a mysterious, lively and sometimes deadly cosmos, with little to no reliance on hoary SF clichés. After growing up with one-trick-pony shows like *Time Tunnel*, this is refreshing in the extreme (or even, dare I say it, "Wormhole X-Treme!").

And the characters of *Stargate SG-1* aren't shiny happy cardboard cutouts, either. Over the past eight seasons Col. Jack O'Neill, Dr. Daniel Jackson (and his season six replacement Jonas Quinn), Maj. Samantha Carter and the Jaffa Teal'c have been mentally and physically tortured, lost people they loved and experienced all the major and minor injuries of real life. But you don't see Jack on a hillside soliloquizing about the death of his son—he's more likely to take it out on a Serpent Guard. The beauty about these fictional characters is that their emotional reactions are realistic; this hooks the audience from the get-go and gets them cheering for O'Neill and company as they continue to fight the good fight against the Goa'uld and other wannabe destroyers of Earth.

> O'NEILL: All right, listen up. There's something you should know before you start shootin' and killin' and ruinin' what could be the start of a beautiful friendship. Our beloved Hathor is dead.
> TROFSKY: What you say is impossible. Hathor is a queen. More than that, she is a goddess!
> O'NEILL: Yeah, okay, ex-goddess, maybe. I killed her myself. You should trust me on this. She's gone. She is no more, she is . . . well, let's face it, she's a former queen.

Another nice thing about the writing team is their reluctance to resort to the bane of thinking SF media fans everywhere: technobabble. Admittedly, the device is a venerable part of media SF—we all know from watching *Dr. Who* that reversing the polarity of the neutron flow solves everything from an impending nuclear explosion to the heartbreak of psoriasis (I only wish it could block spam, too).

And when you get down to it, telling a good story in five acts isn't easy; it requires skill, discipline and the ability to juggle a plot while making sure that the stars get enough air time to earn their paychecks. Telling a story in five acts *and* tossing in something like a wormhole, an alien race or a machine that breaks people into subatomic bits and reassembles them somewhere else just makes the job that much harder. If a writer doesn't have time to explain how a piece of tech works and has to add a couple of lines of scientific gibberish to smooth the way of the plot, so be it (I may bitch about it, but I'll understand).

But the main problem with technobabble is that it's an easy out, and easy outs are, well, easy to use. The *Star Trek* franchise is probably one of the most egregious users/abusers of the device (what *is* a "Level Three diagnostic," anyway?), although shows such as *VR.5* and *TekWar* certainly relied on technobabble to bail their heroes out of the poo when the going got rough. *Stargate SG-1*, on the other hand, stays as far away from technobabble as possible, thanks in large part to Col. Jack "Yadda yadda" O'Neill. When Sam or Daniel start yammering on about the latest alien device/unusual cuneiform/etc., you can count on Jack to listen for roughly five seconds before his eyes glaze over and he growls, "Yeah, whatever—what does it DO?" They give the short answer, and the story keeps moving—beautiful. And once again, it's *realistic*. After all, most military officers don't really want to hang around listening to a long-winded explanation while enemy forces are nearby.

> DANIEL: I did a timeline Boolean search for religion, cult, Set, Setesh, Setek, Set—
> O'NEILL: Yadda.

But one of the best parts about *Stargate SG-1*'s dialogue is that it can be downright funny. Yes, our heroes regularly jump through wormholes and risk death, capture or Goa'uld possession on the other side of the galaxy, but they don't do it with sticks up their butts. In the episode "Prisoners," when SG-1 is mistakenly banished to a desolate penal colony, Jack considers the criminals around them, then mutters to Teal'c, "Look scary and take point." And there's the wondrous "Wormhole X-Treme!", a Klein bottle of a 100th episode where, thanks to a stranded alien posing as a Hollywood advisor, a rip-roaring TV show is based on the Stargate project, complete with actors playing fictionalized versions of SG-1. Much to Jack's disgust, he's portrayed by the particularly over-the-top Nick Marlowe (Michael DeLuise reaching hilariously Kirkian heights of bombastic delivery).

Stargate SG-1 isn't unique in its use of humor—*Farscape*, *Quantum Leap* and *Babylon 5* are also superb SF shows with some hilarious moments. *Quantum Leap*, however, always had a thread of melancholy running through it due to Sam Beckett's inability to leap home, and

Babylon 5 had a tendency to get buried under its own mythology. With *Stargate SG-1*, there's no sense of Homeric heavy-handedness that can form the dark side of epic storytelling; it's probably closest to *Farscape*, in that both shows have a lead character who is a master of sarcasm prone to making snarky comments in the face of impending death. You gotta love that.

> O'NEILL: Hey, Reigar? You know that "we come in peace" business? Bite me.

According to set gossip, a number of Jack's comebacks can also be attributed to the fact that Richard Dean Anderson can't remember his lines and has to ad-lib half of the time (if so, bravo, Rick). Maybe that's the secret of the dialogue—a combination of solid, well-written scripts with skilled actors who don't mind a little extemporaneous exploration of their characters when needed.

Yeah, I know—yadda yadda. Just watch the show and enjoy.

Melanie Fletcher is a woman of simple tastes—she likes to write, preferably for money. Her fiction includes "Star Quality" (Selling Venus, Circlet Press), "Hermaphrodite" (Crossing the Border, Indigo/Gollancz), "Bartok and the Unicorn" (Quantum Muse, July 2002), "The Female of the Species" (Quantum Muse, April 2003) and "A Rose By Any Other Name" (The Four Bubbas of the Apocolypse, Yard Dog Press). She has also produced the chapbooks The Stories That Would Not Die! *and* Dark Matter–Erotica SF and Fantasy *(Belaurient Press).*

Sue E. Linder-Linsley, MA, RPA

EXPLORING THE ARCHAEOLOGY OF *STARGATE SG-1*

From Childhood Westerns to Interstellar Imagination

TELEVISION HAS MADE US ALL, to a certain extent, anthropologists. As a kid, I sprawled on the floor, captivated by black and white Westerns that introduced me to the concept of learning about other cultures. In the narrow confines of those old TV screens, I explored the Old West along with my heroes—part of the landscape, and an observer of it at the same time. I developed a "database" of artifacts: bridle and wagon parts, handmade nails and horseshoes, architecture, town layout and all the items in the general store. By watching those stories, I began to understand how people, their particular place in time and the things they used every day created a culture.

I also learned, at the same time, a lot of the basic tenets of western social values. The best of those shows, like *Have Gun, Will Travel*, even let me question them a little.

But time marched on.

37

As a teenager, I expanded my horizons into the great beyond as the Western transformed into the groundbreaking science fiction space exploration of *Star Trek*. Instead of riding the range, I patrolled the Neutral Zone. I now dreamed of becoming a starship captain and encountering exciting alien cultures. Instead of memorizing items in the local saloon, I was busy cataloging the culture, language and artifacts of cultures that didn't even exist, like the Klingons and Romulans.

Oh, and I could still recognize anything remotely similar to the items from the Old West. That served me well when I found myself light years across the galaxy, but mysteriously on location in the 1800s. (Come on, you know it happens. Even on *Stargate SG-1*.)

As an adult, I see things differently. Space travel at the speed of light, instant matter transportation, time travel and a whole host of other gadgets and concepts are far from impossible, thanks to the rapidly expanding frontiers of science—and sometimes that's as frightening as it is exciting. The cookbook-western-in-space—or "wagon train to the stars"—no longer captures my imagination the way it did when I was younger and (maybe) more innocent. I now have the baggage of higher education to weigh me down. Even when I'm not occupied with matters of science, there's no escaping real life for long: politics, government and other current events just won't go away.

But like all humans throughout history, I still need to warm myself by the fire of imagination. Maybe now more than ever. I could go a lot of places to find that escape . . . but where do I find myself running?

Right into the marathon four-hour block of *Stargate SG-1*, and anticipating the new season's episode later in the week. Why? Because Dr. Daniel Jackson has my dream job.

Stargate SG-1 is the one show that still captures my imagination. It gets the profession of archaeology right, unlike many of the blockbuster movies where the "archaeologist" digs up dinosaur bones. (It sometimes seems like everyone knows that paleontologists dig up dinosaurs except folks in Hollywood.)

Archaeologists study the remains of what people leave behind, and from inference, the culture that created them . . . and very seldom have living people to study. Anthropologists in general study *existing* cultures; archaeology is a sub-discipline of anthropology, as is linguistics, the study of language.

Daniel Jackson is a specialist in all three of these areas. Some laypersons might find this a little unbelievable but in fact, archaeologists are expected to know about many different things—and to operate in a number of interdisciplinary areas. I can easily accept his background in these fields, though his depth of knowledge and fluency with the smallest details are a little much for one man to command.

Now, let's see how he does in applying them . . . .

DR. DANIEL JACKSON: LINGUIST

Daniel's linguistic skills came in handy in the original movie as he solved the initial mystery of the Stargate and helped navigate that first team through the unknown landscape of Abydos. They're somewhat less vital in the television show, because unlike many other science fiction shows, *Stargate* doesn't use the (somewhat tired) universal translator plot device (I myself prefer the marvelous translator microbes in *Farscape*). Instead, they leap straight to the notion that most of the universe speaks English. As a scientist, I wince, but I understand that spending half of an episode either learning a language or having Daniel translating dialogue just isn't dramatically effective.

An interesting fan-proposed theory I've heard is that the Ancients configured the Stargate system to also give travelers the ability to speak and understand the local languages . . . although how they keep up with something so fluid and fast-changing would be a mystery. But it offers a relatively plausible explanation, and I'm perfectly willing to go with it!

Lucky for the team, Daniel reads fluently in many languages when required. He can even learn a new language in a matter of days, human or alien (and if you've ever suffered through a semester of learning a foreign tongue, feel free to grind your teeth in jealousy). This enhanced ability to communicate puts Daniel right in the middle of the action, and gives him a pivotal role of importance even on military or political missions. It's the *archaeologist*, not the soldier, who is chosen by the Tok'ra for a mission to destroy the System Lords . . . because he speaks fluent Goa'uld. (Personally, I think that's very cool. However, I'm not signing up for Goa'uld translation duties, even if I could figure out the syntax.)

All of this is a nice idea, but in reality, if we look at the most famous prehistoric Egyptian archaeologist—who has been doing archaeological research in Egypt for over forty years—it's a well-known fact that he speaks English, and knows only a handful of words of

Arabic. Archaeologists are, in fact, notorious for *not* learning the lingo of the locals. They speak "Archaeologee," which is composed of lots of acronyms and is unintelligible to the average English speaker (and many graduate students).

One hot summer night, an ambitious group of archaeologists (me among them) made this discovery for ourselves when we tried to communicate with the locals. Sadly, our language skills didn't match up to those so dazzlingly modeled by Dr. Jackson. We were lucky to be able to find food, shelter and a working restroom. (I found myself wishing for a totally ubiquitous word, like "kree," to help me along.)

Later we amused ourselves by writing a full page in typical Archaeologee. Other than a few nouns and adjectives, it was all acronyms. "The RFP's SOW to CAA's DOT contract is for an APE . . . ." Very confusing. Then again, maybe that's why Daniel fits so well into the military structure of the SGC, where acronyms surely must be a dialect all their own. A completely new specialty in linguistics . . . .

But I love him most for the moment I can really relate to, from the original *Stargate* movie, when he's confronted for the first time by the living language of the pharaohs. "What's he saying?" asks Col. Jack O'Neil (with one "l"). Daniel replies absently, with the true delight of an archaeologist living his greatest dream, "I have no idea."

Bless him. I can't imagine anyone actually would.

DR. DANIEL JACKSON: ANTHROPOLOGIST

The season seven episode "Grace" is a good example of how anthropology—or at least pure communications—plays a key role in the show, although in an entirely unusual way. Maj. Samantha Carter is actually alone for most of the episode. Her visions of her friends are really hallucinations . . . albeit ones that seemed to channel their abilities and strengths with great accuracy.

It is Daniel's avatar that redirects Sam from her engineering instincts of running diagnostics, when he suggests that the inanimate gas cloud trapping her ship might be a life form.

Sure, we've seen that plot in other space adventures: An apparently hostile life form, whether in the guise of a fuzz ball, blob of goo or gas cloud, tries to communicate with the heroes. Said heroes takes the communication as a hostile action and spend the better part of an episode trying to fight it off before they come to our senses . . . yadda yadda.

SG-1's twist on the story is more realistic than earlier space adventure versions, because Daniel, as an anthropologist (even a dream version of one), is always looking for or suggesting communication in new and unusual situations. He's interpreting data according to completely different rules than those of a physicist or an engineer.

However, it's ironic that Daniel stopped Sam from running and re-running the simulation. Archaeologists also do what is called "modeling," a scientific technique for analyzing data. They run the data over and over again with small manipulations of the parameters. Four times would hardly be a start for most of us. At the same time, we archaeologists are always itching for something new to examine. Given the opportunity to sit in a lab analyzing old data or going in the field to put our hands in the dirt, we'll almost always choose the dirt.

In the episode "Pretense," Daniel uses his anthropological expertise to add context to the facts put into evidence in the Tollan's Triad, or trial, by bringing the plaintiff Skaara's beliefs and culture into the argument. In doing so, he has to give equal recognition to the Goa'uld within Skaara. Although Jack is adamant that the parasites do not have anything like a culture of their own, Daniel is either less convinced, or at least better able to conceal his opinions during the trial. It's his reasoned defense that makes the difference in the end.

This innate anthropological fairness is something he's displayed on other occasions, too. His response to the android Reese in "Menace" is rooted in his ability to look beyond his own cultural biases and see her point of view. It's a two-edged sword. If he'd been wrong about Reese—something we may never know for certain—he might have added Earth to the vast list of worlds destroyed by the Replicators.

Daniel is frequently concerned about the SG units' impact on new worlds. In the episode "Spirits," Daniel specifically wants to know about any indigenous life on PXY-887. According to the military, they have not identified any radio waves, therefore there can't be indigenous life. Well . . . only if we believe that all primitives use radio waves, and even in *Star Trek* radio waves were rarely used by anyone other than the people of 20th century Earth. (We can only assume that Daniel voiced these same concerns . . . off camera.)

In the case of this particular non-radio-emitting world, there is a strong parallel between when Europeans first arrived in the New World and SG-11's actions in mining on a new planet. In both cases, newcomers tried to take an important resource without asking or considering its implication to the culture. Looting is looting, whether it's artifacts or minerals . . . something the Stargate teams learned early and, thankfully, with a minimum of cultural disturbance to the local population. (Okay, in this case, they had to have it thumped into their heads by the local gods, but . . . whatever educational technique works.)

DR. DANIEL JACKSON: ARCHAEOLOGIST

I've never been so convinced that Daniel was a true archaeologist than when he asks Jack, "Not that I mind getting to explore the universe and everything, but we do get paid for this, right?"

Money's important . . . but it's not the best part of the job. Many of my colleagues would probably keep doing what they do even if they *never* got paid for it. Archaeology is sheer fascinating fun, as well as a "day job." (Fun being, in the *Stargate* universe, a relative term. Luckily, not many archaeologists here in our world have to put up with creatures as difficult as the Goa'uld, except in terms of obtaining funding.)

It also rings true in the show that archaeologists aren't infallible. In season seven's "Homecoming," local scientists had identified the most important piece of their collection as nothing but a decorative trinket. The artifact in question was a data crystal with the original Goa'uld research on how to stabilize the inherently unstable naquadria . . . and it was a completely understandable screw-up. The local archaeologists, in predictable fashion, overlooked its real function and value to their investigation—because archaeologists can only categorize items based on their own experience and knowledge. In true interpretative form, with a sometimes narrow mindset, the archaeologist classifies anything "decorative" or "fancy" as an art or religious item, not as a scientific or functional item. If you haven't read it, try the marvelously funny *Motel of Mysteries* by David Macauley to get an idea of just how this phenomenon can occur; in the absence of context, everyday items can assume disproportionate significance. The converse is that discoveries of great meaning can be nothing more attention-getting than a broken stone tablet, like the famous Rosetta Stone, which helped break the code of hieroglyphics.

In "Homecoming," über-villain Anubis knew the importance of that misidentified artifact and went looking for it. This is just like the amateur looter going after something archaeologists overlook due to their preconceived idea about what artifacts are important. *Stargate* has it right.

By the way, Kelowna scientists don't need to shoulder all of the blame. Even though our resident expert Dr. Jackson spent his childhood in museums and dig sites, and certainly has vastly more experience than the local staff, he doesn't make the suggestion that leads to the discovery of the data crystal. (Of course, in his defense, he *does* have little memory of his human past at that point, after just returning from his status as a "glowing jellyfish.") Instead, it's Major Carter's recommendation to review the museum inventory that puts them on the right trail.

So in "Homecoming," factual and realistic characteristics of archaeology are presented . . . just not necessarily offered by SG-1's resident archaeologist.

Daniel's vast archaeological knowledge of ancient Egypt figures helps keep the SGC one step ahead of the evil Goa'uld. Many System Lords take their names from the Egyptian gods—Ra, Hathor, Apophis and Set, among others. The relationship between the Goa'uld and ancient Egypt echoes through the series in place names, character names, dress and hieroglyphs decorating the sets (both building architecture and those marvelous pyramid ships). Daniel's knowledge enables him to remain a key player on SG-1 in the lab and in the field.

Incidentally, although the Goa'uld give them a bad name, ancient Egyptian gods were there to protect and watch over the population, not oppress it. Egyptian beliefs evolved to help people live in a lush narrow strip surrounded by unforgiving desert. This startling contrast is why Hathor, for instance, was such an important figure—not *quite*, as Jack put it, the goddess of sex, drugs and rock 'n roll, but clearly love, music and beauty were her specialties, and very important to a people in such a harsh environment. Climatic change, along with resource availability and conservation, meant life or death for the people of ancient Egypt. Their gods guided their lives and kept them safe through times of drought and hardship. Part of Daniel's initial revulsion toward the Goa'uld—before they made it personal—must have been the perversion of that important balance into a system of tyranny and slavery.

Personally, my favorite episode with archaeological overtones is "2001," involving the Aschen and the Volins. The episode starts with a "previously"—a blood splattered note (in O'Neill's handwriting) comes through the Stargate with a warning about never going to P4C-970.

Do television shows ever take warnings like that seriously? Well, actually, yes. *Stargate SG-1* did, and promptly locked the combination out of the dialing computers, which goes a long way toward establishing their credibility as a show that thinks just as much as it acts.

Unfortunately, events conspire against their best intentions, and SG-1 returns from an unrelated mission to report they may have located important new allies on another world. Of course, *we* know immediately that all is not as it seems, even if we missed that important prequel of "2010." With our vast anthropological database of television adventures, we know that new acquaintances who appear too good to be true usually are. O'Neill has some reservations about the Aschen, but his comments are based on personality, not facts. (He doesn't trust people without a sense of humor.) That's not a very military assessment of the people, by the way; it's more of an anthropological observation. (Maybe Daniel's having an effect on him.)

Instead, it's Daniel who provides the hard evidence of the Aschen's culpability, by picking up on an obscure clue from a farmer who complains about the "ironweed" in his fields and needs the Aschen's assistance to dig it out.

Teal'c would probably assume the ironweed is some plant that a decent weed killer could control, but as an archaeologist, I'm sure Daniel had images (as I do) of fields scattered with small iron rich pebbles (ironstone or hematite). Some places like this, you can't get a shovel into the ground, and when you do, excavation is a tedious process. Some places have large iron deposits strong enough to make your compass point toward the deposit instead of true north. It's a natural assumption that Daniel would want to take a look.

And take a look he does, even at the risk of his life, as he climbs down an iron girder into a hole that may prove to be unstable. He is, after all, an archaeologist on a mission to uncover the unknown; a little danger is acceptable. In the post-*Indiana Jones* school of archaeological thought, it's even required, at least in film and television.

But Daniel's discovery of the Volian newspaper archive is a little more precious than fortuitous. How could he possibly know that a tube he so easily found would have newspaper copies from the final days of the original civilization? Believe me, this is the way we archaeologists wish it would happen, but never does. If we did find a buried city, we couldn't just climb down a ladder into it. We would have to spend months or even years removing all the dirt by hand, sifting and cataloguing . . . and then when we got down to the floor level we wouldn't find a newspaper conveniently dated just prior to abandonment, containing headline articles of everything we need to know.

Real archaeologists uncover information that raises more questions than it answers. Don't worry. We find it just as frustrating as you do.

Daniel is right in his response to Teal'c's warnings that the cavern is dangerous and they should return to the surface. He says that the papers may be their only chance to figure out what has happened . . . and just as Jack can leave no soldier behind, giving up an artifact is difficult if not impossible for Daniel Jackson. Not only that, but Daniel's brain is spinning with a vast knowledge of civilizations and time scales for change, and the information simply doesn't fit with what his training and experience are telling him.

It's Daniel and his archaeological appetite for looking into ruins, exploring the unknown, ignoring danger in pursuit of adventure and asking questions outside the box that give the SG-1 team the information they need to figure out just how much trouble they're really facing.

Every archaeologist wants to make that great find. To make that great discovery . . . track down that lost city . . . except in reality, there is no such thing as a "lost city." A city can't really be lost. It's still right where we left it, in the same geographic location; it's only that living people have lost the knowledge of how to find it. In season seven we learn that the Ancients made a city "lost" from other people who might want to find it. Now, normally a city can't be "made lost" because all the people who know of it would have to die off, but from the Ancients, we'll believe it.

Enter Daniel's old girlfriend Sarah as the host for the Goa'uld Osiris, in "Chimera."

Sarah, needing key information that has disappeared from living human memory, enters Daniel's dreams and tries to lead him to recover knowledge he may have retained from his time as an Ascended Being.

For the purpose of jogging Daniel's memories, Osiris introduces a tablet that is supposedly a guide to the Lost City. She claims that it was found in Morocco, and that it was radiocarbon dated to 10,000 years ago.

Hmm. I kept waiting for Daniel—even in dream-logic—to take exception to this assertion, but maybe he was distracted by being, er, asleep. Composition of the tablet is not discussed, but the artifact appears to be a slate or dark stone with carved writing. The problem is that stone can't be radiocarbon dated! It has to have plant or organic content for that to work.

My other objection is a bit less obvious and more pervasive. While the Goa'uld's culture is based on ancient Egyptian culture (or perhaps the other way around), Ancient writing (like that on the tablet) is the root from which Medieval Latin was derived. But if the Ancients were here long before the Egyptians, and the medieval period is far removed, why doesn't the language of the Ancients give rise to hieroglyphics rather than Latin? Another linguistic puzzle, rivaling that of why cultures all over the galaxy speak modern English . . . .

But I digress.

Daniel is a widely acknowledged expert on Ancient Egypt, but he's full of hidden depths, too. In the episode "Demons," we learn that Daniel also has a pretty fair working knowledge of the Middle Ages. If so, he's exceptionally gifted; real-world archaeologists usually specialize or focus their study on a particular culture or time period. This is just because it takes so much time to gain all the necessary education. Daniel, however, doesn't have a limit on the range of his knowledge. He's a walking encyclopedia of all cultures, from all time periods, and even knows about alien cultures with a minimum of study. Then again, who can explain Sam Carter's miraculous ability to master every discipline of science and technology? The breadth and depth of his knowledge just make Daniel all the more fascinating . . . if more daunting to those of us who have to live up to his image.

ANTHROPOLOGY AND ARCHAEOLOGY BEYOND THE STARGATE—INTO THE GREAT UNKNOWN

In *Stargate SG-1*, Egyptian mythology has leapt right off the pages of the *Book of the Dead*—and transformed itself. What we thought was legend becomes a history lesson of the Goa'uld's previous interference with cultural development on Earth. The fact that humans from Earth have been abducted to populate the universe does away with any potential *Star Trek*-like prime directive about non-interference at first contact with a new species—but that doesn't mean there aren't plenty of moral and ethical dilemmas to go around.

Unlike the settlers "civilizing" the untamed West in those black and white dramas I grew up with, the Stargate teams don't set out to conquer the natives, or even bring the local population around to their way of thinking. In fact, the spirit of colonialism and Manifest Destiny is embodied by our favorite human bad guys: the NID, Maybourne and (of course) Senator (and later Vice President) Kinsey.

There is an overlay of politics to interactions with and between alien cultures that is reflective of international treaty and trade agreements right here on Earth. Even the Goa'uld—bad guys though they are—have to abide by the legal fine print. In fact, one of the most interesting aspects is that they exist in an uneasy ceasefire with each other, and collectively, with the Asgard.

You're probably thinking, "But that sounds more like modern day life than ancient history!" And, of course, you're right—and wrong. Kings and gods have been making treaties (and breaking them) for thousands of years. In fact, Ramses II (technically a god), who ruled Egypt for 67 years during the 12th century B.C., is the first ruler we know of to actually put in writing a peace treaty (with the Hittites). Interestingly, both copies of this treaty—written in both hieroglyphics and the Hittite language Akkadian—survive to prove that the rulers really did reach a lasting accord. (Although, predictably, both claimed credit for brokering the deal.)

A discussion of the relationship between SG-1 and archaeology can't be complete without a discussion of "ascending." In the *Stargate* universe, ascending isn't necessarily death—an idea that might have sounded familiar to many ancient cultures.

The ancient Egyptians believed that the living ruler (Pharaoh) was born just like any of us, but was also the living manifestation of a god during his lifetime. Just when the Pharaoh officially obtained his status as a deity during the process is uncertain, since rulers frequently changed due to civil disputes and family politics . . . presumably before godhood took effect.

At death, the Pharaoh "ascends" and becomes the non-corporeal spirit that rules the world from above.

This is actually similar to being chosen by the Goa'uld as a host. On being infected with the parasite, a human metamorphoses into a Goa'uld—a warrior in battle to conquer and control while on the path to become a System Lord. They rule from above and control the economics of their planets. The similarities to this type of ascending are the basis for the *SG-1* story line.

When Daniel ascends-with-a-capital-"A," it's something like the Egyptian theory of Pharaoh transcending his human origins to become a god, watching over his people—and it's also a classic life-after-death ascension as well. We've seen Ascended Beings before in science fiction . . . remember the glowing, more-than-human Ambassador Kosh of *Babylon 5*? The implication on *B5*, as in *SG-1*, was that there was a species that watched over us and cared for us but rarely interfered with our development. In the case of the Ascended on *Stargate*, they're also what we aspire to become—the next step in our development.

As archaeologists, our work brings long-dead cultures back to life. For my money, there could be no better end for an archaeologist than to become an all-knowing godlike being who has the power and knowledge to help protect developing cultures. I envy Daniel his stint on the higher planes, unrestricted by human boundaries. Yet it was that very quality that made Daniel so exceptional as an anthropologist and archaeologist that proved his undoing as an Ascended—he couldn't just sit by and watch things go wrong.

And he paid the price for it.

We've come a long way from those early anthropology lessons in front of flickering black and white TV screens. Good still triumphs over evil . . . but in *Stargate SG-1*, it does so at a cost. Nothing demonstrates the point better than the moral and ethical dilemmas of episodes like "Beast of Burden" and "Scorched Earth." Anthropology helps us frame the questions those dilemmas pose: Do we help the Unas win freedom from slavery at the cost of innocent human lives? Do we destroy an alien culture to allow a human one to flourish? Science can't provide those answers, but anthropology and archaeology can at least help teach us the mistakes others have made in the past. George Santayana's quote is more apropos now than ever: "Those who cannot learn from history are doomed to repeat it."

Stargate SG-1 uses science to help us learn not just from history, but from our potential future as well.

One last thought: If one day we do discover a working Stargate, and find the universe beyond the wormhole to be anything like the one Dr. Daniel Jackson is exploring, archaeologists will have a whole new frontier of work to be done. Not just uncovering the secrets of our lost colonies in the stars, but the archaeological record of the Ancients, the Furling, the Nox, the Asgard. Maybe Thor will let us turn the first spadeful of dirt to uncover the secrets of his ancestors, uncounted millennia ago.

Now *that* will be a dig site to look forward to.

Sue Linder-Linsley is currently the Executive Director for the Chickasaw Cultural Center, which is presently being built by the Chickasaw Nation in Sulphur, Oklahoma, and will open in the fall of 2006. She has an MA from Southern Methodist University, and specializes in the conservation, preservation and care of collections, as well as North American historic and prehistoric archaeology. She is a member of the Register of Professional Archaeologists (RPA), and the Managing Editor of their professional publication, RPA Notes, *as well a Communications Committee Member, Archives Committee Chair and Web site developer. She is a member of the Society of Professional Archaeologists and the Council of Texas Archaeologists.*

Jim Butcher

ARTIFICIAL INTELLIGENCE AND GENUINE STUPIDITY

The Role of Intelligence in Stargate SG-1

DANIEL (to Thor): Wait a minute. You're actually saying that
   you need someone dumber than you are.
JACK: You may have come to the right place.
CARTER: I could go, sir.
JACK: I dunno, Carter. You may not be dumb enough.

STARGATE SG-1: A SERIES APART

T HE MOST WONDERFUL ASPECT OF SCIENCE FICTION, to me, has always
      been its reverence for intelligence. From the beginning, in
      written, artistic and motion-picture presentations the role of a
protagonist's intelligence in science fiction has been one of paramount

dominance. SF abounds with brilliant scientists, brilliant engineers, brilliant military commanders, brilliant *et cetera*, *ad nauseum*.

And then there is *SG-1*.

The role of intelligence in *SG-1* reflects a profound statement from the *Tao of Yakko, Wakko and Dot*: It's a big universe, and we're not. Humans are not presented as an ultimate species, but only as a little fish in a great big pond. They face challenges and dangers both petty and almost entirely beyond their comprehension, and all too often fall prey to chance, a foolish miscalculation or a clever foe. This humbler, more pragmatic portrayal of human intelligence as it relates to exploring the galaxy is what sets *SG-1* apart from most classic science fiction.

Too often, intelligence in science fiction is portrayed as a single characteristic, a definitive measure of raw brainpower. In the universe of *SG-1*, however, intelligence is presented in a great many shades and colors. No single form of intelligence is sufficient to face the challenges of an enormous and unfriendly universe on its own, and must instead rely upon complementary forms of intelligence in order to survive and prosper.

That basic theme is reflected within the personalities of the team members of SG-1 and, more importantly, within the presentation of the lead characters as a group.

THE EGGHEAD

Let's call the most overt and commonly considered form of intelligence portrayed in the series the egghead mentality. Reason, logic, learning and employing the scientific method to discover new things all fall under this form of intelligence. It's book learning, and its poster child is Maj. Samantha Carter.

The eggheads are the ones with all the really cool gadgets. They reverse-engineer alien gizmos, design entirely new technologies, write big papers about what they've done and confuse everybody who isn't a fellow egghead. When the chips are down and something has gone horribly wrong with a major piece of hardware, it's Carter who will be frantically repairing, disarming, translating, hacking, bypassing, reversing polarity, calculating or rerouting something. Carter's science-based intellect has saved SG-1 and the SGC on multiple occasions, and includes such feats as designing hyperspace travel technology (okay, so, it didn't work all that great; it's still a lot closer than *you've* gotten to a working hyperdrive), working out the physics related to Stargate-based time travel, countering the activities of micro cellular nanites, repairing Goa'uld technology based upon the interaction of plastic slots and primary colored crystals, and sending a freaking star into spontaneous supernova.

An egghead like Carter is not, however, limited to figuring things out with a calculator and a slide rule. You can rely upon Carter's steady logic and calculation to spot patterns in behavior or to predict the behavior of a given individual, provided there is enough data to give her a decent baseline. Carter has puzzled out the behavior of an entire town of narco-Goa'uld and accurately predicted the betrayal of multiple Goa'uld bad guys.

Granted, eggheads such as Carter do have some weaknesses that come along with their abilities. Reliance upon the scientific method as a base model for reason sometimes renders them less capable of thinking quickly or of making intuitive leaps ahead in their chains of thought. It can also make them less adept than others at predicting irrational or illogical behavior in their fellow beings. Similarly, at times of crisis they may be prone to relying too heavily upon their proven methods of applying their intelligence, proceeding blindly upon their chain of logic and giving insufficient weight to the arguments of others. That weakness in Carter's intellect led her to a plan of action that nearly allowed Anubis to melt the iris on the SGC's gate, which would have wiped out the SGC, Cheyenne Mountain and most of Colorado.

Other eggheads presented in the series include Dr. Janet Fraiser, the Mengele-esque Goa'uld Nirrti and Chancellor Travel of the Tollans.

THE EMPATH

A second form of intelligence presented in the series can be represented by what I call the Empaths. It is a more intuitive sort of intellect, one adept at examining and understanding the thoughts, emotions and motivations of other beings. Lest there be any doubt as to who of the Big Four in SG-1 is the empath, I'll spell it out—Dr. Daniel Jackson.

The true strength of the empath is best shown in personal interactions and conflicts. When conflict arises, it is the empath who is best suited to understanding the emotional core at the heart of the situation. It is the empath who can understand the source of the grief, the hatred, the anger or the desire that fuels the conflict, and thus the empath who has the best opportunity to resolve it. Often, it is the empath whose close association with his own emotions, as well as those of others, gives him the kind of strength of character and resolve that could not be provided by mere rationality.

In his tenure with SG-1, Dr. Jackson's ability to empathize with others has both repeatedly brought him into conflict with his own team members and enabled him to possess insights and knowledge that have saved them from multiple threats. This is demonstrated most overtly during such incidents as the Asgard-Goa'uld negotiations involving the protected status of the planet Earth, where Dr. Jackson constantly managed to smooth over hostile tensions so that the talks could proceed. Other sterling examples of Dr. Jackson's brand of intellect at its best include his part in deciphering the riddles that initially led to first contact with the Asgard, establishing friendly (or at least non-murderous) relations with the Unas and preserving the Enkaran civilization from destruction by the Gadmeer terraforming ship.

The empath, while undeniably a formidable intellect in the right circumstances, is plagued with its own weaknesses. By focusing so intently upon the thoughts, emotions and intentions of other beings, an empathic intellect can often be blinded to the practical effects of that being's actions. In addition, an empathic intellect's reliance upon emotion as both a conduit to communication with others and a source of personal strength can be easily manipulated by others—such as when Anubis deceived Dr. Jackson into betraying his comrades by turning over the powerful artifact known as the Eye of Ra, only to betray Dr. Jackson, destroy the world of Abydos he'd been trying to protect *and* force Dr. Jackson to act against Anubis, resulting in his expulsion from the society of energy-beings known as the Ascended.

Other empaths presented in the series include Lya of the Nox, Narim of the Tollans and the Goa'uld Hathor.

THE PRACTICAL PHILOSOPHER

Another breed of intelligence specializes less in the abstract estimation of logic or emotions and more in tangible problems faced on a daily basis. This kind of practical philosopher has a much narrower and more immediate focus than either an egghead or an empath, and while they aren't going to be reconfiguring a quantum transdoohickey any time soon, if there's a firefight raging, a building burning down around your ears, an enraged Jaffa bent on ripping your nose off or an alien deathbeast hunting down your team, you'd better have one along for the ride. The most prominent practical philosopher on *SG-1* is Teal'c.

In some ways, Teal'c is the most adaptable member of the team. Whether the task is raw physical labor, combat, gathering intelligence or comforting a friend, Teal'c can apply himself ably to a broad variety of situations. Equally as able to rely upon intuition as to employ cool logic, the practical philosopher addresses problems based upon his current resources, environment and relative capabilities, and often serves as a foil to ultimately strengthen one of the more intricate plans provided by others. Teal'c repeatedly provides criticism and alternative suggestions to the problem at hand, often supplying his team members with knowledge they do not possess. He is an able planner when a tactical problem needs to be solved, but is even more skilled following orders as a part of a team.

There is little need to cite specific instances of Teal'c's applications of practical intelligence. He demonstrates them in virtually every single mission (which means pretty much every episode). Outside of combat, though, he has made stirring speeches to his fellow Jaffa, tunneled his way from the buried Stargate on Edora and taken heroic and innovative action by sharing his symbiote with the dying Bra'tac.

Practical thinkers like Teal'c, however, face certain shortcomings. In solving the immediate problems, the practical philosopher often does not sufficiently take the long-term consequences of their decisions into account. Teal'c's very presence in the SGC is a perfect example of a lack of long-term foresight. In the critical decision to help O'Neill, SG-1 and the captive human prisoners escape from the slaughter ordered by Apophis, Teal'c did not foresee the consequences of his actions beyond, of course, the bleak prospects for his career as First Prime of Apophis. O'Neill had to all but carry him bodily back to the Stargate. Teal'c had not considered his long-term options, the potential consequences to his wife and child or the broader implications of his actions for the Jaffa as a whole.

Other practical philosophers in the series include Master Bra'tac (naturally), the renegade Asgard Loki and the offworld inventor Ma'chello.

THE KNIGHT

The last form of intellect portrayed within the members of SG-1 differs significantly from the previous three. While eggheads, empaths and practical philosophers engage their minds to determine *how* to accomplish a specific goal, the knight's focus is more upon determining *why* (or even *if*) to accomplish it. The knight faces the daunting task of assimilating his options and actions and weighing them against a code of morality from which he refuses to deviate. This sense of moral caution, this quality of honor, is what sets a knight apart from the others, and is a form of intellect every bit as significant as the other three. Within the framework of *SG-1*, Col. Jack O'Neill is the embodiment of the knight mentality.

The code of honor Jack pursues bears little resemblance to what one traditionally associates with the word—duels of honor, the field of honor, the loss of honor, et cetera. Instead, Jack's principles are grounded in a military officer's mentality—lead from the front, stay loyal to your friends, do what you say you will and never, ever leave anyone behind.

Jack's sense of honor has compelled him to make more than a few seemingly rash decisions—many of which have paid off in the long run. Going to the assistance of the Asgard when besieged by the Replicators offered less than sanguine chances of survival, but O'Neill refused to abandon the allies who had helped the SGC so often before. In a similar fashion, he has gone to the aid of the Tollans despite their best efforts to prevent him, sacrificed his very life in an alternate future in order to prevent the sterilization of the human race and generally laid his own butt on the line whenever his sense of honor compelled him to do so.

As a result, O'Neill and the SGC have built a formidable network of allies, based in large part upon the actions of the team led by O'Neill. O'Neill's sense of honor and loyalty have repeatedly impressed and benefited other societies, who have repaid his assistance in turn. Most notable of these allies are of course the Asgard, but many other societies, while not as advanced as the Asgard, have staunchly offered whatever support they are able to give. This network of allies is almost entirely the result of SG-1 dealing with them within the framework of honor and sincerity captained by O'Neill.

The pitfalls of the knight intellect are myriad. Failing to measure up to one's own code of honor can be a wrenching experience. Similarly, the extra burden of responsibility in making choices that will effect others can weigh very heavily on the knight's mind, and it is far too easy for the knight to accept too much personal responsibility for grievous outcomes as a result of his decisions. Finally, the knight's sense of honor can sometimes be pitted against his own best interests or the best interests of others, given an opponent heartless enough to manipulate the situation.

Besides O'Neill, other knight intellects in the series include the ascended being Oma Desala, the Goa'uld Lord Yu, General Hammond and Thor of the Asgard.

OUT OF MANY, ONE

Hey look, four neat pigeonholes!

Does this mean that any given character in SG-1 possesses only one form of intellect? No, naturally not. Dr. Jackson clearly has a strongly defined set of principles, for example, and Carter is certainly not incapable of getting her hands dirty to apply a practical intellect to a problem at hand. Colonel O'Neill is obviously capable of performing calculus when necessar . . . .

Hmm. Okay, bad example.

The point is that *Stargate SG-1* presents each varying form of intellect as one that has its own merits and flaws; no single one of them grossly surpasses the others. In fact, each form must have the others to balance out its own weaknesses, and though tensions and frictions often arise because of their differences, in the final analysis their differences make the whole team stronger, more dynamic and more capable than any member would be alone.

Book learning simply isn't enough. Neither is intuition, or practical experience.

Honor alone will accomplish little. If it hopes to prevail, knight intellect must take the foremost role in leading, balancing and supporting the others. Honor is what separates Major Carter from Nirrti. A sense of personal conscience is what makes the difference between

Dr. Jackson and the emotionally manipulative Hathor. That personal sense of morality is what makes the difference between Teal'c and the stereotypical Goa'uld-loyal Jaffa. Honor itself needs contact and interaction with the other forms of intellect to remain true to its own. The knight who refuses to stand beside others becomes a dark reflection of the ideal, like the merciless, vicious, but ultimately honest and honorable Goa'uld Yu.

In the final analysis, that is one of the core values of *Stargate SG-1*: People need one another. The universe is an enormous, dangerous, wonderful and terrifying place, and no one can handle it all by themselves, regardless of how intelligent they may be, what kind of gadgets they own or where their talents might lie. This fundamental acknowledgment of our inherent flaws, the strength of united purpose and mankind's relative insignificance sets the series apart from more Utopian models of science fiction and creates a far more passionate, dynamic and engaging story universe.

Now if you'll excuse me, I have to get some chores out of the way. I want to make sure that my schedule is clear for this week's episode.

Jim Butcher is a martial arts enthusiast with fifteen years of experience in various styles, including Ryukyu Kempo, Tae Kwan Do, Gojo Shorei Ryu and a sprinkling of Kung Fu. He enjoys fencing, singing, bad science fiction movies and live-action gaming. He is the author of the Dresden Files series, which includes Storm Front, Fool Moon, Grave Peril, Summer Knight, Death Masks *and* Blood Rites, *and the forthcoming Codex Alera series, the first of which,* Furies of Calderon, *will be released in hardcover in late 2004. He lives in Missouri with his wife, son and a vicious guard dog.*

Fran Terry, M.D.

HELP! THE ALIENS HAVE LANDED AND TAKEN OVER MY BRAIN

Parasitology and the Goa'uld

ALIEN MIND CONTROL is a familiar theme in science fiction. Its popularity may be because mind control—and its attendant loss of autonomy, free will and self-determination—is truly terrifying to humans. Exploring the conflicts between the controlling alien and controlled human makes for good drama and interesting fiction. In real-life situations, mind control (brainwashing, etc.) has application as a tactical and terror weapon. The concept of mind control creates a reaction—in both observers and victims—that is strong, visceral and disorienting.

In science fiction, alien mind control usually occurs by one of three routes: 1) an alien "chip" directly implanted into the human brain; 2) total takeover of the human body and mind, sometimes leaving the exterior intact and recognizable as human, other times drastically changing the outward appearance; or 3) invasion by some parasite that attaches to or overwhelmingly influences the brain and takes over the human's thoughts and actions.

For *Farscape*'s John Crichton and *Earth: Final Conflict*'s Boone and Sandoval, the alien is an implant surgically embedded into the brain. John Crichton cruised the galaxy always dogged by Scorpius's implant; thought signals from the chip would invariably come to the forefront at the most inopportune times. Those images were usually some combination of repressed memories of torture in the Aurora chair, fragments of events from his teen and young adult years on Earth and a cartoon-ish manifestation of Scorpius himself in some bizarre costume (loud Hawaiian shirt, "Harvey the 6-foot rabbit," etc.). Companion agents in the *E:FC* universe received the CVI—cyberviral implant—to ensure that Companion interests always took precedence . . . although the absolute penetration of that allegiance was always in some question with Boone. Some of his former self-determination seemed to be left intact, even if it did need to remain hidden from the Companions and their other agents.

Men In Black's "bug" terrorized New York "in a brand new Edgar suit" (alien mode of entry into Edgar unspecified; the bug alien did not move among human hosts). The giant slug/squid alien in *The Hidden* entered through the mouth but left the rest of the body (mostly) intact. Both of the melded alien-inside human creatures looked somewhat like the original human, but certainly didn't act like him/her.

Parasites, often portrayed as really hideous worm or insect-like creatures, enter the body in various ways. In *Star Trek: The Wrath of Khan*, a hard-shelled worm making loud chewing noises bored through the ear into the brain. In *Babylon 5*'s episode "Grail," a lobster-like crustacean attached to the back and sank through the skin to bond with the spine (and presumably with the spinal cord and brain). In *Stargate*, the larval Goa'uld occupy a pouch in the host humanoid's abdomen, and from there supplant the host's immune system. The host will die if the larva is removed; thus the parasite "persuades" the host to leave it in place. Mature adult Goa'uld leave the larval host's abdominal pouch and enter their new host through the anterior (front) neck or base of the skull, leaving a non-healing wound or obvious scar, to wrap around the spine and attach to/control the brain. In most cases, the story either implies or explicitly states that attempts to remove the parasite will result in the host's certain death. In all cases, regardless of the specific form or mechanism of control or the route of entry/take-over, the alien controls the host's thoughts and actions, and there are usually obvious external signs of infestation.

Science fiction parasites are sometimes known as "symbiots." True parasites—such as any intestinal worm—live by obtaining all nourishment from their host, usually at some cost to the host's health. Infection may eventually lead to the host's death, as well as the death of the parasite, unless it moves on to another host. Symbiots (also spelled "symbiote" and "symbiont") by definition have a mutually beneficial relationship with the host; the presence of each provides nourishment or protection for the other. Certain bacteria in the human gut are considered symbiotic—they derive nutrients from the host human's diet and help digest that food into forms usable by the human. Their absence—usually after high doses of broad-spectrum antibiotics—can lead to short-term malnutrition until enough of them re-colonize the gut to resume proper digestion. Commensals have a variant symbiotic relationship in which one entity benefits from the other's presence, but second entity is unaffected. Remoras, for instance, attach to sharks. The sharks provide transportation and the remoras eat "leftovers" when the sharks are finished feeding. It is not clear that the shark benefits from this relationship, but it is apparently not harmed by it.

It is arguable whether the Goa'uld are symbiots as they claim. Forcible take-over, host enslavement for the alien cause and certain host death if the larva or adult are removed hardly describes a "mutually beneficial" relationship. *Star Trek's* Trill species and the Tok'ra in *Stargate SG-1* have a more symbiotic relationship with their hosts than the Goa'uld do. Even though the Goa'uld and Tok'ra are the same species, the Tok'ra creature enters the host's body via the mouth, leaving no external scar. The joining is done when the host is near death, with the joined pair then living a long, healthy and productive life together. Although it certainly would be an advantage for the Tok'ra to enter a healthy host, one not in dire need of immediate repair, the story line never shows a Tok'ra symbiot forcibly invading an unwilling human host. Dramatically, this provides a distinct difference between the Tok'ra and Goa'uld, showing that some members of the symbiot species can be cooperative and beneficial, while others apparently choose to be quite evil.

Real parasitic infections are well known in human and animal medicine. A variety of parasites, plus assorted other infectious agents like bacteria, viruses, protozoa and abnormal proteins known as prions, can infect the human brain. However, none are known to turn an otherwise law-abiding human into a rampaging killer with primary allegiance to the invading agent, bent on the destruction or control of the host's native race. In fact, most humans with advanced brain infections/infestations (e.g., encephalitis, cerebritis, meningitis), abscesses or tumors are generally too sick to move, eat or talk. They certainly cannot travel the galaxy, wielding deadly weapons and terminally bad attitudes.

The human brain has a number of defense mechanisms that protect against infection/invasion, but these are not totally impenetrable. Specific human brain defenses include specialized cells that wrap around blood vessels within the brain, forming the "blood-brain barrier." This prevents some drugs and other foreign materials in the blood stream from affecting brain cells. The brain's immune system acts to inactivate, destroy, scavenge or wall-off any invading organisms. At best, any real chemical, biological or mechanical invasion of the brain produces thought and behavior changes that would make the victim less efficient as a fighting machine, rather than create a fighter totally committed to the alien cause. At worst, brain infection is fatal. Alcohol induces poor judgment and sloppy muscle control, nerve gas paralyzes and parasites/viruses/bacteria/protozoa in the brain cause delirium and death.

Drugs like cocaine and PCP (phencyclidine) alter perception and can transiently increase strength and reduce inhibitions to violence. Long-term use causes chemical changes in the brain that can lead to paranoia and psychosis. While users may briefly feel and act stronger and commit horrific acts of violence, over the long term these users do not become effective soldiers who are good at following orders.

Biologically, a really efficient alien bent on converting humans into servant soldiers via brain invasion would have to get past all of these mechanical and biochemical immune defense mechanisms to then supercharge those affected/infected, rather than inducing the usual "shut down and repair" sick mode. Sick humans are completely useless as a fighting force. Aliens intent only on subjugation, annihilation and planetary acquisition may have an easier time achieving that goal—massive numbers of sick or injured humans can't put up much resistance. This is one basis for biological warfare.

The Goa'uld, as portrayed, are very effective as parasites from a biological and medical standpoint. The larvae are implanted into Jaffa starting at the age of eight years. Early adolescent Jaffa hosts have already survived childhood illnesses and accidents, and have a good chance of survival into adulthood.

By supplanting the Jaffa immune system, Goa'uld ensure both their own and their host's growth and survival—presumably no Jaffa would want to kill himself by killing or removing his Goa'uld larvae, and death of the Jaffa host does not ensure death of the larva if a new host can be located promptly. Psychologically, some races can justify self-sacrifice for a "good" cause, but few (perhaps none?) will pursue suicide if obviously futile.

While it's shown that only one larva can inhabit a Jaffa host's pouch and only one adult Goa'uld lives in a given host, are there ever situations in which two Goa'uld might briefly need to share a host? Might there be a combat situation in which the Jaffa, despite the larva's strengthening effect, suffers a fatal traumatic injury and the now host-less larva needs a temporary home until a new Jaffa becomes available? Larva are shown as living in jars full of liquid (presumably nutrient media) prior to implantation, but there may be times when those are not immediately available, and it is not clear that a larva—once implanted into a Jaffa—can survive being put back into the jar again. Would two larvae tolerate each other for the overall benefit of their race? This assumes that survival of each individual larva is important to the Goa'uld race as a whole. Or would they battle it out (inside the pouch) for "survival of the fittest"? What would the Jaffa host feel if there were two larvae in the pouch instead of one, especially if they're fighting for their lives Goa'uld-style . . . ? Ouch! What would be the biological effects of two larvae in the same pouch— a temporarily supercharged host immune system, extreme weakness due to competing larvae or a roller coaster of raging hormones? Only the Goa'uld know for sure, and they're certainly not inclined to share that information.

Several episodes of *Star Trek: The Next Generation* and *Star Trek: Deep Space Nine* dealt with displaced Trill hosts. In each case, only one symbiot can inhabit a host at a time, and a symbiot can temporarily survive within a host of a different species than the preferred or "usual" host. This comes at some cost to the new host's health. If the Goa'uld follow this model, the larva from a mortally wounded Jaffa would likely seek out the nearest warm body, regardless of genetic or species-specific compatibility. Recall that Major Kawalsky was infected this way.

Biologically, becoming the host's immune system ensures the invader's survival and eliminates any chance of rejection or inducing illness/weakness in an otherwise strong and useful host. Presence of the larva is portrayed as making the host stronger and more resilient, which has some physical advantages for both the host and larva.

Adult Goa'uld are at least equally resilient and resistant to outside intervention, though they may be killed if the host is killed and if a new host—or sarcophagus for the injured old one—is not found within a critical time frame.

Attaching to the host's brain makes controlling the host's thoughts and actions apparently easy (from a story line standpoint), and makes host death believable if removal is attempted. Brain surgery is a tremendously frightening concept and is the only apparent way that an adult Goa'uld may be removed. Host death following some surgical complication during craniotomy (opening the skull) is also mostly believable. Treatments such as high-dose radiation or some sort of anti-Goa'uld super-antibiotic or other biology-based therapy weren't discussed or shown. However, none of those treatments is without obvious potential harm to the host as well.

Goa'uld act to preserve themselves at all costs. A species who function by taking over the bodies, immune systems and minds of their hosts would have little or no ethical difficulty killing that host if the situation became a matter of "me or him." In that context, it is entirely believable that a threatened Goa'uld would sacrifice the host and move on, rather than try to preserve both itself and the host. In the case of Major Kawalsky's post-operative death, it is interesting that the Goa'uld appeared to slither away rather than immediately leap into the nearest member of the medical care team. As a physician, I prefer to consider this an inconsistency in Goa'uld behavior, rather than an alien commentary on the relative value of human medical personnel as potential Goa'uld hosts. However, if the creature considers me unsuitable for invasion, that's not entirely bad.

Goa'uld live in multiple hosts during their life cycle. Goa'uld larva are produced when a Goa'uld queen mates either with another (male) Goa'uld, or with a male of the target species (although Goa'uld *hosts* are forbidden from mating with each other). Some sources state that larvae are birthed from asexual mothers, but Hathor is decidedly female and seduces a male human to produce larvae capable of infecting other humans. This indicates that Goa'uld may be more efficient at infecting a population if they share some of the same DNA. However, they are still apparently capable of taking hosts by force even if there is no common genetic material.

The Goa'uld themselves have sex-specific features, such as the female's large dorsal fin, and appear to prefer—though not require—hosts of the same gender. Larval Goa'uld grow and mature in one host (Jaffa or other target species), then transfer to another host to live out their adult lives.

Many parasites that commonly affect humans also have a multi-host life cycle. These parasites spend part of their life cycle in an insect (as with malaria), or in another animal (as with hookworms or roundworms). The immature form develops in the insect or other animal, then is either directly injected into the human, or is deposited into an environment where humans come into contact with it and are then infected.

Parasites may enter the human body through intact skin via a bite from an insect, through non-intact skin or breaks in mucus membranes, or by ingestion of food contaminated with infective larvae or parasite eggs (parasites develop in the gut then spread into muscle, or travel through bloodstream or via nerves to other tissues). In all cases, infection is not immediately apparent and insect-generated pheromones do not immediately lull the victim into an immobile trance, in which the victim does not struggle against further invasion. There is no "X" marking a repugnant nutrient slime-lined pouch in the abdomen, no non-healing wound at the front of the neck and no distinct scar at the base of the skull or other point of entry. Entering undetected gives the parasite a chance to grow and multiply before producing obvious signs of infection that could lead to discovery. Obvious clinical illness leads the host to seek medical treatment, which may then kill the invading parasite.

Could a species like the Goa'uld really infect humans, turning them into slaves for the Goa'uld cause? What would it take for a parasite (ahem . . . symbiot), to infect a human, then induce the desired behavior change?

In Hathor's meeting with O'Neill, and most every other male on the base, all of the strict military discipline and trained (male) reasoning minds are no match for a waft of alien feminine pheromones. (Apparently, estrogen provides some resistance to this effect since every female on base can immediately determine the presence and cause of the males' behavior changes and understand how to use that to their advantage to regain control of the base.) Once past the emotional resistance the parasite would encounter, possibly by a similar use of pheremones, it would then have to subdue or evade the host human's immune system. The Goa'uld parasite invades, then simply eliminates, and later replaces, the host's entire immune system. There is no known human parasite that attracts or invades in this way. Some insect parasite vectors (insects that carry infective viruses, bacteria, etc) may use pheromones to seduce others of their own species (usually for reproduction), but none exude a chemical that humans find irresistibly attractive. *All* parasites that infect humans evoke some sort of immune response—fever, open skin lesions at the site of entry, vomiting or diarrhea, delirium or behavior changes— depending upon route/site of entry and which organ(s) the parasite infects.

For the Goa'uld to survive in a human and replace its host's immune system, there would need to be some physiological/biochemical connection between the Goa'uld larva in its pouch and the host's blood stream. The humanoid immune system is predominantly located in the blood stream (also in the bone marrow and in other organs directly connected to the blood stream). "Replacing the immune system" is akin to a whole-body transfusion or a massive dose of whole-body radiation. Therefore, the larva cannot simply be walled-off and isolated inside the host's abdominal pouch, but must have some biochemical connection to the rest of the host's body via the blood stream, even if the larval form of the parasite does not otherwise "communicate" with its host.

The only known structure that allows such a connection between an otherwise self-contained resident creature and its surrounding host is the placenta in a pregnant female mammal. Some biochemical compounds cross the placenta; whole cells generally do not. The specific logistics of replacing a host human's entire immune system— cells, antibodies and other immune system organs—would be incredibly complex, boring in the real biochemical details and thus left to the sweeping imagination of the science fiction viewer.

Adult Goa'uld, in attaching to the brain and spinal cord, must also evade or replace the host's immune system. In humans, any foreign body in the nervous system provokes a significant immune response—including fever, pain and behavior changes. Foreign bodies always enter the human brain via a traumatic injury—stab wound, gunshot, blow to the head, motor vehicle accident, etc. Entry of an adult Goa'uld is portrayed as equally traumatic, leaving an open wound or obvious unique scar and causing some pain and deformity of the neck while the entry and transit are in progress.

Following a traumatic brain injury, humans may demonstrate violent outbursts and aggression. Behavior after the brain injury varies, depending upon which parts of the brain are affected. However, there are no known cases (at least not yet!) in which the victim instantly gained knowledge of alien weaponry or strategy, suddenly demonstrated the motor skills to aim a weapon or developed an immediate, total and unwavering allegiance to the source of the assault.

Adult Goa'uld conveniently enter their host close to the site of their final "working" location. To get from the front of the neck to the rear base of the skull requires tunneling through an area loaded with vital nerves, blood vessels, respiratory structures, muscles and bones. Disruption of any of these can mean sudden death for the host, although the Goa'uld evidently know this and know how to transit without killing the new host . . . or at least know how to immediately repair any damage. Although dangerous, entry near the brain is likely the most efficient means for the Goa'uld to achieve dominance over the host.

A brief review of host human anatomy: the trachea and esophagus, connecting the mouth to the lungs in the chest and stomach in the abdomen, respectively, are in the front of the neck. The trachea lies directly in front of the esophagus, and both start behind the base of the tongue. The thyroid lies just above the Goa'uld's site of anterior (front) neck entry; the gland should be left intact if the host is to remain in the best possible physical condition. Of course, any parasite that can replace a host's immune system probably would have little difficulty providing total replacement for thyroid gland function as well. Major blood vessels between the heart and the brain (carotid arteries and jugular veins) course vertically through the neck. Two major nerves from the brain to the tongue (cranial nerve XII) and to the heart and stomach (cranial nerve X, or vagus nerve) follow these vertical blood vessels closely. Nerves from the spinal cord into the arms (brachial plexus) are on both sides of the neck, and spread through the lateral (side) neck muscles in a complex fan pattern.

Surprisingly, human anatomy does provide a path of travel from the front of the neck to the back of the skull. All of the human neck structures are arranged in layers separated by sheets of tough connective tissue called fascia (pronounced *faa' sha*). Spaces between bundles of muscles, blood vessels or nerves are lined with fascia on both sides and are called fascial planes. Dissecting through these fascial planes is traveling the path of least resistance.

It is possible to move between the anterior neck and the base of the skull solely by traveling within fascial planes; this can be done without disrupting any of the vital neck structures, but will result in obvious visible deformity of the neck while the parasite is moving. Again, there is no known real parasite that operates exactly like this. There are parasites that enter through a cut or other break in the skin in one part of the body, then travel to and reside in another area, and some leave obvious tracks or traces in the skin as they go, but none are known to enter the neck and then attach to the brain or spine.

Once at the base of the skull, there is easy access to the brain and spinal cord. At the base of the skull is an opening called the foramen magnum (literally, "big opening"). The bottom of the brain connects to and becomes the spinal cord. The spinal cord exits the skull and enters the spinal canal in the bones of the neck (cervical vertebrae) through the foramen magnum. The bottom of the skull bones (base of the skull) rests on the first neck bone (first cervical, or 'Atlas' vertebrae). A small but flexible space between the two bones can be exploited by mercenaries, executioners and parasites, er . . . symbiots. There are also spaces between the posterior (back) portions of the neck bones (cervical vertebrae). This is where the nerves exit from the spinal cord to go to the muscles in the neck, shoulders and arms. Again, a creative parasite/symbiot could use these spaces as relatively unobstructed entry points.

The brain is encased within the bones of the skull and the spinal cord is contained within the bones of the cervical (neck), thoracic (truck) and lumbar (low back) spine. Both the brain and spinal cord are covered by three layers of protective tissue called meninges (pronounced *men in' geez*). The dura is the most exterior and toughest of the three, the arachnoid is the middle layer and the pia is the innermost, directly attached to the brain and spinal cord. There are thin spaces between all three and there is a layer of fluid circulating in the space between the arachnoid and pia.

To reach brain cells, any projection from the parasite would most likely enter through the foramen magnum or through a space between two of the cervical vertebrae. Color-enhanced MRI (magnetic resonance images) of the adult Goa'uld living within Major Kawalsky showed the body of the parasite/symbiot located outside the posterior skull and upper cervical spine. Some tentacle or other projection must actually get inside the skull and contact or penetrate the brain to exert its mind-controlling effects. That tentacle would then have to pass through the three layers of meninges to get to the brain. The surface of a live human brain is solid, but very soft. It would offer no mechanical resistance to a Goa'uld.

Controlling the host's muscle motion is simply a matter of activating the correct spot on the motor cortex of the brain or stimulating the correct nerve from the spinal cord to send a chemical/electrical impulse into the muscle to make it move. The physiology of human nerve conduction and muscle motion is fairly well understood and is a cascade of ion channels responding to chemical concentrations in the surrounding tissue fluid. The presence of various chemical ions (sodium, potassium, calcium, etc.) creates an electrical charge. Coordinating complex motions requires synchronized impulses, something that a normal human learns and generally performs without specific conscious thought or direction. Research has shown that electrodes implanted in the muscles of someone with a spinal cord or nerve injury can help them walk or move again. *Stargate's* writers hope that the viewers believe that a complex and diabolical race like the Goa'uld could also master similar control.

Making the host's eyes glow, particularly when the resident Goa'uld is annoyed or aroused, is an effect unique to the Goa'uld parasite. There is no known agent or parasite that causes a similar glowing effect in humans or animals. Fatigue, drug use and irritation of the eye cause a "bloodshot" appearance of the schlera (pronounced *sklair' a*), the white part of the eye. Liver or gallbladder disease can make the same area appear almost fluorescent yellow, but nothing has been identified yet that can turn a brown or blue iris (the colored portion of the eye) to glowing gold and then back to its original appearance. Apparently the host's vision is not affected during the glow. None of the hosts complain of sudden blindness, which is certainly frightening enough to humans to elicit some remark. Perhaps the symbiot's naquadah can flood the host's circulation (or reach high enough concentrations in the host's head and neck, given the location of the symbiot in/on the brain) to cause a brief flush and glow that promptly dissipates, as it is metabolized to some compound that does not cause any change in the host's outward appearance.

Human thought, memory and motivation are complex biochemical and neurologic/electrical processes that are less well understood than muscle motion or body action. Exactly how an invading alien would take over the host's thought processes is a matter for speculation.

Currently, it is known that sustained physical and emotional stress, including sleep deprivation, hunger, physical illness, threats against self or loved ones, etc., can make a person's thoughts more susceptible to outside influence. Having an alien take up residence just outside one's skull, probing tentacles, secreting foreign chemicals and firing alien electrical impulses into one's brain, and forcing muscle action that the host does not initiate would certainly qualify as "stressful." Under those circumstances, human host thought processes, beliefs and motivations might be more likely to fall under the influence of the resident alien consciousness. The creature could make the host do something it otherwise would not consider or desire. Specifics of the mechanics or biochemistry of this kind of mind control is obviously not yet known with certainty. Leaving the matter open for interpretation by the viewer's imagination probably produces more vivid and frightening images than if the precise mechanism of this mind control were presented in detail.

As stated previously, any agent known to infect or infest the mammal (human or animal) brain or spinal cord causes a noticeable inflammatory/immune reaction, behavior changes and usually symptoms severe enough to incapacitate the "host." That host may present an infectious threat to others close by but, with rare exception (such as rabies or heavy metal poisoning causing psychosis), it is usually not a physically violent threat. Fortunately, there is no agent or parasite yet known that invades, energizes, strengthens and then turns the host into an efficient, effective and totally obedient fighting machine.

The Goa'uld race, as portrayed through the feature film and television episodes of *Stargate*, are a formidable adversary—terrifying, merciless and ruthless. They attack humanoids at a most fundamental level, taking control of their thoughts and actions and depriving them of even basic self-determination. According to some references, the Goa'uld take over the mind and body, but leave the hosts aware that, while their thoughts and actions are not their own, they are powerless to do anything about it. The species is written with an element of medical plausibility, so that viewers cannot automatically dismiss it as "fluff," unworthy of further attention.

Our limited forays into the galaxy so far have not identified any race or creature as threatening as the Goa'uld. However, science fiction fans are always open to the possibility of believing, even if we hope this particular threat couldn't really exist.

Say . . . how long have you had that scar on your neck . . . ?

BIBLIOGRAPHY

Babylon 5. Babylonian Productions. www.babylon5.com

Earth: Final Conflict. Gene Roddenberry Productions. www.efc.com

Farscape. Jim Henson Productions. www.farscape.com

The Goa'uld Homeworld. www.systemlords.hypermart.net

Guyton AC, Hall JE. *Textbook of Medical Physiology*, WB Saunders, Tenth Edition, August 2002.

The Hidden. New Line Cinema 1987.

Langman J, Woerdeman MW. *Atlas of Medical Anatomy*, The Saunders Press, 1982.

Men In Black. Columbia Pictures, Amblin Entertainment 2000.

Netter FH, Hansen JT. *Atlas of Human Anatomy*, Novartis Medical Education, Third Edition, January 2003.

Roitt IM, Brostoff J, Male DK. *Immunology*, Gower Medical Pub, C V Mosby, 1985.

Roitt IM, Delves PJ. *Roitt's Essential Immunology*, Blackwell Science Inc., Tenth Edition, August 2001.

Sci-Fi Channel. www.scifi.com

Stargate SG-1. www.stargate-sgl.com

The Stargate Omnipedia. www.gateworld.net/omnipedia

Star Trek: The Next Generation and *Star Trek: Deep Space Nine*. www.startrek.com

Francine Terry, MD, MPH, is a lifelong science fiction reader, more recently a writer on topics bridging science fact and fiction and a speaker on hard science topics at many science fiction gatherings. In the "real world," she works as an emergency physician in Cleveland, Ohio, operates a small farm with her husband Steve Brownfield and is the founder and chief operating officer of an animal welfare non-profit, AlterPet Inc. Her science writings have appeared in science fiction publications in both Ohio and Colorado and in national publications such as the Starfleet Communiqué *and the* UFPI Universal Translator. *She and Dr. Howard Scrimgeour, DVM, comprise the "Paradox (pair of docs) Traveling Science Show," frequently seen presenting biological topics to science fiction fans at Marcon and Toronto Trek. In her spare time, she reads scientific journals, seeking fact-out-of-fiction discoveries to share with fellow fans.*

Dr. John Gribbin

TIME TRAVEL FOR BEGINNERS

Since time travel and wormhole travel play such an important role in Stargate SG-1, *we thought we'd ask an expert about exactly how all that works in real-world terms: what are the chances that practical time travel could actually exist? Dr. John Gribbin, Visiting Fellow in Astronomy at the University of Sussex, and author of* Companion to the Cosmos, *takes a stab at making it all understandable—and fun—for those of us who (like Col. Jack O'Neill) might need it explained in beginner's terms.*

"Look, I know I should know this by now. I swear it'll be the last time I ask. But these wormholes we go through, they're not always there, right?"

—Col. Jack O'Neill, "A Matter of Time"

A LMOST EXACTLY ONE HUNDRED YEARS AGO, in 1905, Albert Einstein published his special theory of relativity. It was Einstein, as every schoolchild knows, who first described time as "the fourth dimension"—and every schoolchild is wrong. It was actually H. G. Wells who wrote, in his classic novel *The Time Machine*, that, "there is no difference between Time and any of the three dimensions of Space, except that our consciousness moves along it." H. G. Wells' story was first published in book form in 1895. That was the minus tenth anniversary of the first publication, in 1905, of Albert Einstein's special theory of relativity.

Since the time of Wells and Einstein, there has been a continuing literary fascination with time travel and especially with the paradoxes that seem to confront any genuine time traveler (something that Wells neglected to investigate). The classic example is the so-called "granny paradox," where a time traveler inadvertently causes the death of his granny when she was a small girl, so that the traveler's mother, and therefore the traveler himself, were never born. In which case, he did not go back in time to kill granny . . . and so on.

A less gruesome example was entertainingly provided by the science fiction writer Robert Heinlein in his story "By His Bootstraps" (available in several Heinlein anthologies). The protagonist in the story stumbles on a time travel device brought to the present by a visitor from the far future. He steals it and sets up home in a deserted stretch of time, constantly worrying about being found by the old man he stole the time machine from—until one day, many years later, he realizes that he is now the old man, and carefully arranges for his younger self to "find" and "steal" the time machine. Such a narcissistic view of time travel is taken to its logical extreme in David Gerrold's *The Man Who Folded Himself* (Random House, 1973; BenBella Books, 2003).

Few of the writers of *Dr Who* have had the imagination to actually use his time machine in this kind of way. It would, after all, make for rather dull viewing if every time the Doctor had been confronted by a disaster he popped into the TARDIS, went back in time and warned his earlier self to steer clear of the looming trouble. But the implications were thoroughly explored for a wide audience in the *Back to the Future* trilogy, ramming home the point that time travel runs completely counter to common sense. Obviously, time travel must be impossible. Only common sense is about as reliable a guide to science as the well known "fact" that Einstein came up with the idea of time as the fourth dimension. Sticking with Einstein's own theories, it is hardly common sense that objects get both heavier and shorter the faster they move, or that moving clocks run slow. Yet all of these predictions of relativity theory have been borne out many times in experiments, to an impressive number of decimal places. And when you look closely at the general theory of relativity, the best theory of time and space we have, it turns out that there is nothing in it to forbid time travel. The theory implies that time travel may be very difficult, to be sure, but it's not impossible.

> "Do we really think anyone's going to believe that woman if she goes around blabbing about a 'Stargate?' I mean, I have a hard enough time believing that woman down on 73rd who walks around talking about these little devil people who live in her hair. Even though she could use a little conditioner."
>
> –Col. Jack O'Neill, "Hathor"

Perhaps inevitably, it was through science fiction that serious scientists finally convinced themselves that time travel could be made to work, at least by a sufficiently advanced civilization. It happened like this: Carl Sagan, a well-known astronomer, had written a novel in which he used the device of travel through a black hole to allow his characters to travel from a point near the Earth to a point near the star Vega. Although he was aware that he was bending the accepted rules of physics, this was, after all, a novel. Nevertheless, as a scientist himself Sagan wanted the science in his story to be as accurate as possible, so he asked Kip Thorne, an established expert in gravitational theory, to check it out and advise him on how it might be tweaked up. After looking closely at the non-commonsensical equations, Thorne realized that such a wormhole through spacetime actually could exist as a stable entity within the framework of Einstein's theory.

Sagan gratefully accepted Thorne's modification to his fictional "star gate," and the wormhole featured in the novel, *Contact*, published in 1985. But this was still only presented as a shortcut through space. Neither Sagan nor Thorne realized at first that what they had described would also work as a shortcut through time. Thorne seems never to have given any thought to the time travel possibilities opened up by wormholes until, in December 1986, he went with his student Mike Morris to a symposium in Chicago, where one of the other participants casually pointed out to Morris that a wormhole could also be used to travel backwards in time. Thorne tells the story of what happened then in his own book, *Black Holes and Time Warps* (Picador). The key point is that space and time are treated on an essentially equal footing by Einstein's equations—just as Wells anticipated.

So a wormhole that takes a shortcut through spacetime can just as well link two different times as two different places. Indeed, any naturally occurring wormhole would most probably link two different times. As word spread, other physicists who were interested in the exotic implications of pushing Einstein's equations to extremes were encouraged to go public with their own ideas once Thorne was seen to endorse the investigation of time travel, and the work led to the growth of a cottage industry of time travel investigations at the end of the 1980s, and continued into the 1990s. The bottom line of all this work is that while it is hard to see how any civilization could build a wormhole time machine from scratch, it is much easier to envisage that a naturally occurring wormhole might be adapted to suit the time traveling needs of a sufficiently advanced civilization. "Sufficiently advanced," that is, to be able to travel through space by conventional means, locate black holes and manipulate them with as much ease as we manipulate the fabric of the Earth itself in projects like the Channel Tunnel.

> "I'm obviously no scientist, but, ah . . . couldn't we use
> that Ben Franklin thing?"
> –Col. Jack O'Neill, "The Torment of Tantalus"

There is still one problem with wormholes for any hyperspace engineers to take careful account of. The simplest calculations suggest that whatever may be going on in the universe outside, the attempted passage of a spaceship through the hole ought to make the star gate slam shut. The problem is that an accelerating object, according to the general theory of relativity, generates those ripples in the fabric of spacetime itself known as gravitational waves. Gravitational radiation, traveling ahead of the spaceship and into the black hole at the speed of light, could be amplified to infinite energy as it approaches the singularity inside the black hole, wrapping spacetime around itself and shutting the door on the advancing spaceship. Even if a natural traversable wormhole exists, it seems to be unstable to the slightest perturbation, including the disturbance caused by any attempt to pass through it.

But Thorne's team found an answer to that for Sagan. After all, the wormholes in *Contact* are definitely not natural, they are engineered. One of his characters explains:

> There is an interior tunnel in the exact Kerr solution of the Einstein Field Equations, but it's unstable. The slightest perturbation would seal it off and convert the tunnel into a physical singularity through which nothing can pass. I have tried to imagine a superior civilization that would control the internal structure of a collapsing star to keep the interior tunnel stable. This is very difficult. The civilization would have to monitor and stabilize the tunnel forever.

But the point is that the trick, although it may be very difficult, is not impossible. It could operate by a process known as negative feedback, in which any disturbance in the spacetime structure of the wormhole creates another disturbance, which cancels out the first disturbance. This is the opposite of the familiar positive feedback effect, which leads to a howl from loudspeakers if a microphone that is plugged in to those speakers through an amplifier is placed in front of them. In that case, the noise from the speakers goes into the microphone, gets amplified, comes out of the speakers louder than it was before, gets amplified . . . and so on. Imagine, instead, that the noise coming out of the speakers and into the microphone is analyzed by a computer, which then produces a sound wave with exactly the opposite characteristics from a second speaker. The two waves would cancel out, producing total silence.

For simple sound waves, this trick can actually be carried out here on Earth; you can even buy headphones that cancel out the noise from jet engines, to the benefit of long-haul fliers. So it may not be completely farfetched to imagine Sagan's "superior civilization" building a gravitational wave receiver/transmitter system that sits in the throat of a wormhole and can record the disturbances caused by the spaceship's passage through the wormhole, "playing back" a set of gravitational waves that will exactly cancel out the disturbance before it can destroy the tunnel.

But where do the wormholes come from in the first place? The way Morris, Yurtsever and Thorne set about solving the problem posed by Sagan was the opposite of the way everyone before them had thought about black holes. Instead of considering some sort of known object in the Universe, like a dead massive star or a quasar, and trying to work out what would happen to it, they started out by constructing the mathematical description of a geometry that described a traversable wormhole, and then used the equations of the general theory of relativity to work out what kinds of matter and energy would be associated with such a spacetime. What they found is almost (with hindsight) common sense. Gravity, an attractive force pulling matter together, tends to create singularities and to pinch off the throat of a wormhole. The equations said that in order for an artificial wormhole to be held open, its throat must be threaded by some form of matter, or some form of field, that exerts negative pressure, and is associated with antigravity.

Now, you might think, remembering your school physics, that this completely rules out the possibility of constructing traversable wormholes. Negative pressure is not something we encounter in everyday life (imagine blowing negative pressure stuff into a balloon and seeing the balloon deflate as a result). Surely exotic matter cannot exist in the real universe? But you may be wrong.

The key to antigravity was found by a Dutch physicist, Hendrik Casimir, as long ago as 1948. Casimir, who was born in The Hague in 1909, worked from 1942 onwards in the research laboratories of the electrical giant Philips, and it was while working there that he suggested what became known as the Casimir effect. The simplest way to understand the Casimir effect is in terms of two parallel metal plates, placed very close together with nothing in between them. The quantum vacuum is not like the kind of "nothing" physicists imagined the vacuum to be before the quantum era. It seethes with activity, with particle-antiparticle pairs constantly being produced and annihilating one another. Among the particles popping in and out of existence in the quantum vacuum there will be many photons, the particles that carry the electromagnetic force, some of which are the particles of light. Indeed, it is particularly easy for the vacuum to produce virtual photons, partly because a photon is its own antiparticle, and partly because photons have no "rest mass" to worry about, so all the energy that has to be borrowed from quantum uncertainty is the energy of the wave associated with the particular photon. Photons with different energies are associated with electromagnetic waves of different wavelengths, with shorter wavelengths corresponding to greater energy; so another way to think of this electromagnetic aspect of the quantum vacuum is that empty space is filled with an ephemeral sea of electromagnetic waves, with all wavelengths represented.

This irreducible vacuum activity gives the vacuum energy, but this energy is the same everywhere and so cannot be detected or used. Energy can only be used to do work, and thereby make its presence known, if there is a difference in energy from one place to another. Between two electrically conducting plates, Casimir pointed out, electromagnetic waves would only be able to form certain stable patterns. Waves bouncing around between the two plates would behave like the waves on a plucked guitar string. Such a string can only vibrate in certain ways, to make certain notes—ones for which the vibrations of the string fit the length of the string in such a way that there are no vibrations at the fixed ends of the string. The allowed vibrations are the fundamental note for a particular length of string, and its harmonics, or overtones. In the same way, only certain wavelengths of radiation can fit into the gap between the two plates of a Casimir experiment. In particular, no photon corresponding to a wavelength greater than the separation between the plates can fit into the gap. This means that some of the activity of the vacuum is suppressed in the gap between the plates, while the usual activity goes on outside. The result is that in each cubic centimeter of space there are fewer virtual photons bouncing around between the plates than there are outside, and so the plates feel a force pushing them together.

It may sound bizarre, but it is real. Several experiments have been carried out to measure the strength of the Casimir force between two plates, using both flat and curved plates made of various kinds of material. The force has been measured for a range of plate gaps from 1.4 nanometers to 15 nanometers (one nanometer is one billionth of a meter) and exactly matches Casimir's prediction.

In a paper they published in 1987, Morris and Thorne drew attention to such possibilities, and also pointed out that even a straightforward electric or magnetic field threading the wormhole "is right on the borderline of being exotic; if its tension were infinitesimally larger . . . it would satisfy our wormhole-building needs." In the same paper, they concluded that "one should not blithely assume the impossibility of the exotic material that is required for the throat of a traversable wormhole."

The two CalTech researchers make the important point that most physicists suffer a failure of imagination when it comes to considering the equations that describe matter and energy under conditions far more extreme than those we encounter here on Earth. They highlight this by the example of a course for beginners in general relativity, taught at CalTech in the autumn of 1985, after the first phase of work stimulated by Sagan's enquiry, but before any of this was common knowledge, even among relativists. The students involved were not taught anything specific about wormholes, but they were taught to explore the physical meaning of spacetime metrics. In their exam, they were set a question which led them, step by step, through the mathematical description of the metric corresponding to a wormhole. "It was startling," said Morris and Thorne, "to see how hidebound were the students' imaginations. Most could decipher detailed properties of the metric, but very few actually recognized that it represents a traversable wormhole connecting two different universes."

> "Cultures with advanced technology tend not to like to share it."
>
> –Col. Jack O'Neill, "The Nox"

For those with less hidebound imaginations, there are two remaining problems—to find a way to make a wormhole large enough for people (and spaceships) to travel through, and to keep the exotic matter out of contact with any such spacefarers. Any prospect of building such a device is far beyond our present capabilities. But, as Morris and Thorne stress, it is not impossible, and "we correspondingly cannot now rule out traversable wormholes." It seems to me that there's an analogy here that sets the work of such dreamers as Thorne and Visser in a context that is both helpful and intriguing. Almost exactly 500 years ago, Leonardo da Vinci speculated about the possibility of flying machines. He designed both helicopters and aircraft with wings, and modern aeronautical engineers say that aircraft built to his designs probably could have flown if Leonardo had had modern engines with which to power them—even though there was no way in which any engineer of his time could have constructed a powered flying machine capable of carrying a human up into the air.

Leonardo could not even dream about the possibilities of jet engines and routine passenger flights at supersonic speeds. Yet Concorde and the jumbo jets operate on the same basic physical principles as the flying machines he designed. In just half a millennium, all his wildest dreams have not only come true, but have been surpassed. It might take even more than half a millennium for designs for a traversable wormhole to leave the drawing board, but the laws of physics say that it is possible—and, as Sagan speculates, something like it may already have been done by a civilization more advanced than our own.

Physicists have even found the law of nature which prevents time travel paradoxes and thereby permits time travel. It turns out to be the same law that makes sure light travels in straight lines and which underpins the most straightforward version of quantum theory, developed half a century ago by Richard Feynman.

Relativists have been trying to come to terms with time travel ever since Kip Thorne and his colleagues at CalTech discovered— much to their surprise—that there is nothing in the laws of physics (specifically, the general theory of relativity) to forbid it.

The worry for physicists is that this raises the possibility of the paradoxes, familiar to science fiction fans, discussed earlier. The equivalent paradox in the relativists' calculations involves a billiard ball that goes in to one mouth of a wormhole, emerges in the past from the other mouth, and collides with its other self on the way in to the first mouth, so that it is knocked out of the way and never enters the time tunnel at all. But, of course, there are many possible "self consistent" journeys through the tunnel, in which the two versions of the billiard ball never disturb one another.

If time travel really is possible—and after all these years' intensive study all the evidence says that it is—there must, it seems, be a law of nature to prevent such paradoxes arising, while permitting the self-consistent journeys through time. Igor Novikov, who holds joint posts at the P. N. Lebedev Institute in Moscow and at NORDITA (the Nordic Institute for Theoretical Physics) in Copenhagen, first pointed out the need for a "Principle of Self-consistency" of this kind in 1989. Later, working with a large group of colleagues in Denmark, Canada, Russia and Switzerland, he found the physical basis for this principle. It involves something known as the principle of least action (or principle of minimal action), and has been known, in one form or another, since the early seventeenth century. It describes the trajectories of things, such as the path of a light ray from A to B, or the flight of a ball tossed through an upper story window. And, it now seems, the trajectory of a billiard ball through a time tunnel.

Action, in this sense, is a measure both of the energy involved in traversing the path and the time taken. For light (which is always a special case), this boils down to time alone, so that the principle of least action becomes the principle of least time, which is why light travels in straight lines.

You can see how the principle works when light from a source in air enters a block of glass, where it travels at a slower speed than in air. In order to get from the source A outside the glass to a point B inside the glass in the shortest possible time, the light has to travel in one straight line up to the edge of the glass, then turn through a certain angle and travel in another straight line (at the slower speed) on to point B. Traveling by any other route would take longer.

The action is a property of the whole path, and somehow the light (or "nature") always knows how to choose the cheapest or simplest path to its goal. In a similar fashion, the principle of least action can be used to describe the entire curved path of the ball thrown through a window once the time taken for the journey is specified. Although the ball can be thrown at different speeds at different trajectories (higher and slower, or flatter and faster) and still go through the window, only trajectories which satisfy the principle of least action are possible.

Novikov and his colleagues have applied the same principle to the "trajectories" of billiard balls around time loops, both with and without the kind of "self collision" that leads to paradoxes. In a mathematical *tour de force*, they have shown that in both cases only self-consistent solutions to the equations satisfy the principle of least action—or in their own words, "the whole set of classical trajectories which are globally self-consistent can be directly and simply recovered by imposing the principle of minimal action."

The word "classical" in this connection means that they have not yet tried to include the rules of quantum theory in their calculations. But there is no reason to think that this would alter their conclusions. Richard Feynman, who was entranced by the principle of least action, formulated quantum physics entirely on the basis of it, using what is known as the "sum over histories" or "path integral" formulation, because like a light ray seemingly sniffing out the best path from A to B, it takes account of all possible trajectories in selecting the most efficient. So self-consistency is a consequence of the principle of least action, and nature can be seen to abhor a time travel paradox. Which

removes the last objection of physicists to time travel in principle—
and leaves it up to the engineers to get on with the job of building a
time machine.

> "All right, so it's possible there's an alternate version of
> myself out there that actually understands what the hell
> you're talking about?"
> —Col. Jack O'Neill, "Point of View"

There is another way out of all the difficulties, if you don't like
that one. It involves the other great theory of physics in the twentieth
century, quantum mechanics, and another favorite idea from science
fiction, that of parallel worlds. These are the "alternative histories,"
in which, for example, the South won the American Civil War (as
in Ward Moore's classic novel *Bring the Jubilee*), which are envisaged
as in some sense lying "alongside" our version of reality. According
to one interpretation of quantum theory (and it has to be said that
there are other interpretations), each of these parallel worlds is just as
real as our own, and there is an alternative history for every possible
outcome of every decision ever made. Alternative histories branch out
from decision points, bifurcating endlessly like the branches and twigs
of an infinite tree. Bizarre though it sounds, this idea is taken seriously
by a handful of scientists (including David Deutsch, of the University
of Oxford). And it certainly fixes all the time travel paradoxes. It is
also the basis of one of the best modern fantasies, Philip Pullman's *His
Dark Materials* trilogy.

In this theory, if you go back in time and prevent your own birth
it doesn't matter, because by that decision you create a new branch of
reality, in which you were never born. When you go forward in time,
you move up the new branch and find that you never did exist, in that
reality; but since you were still born and built your time machine in
the reality next door, there is no paradox.

There's one last snag. It seems you can't use a time machine to
go back in time to before the time machine was built. You can go
anywhere in the future and come back to where you started, but no
further. Which rather neatly explains why no time travelers from our
future have yet visited us—because the time machine still hasn't been
invented!

Hard to believe? Certainly. Counter to common sense? Of course. But the bottom line is that all of this bizarre behavior is at the very least permitted by the laws of physics, and in some cases is required by those laws. I wonder what Wells would have made of it all.

> "Sounds like a good idea for a TV show, if you're into that sort of thing."
> 　　　　　　　　　　–Col. Jack O'Neill, "Point of No Return"[1]

John Gribbin trained as an astrophysicist but makes his living writing science books for non-scientists. His best known is In Search of Schroedinger's Cat, *and his latest is* Deep Simplicity. *His science fiction books are less well known and mostly out of print, but older readers may have come across* The Sixth Winter *(co-written with Douglas Orgill). Gribbin lives in his county of East Sussex, in England, and has an honorary post at the University of Sussex, which provides him with agreeable company and involves no duties at all.*

---

[1] Editor's Note: We don't know what Wells would have made of it, but we have a hunch that he—like the creators of *Stargate SG-1*—would be delighted to know that science has tentatively validated some of our fondest, wildest dreams. Dr. Gribbin has offered an amazing glimpse of how the Stargate actually could work. And whether wormhole travel—and time travel—actually does exist outside of *Stargate SG-1*, we're sure you're happy to know that it's not all science fiction.

J.C. Vaughn

WE NEED YOU BACK

I F THERE IS A MORE TRITE, worn out, or just plain stupid phrase than this in the fiefdoms of fiction, will it please stand up?

"We need you back."

Put down the book. Leave the movie. Stop playing the video game. Flinch, squirm, writhe. Change the channel, step away from the television. There's nothing to see here. Move along.

Whether it's science fiction, action adventure, espionage or just about anything except family drama or romance, when one hears those four words, one should in general consider oneself insulted.

Why? Because things normally just don't work that way in real life. It destroys the willing suspension of disbelief faster than Shelley Winters surviving a disaster film.

And yet, we keep hearing it. Producers, directors and writers keep thinking they're cool for bludgeoning us with it, and they unfortunately are regularly rewarded for doing so. It is a one of those proverbial vicious cycles waiting for Susan Powter to scream, "Stop the insanity!" or at least, "Stop the mediocrity!"

Think about the steely looks, the desperate you're-the-only-one-who-can-do-it requests, the eleventh hour pleadings. They're a staple of entertainment, aren't they? Whether it's second-rate James Bonds or fourth-rate army heroes, it's as ubiquitous as guys in red shirts being stupid enough to beam down with Captain Kirk.

"We need you back."

Thank goodness that *Stargate SG-1*, the most intelligently written science fiction television series in many, many years, has never used that phrase.

Oh, wait.

Jack O'Neill. They needed him back, didn't they? After the movie and in order to get the pilot episode of the series going . . . .

Uh-oh.

No. No "uh-oh."

Jack O'Neill is someone they needed and there's good reason they would have gone and brought him back to the Cheyenne Mountain complex. So, relax, take a breath, and let's take a look at what makes the good colonel such an exception.

WE NEED YOU BACK—THE EARLY YEARS

First a little history. The first time it happened, it wasn't the most stupid idea ever.

It wasn't Neville Chamberlain's "Peace In Our Time" foreign policy. It wasn't thinking *Cop Rock* would be a great TV series. It wasn't even Fisher Price producing angry-looking Donald Duck toys as Easter gifts for toddlers in the '30s.

It was dumb, but it was understandable.

There are probably older examples, but flash back if you will to the movie serials of the '30s and '40s. The serials were almost exclusively aimed at kids—*Flash Gordon, Buck Rogers, Spy Smasher, Captain Marvel*—and kids by and large wanted heroes they could be amazed by and admire. It was up to Flash, Buck and company to save the world or the universe. They were the only ones who could do it: *You're the only one who can save us*, or if you're slightly younger, *Help me, Obi-Wan Kenobi. You're my only hope.*

Feature movies of the period weren't much more sophisticated, at least on average. By the time war movies were in full swing, the cliché was deeply entrenched in the minds of many moviegoers, radio listeners and readers.

Like today's twenty-year-olds who have grown up with the X-Men in cartoons, videogames and more recently feature films, but who have never seen them in a comic book, entertainment enthusiasts by the 1950s had no idea they were watching child-like assumptions that the military or the government or space command would get this *one special person* who didn't even really want to come back to agree to come back to save all of us, usually griping about it as they agreed to return.

Whatever the reason, the cliché struck and stuck. Maybe it was a function of wanting to believe that the individual is that important. Maybe it was the unsophisticated nature of the then-new media. Maybe it was the smaller population base.

The population of the United States of America in the 1930s and early '40s, during the heyday of movie serials and radio shows, was about 120-140 million people. That means that if you were one in a million, there were only 120-140 of you to go around. That means that there were only 2.5 or so of you per state (in forty-eight states). You'd be pretty easy to miss. I would, too, if it makes you feel any better.

WHAT THE HECK DOES THIS HAVE TO DO WITH *STARGATE*?

Glad you asked. In 1994, writer-producer Dean Devlin and writer-director Roland Emmerich had given us a very compelling thrill ride with their film, *Stargate*. Kurt Russell and James Spader, as Col. Jack O'Neil and Dr. Daniel Jackson, respectively, sparked quite a bit of imagination with the fierce dynamic of their interplay as they viewed the story's tumultuous experience through distinctly different eyes.

At the end of the film, O'Neil was back on Earth and Jackson stayed behind on the planet Abydos. There was a world of redemption waiting for O'Neil and one of adventure and exploration awaiting Jackson, and that was pretty much that.

The film was great, but certainly its $71,567,262 total box office take didn't begin to compare with Devlin and Emmerich's 1996 blockbuster, *Independence Day*, which took in $306,169,255.[1] It seemed as if the Stargate, or *la porte des étoiles* as the French might call it before surrendering to the Goa'uld, was closed for good.

And maybe it even seemed better that way.

By that point the original *Star Trek* crewmembers were in their late 870s (some as old as 950) and it was getting pretty ridiculous to think

---

[1] Results retrieved February 24, 2004 from www.boxofficeMojo.com (2004)

that one crew could serve together on forty-seven successive ships with the same name without getting on each other's nerves. Seriously, George Takei only had to *act* with William Shatner and they couldn't get along. Sulu had to save the universe with Kirk.

We loved the characters, but we didn't really love them enough to let them go. So when a good science fiction movie came and went, and it didn't look like there would be a sequel, that seemed like it would be okay. (And I'm not even mentioning the third and fourth *Alien* movies to prove my point.)

Then came the words: "*Stargate* TV series."

It debuted July 27, 1997, on the Showtime cable network, the place the Viacom media conglomerate hides things like *The Reagans* mini-series. It wasn't an immediate hit and things didn't instantaneously click, but the show worked. And it worked because it had some seriously strong underpinnings.

First was that they made the story work for the characters.

Episode One, "Children of the Gods" (written by Jonathan Glassner & Brad Wright, directed by Mario Azzopardi), established that in this case the United States Air Force did indeed need Col. Jack O'Neill back. (The same did not go, obviously, for the spelling of his name.)

This kind of thing happens in the case of a person having a specific talent for the job at very high levels (Gen. Pete Schoomaker was recalled to active duty to become the Army's Chief of Staff) and in the case of mass need generally at the lower levels (thousands recalled in times of war). It happens very, very sparingly in between.

And specific, unique knowledge and experience can make it happen.

Jack O'Neill definitely had unique experience. He was the only officer to have commanded a team through the gate and back. If that's not "we need you back" material, then nothing is. So Kurt Russell gave way to MacGyver, and James Spader gave way to . . . that guy who looked a lot like James Spader.

Second, the show's creative staff found the internal logic of the series right away. Inherent in the Stargate's design was the possibility of numerous worlds beyond Earth, so O'Neill returns to Abydos, swings by Daniel Jackson's place and heads out for a spin around the galaxy. Not only did they actually need him back for this, they ended up needing him around for a long time.

YOU MUST REMEMBER THIS (NO, REALLY)

It was Mr. Spock who said, "Remember," but it was the characters populating *Stargate SG-1* who actually remembered things between episodes and from season to season.[2] As Jack O'Neill and the SG-1 team gained new experiences, it wasn't just so they could show us cool action, get a laugh or tell us the moral of that week's very special episode. They accumulated knowledge and memories that would come into play in future adventures and informed the thought processes of the characters just as they informed the viewers.

Related stories such as "In The Line Of Duty" (early in season two), "Serpent's Song" (later in season two) and "Jolinar's Memories" (midway through season three) wove distinct elements together, but occurred many episodes apart . . . and yet the characters remembered what had happened previously.

"Carter remembers the pain and torture when the Ashrak, a Goa'uld assassin, killed Jolinar, the Tok'ra Goa'uld who possessed her. She believes the same device was used on Apophis. The device is not used to extract information, but is a method of torture," read an episode description on the Gateworld.net website (a site dedicated to the show).[3]

"Well, of course," you say. (Go ahead, say it.)

No, not of course. *SG-1* isn't the first show or even the first science fiction show with good continuity, but it certainly may be one of the best. The experience that warranted Jack O'Neill staying in the service was just for starters. This is still a new enough development in television land that we should definitely be celebrating it. Just ask Chuck Cunningham.

Of course you don't remember Chuck Cunningham on *Stargate*. He wasn't on *Stargate SG-1*. And he wasn't on *Happy Days* for long either. Chuck was Richie's older brother, who always played basketball. Sometimes he just answered with a dribble, much like the French. Think I'm making it up? Check IMDB.com for Gavan O'Herlihy and Randolph Roberts. Chuck Cunningham wasn't around long, but he was played by two guys. Old Chuck was sent off to play basketball and never mentioned again, sort of like Roberts' post-Chuck acting

---

[2]*Star Trek II: The Wrath of Khan.* But you knew that.
[3]Gateworld.com fan website (2004). Retrieved February 26, 2004 from http://www.gateworld.net/
sg1/s2/218.shtml

career. O'Herlihy at least worked steadily, but no one ever said, "We need you back, Chuck Cunningham."

On *SG-1*, though, you never know who's going to become an important character. Col. Harold "Harry" Maybourne, for instance, went from obsequious opposition to serious threat to grudging ally, all the while pursuing his own agenda as he popped up from time to time. Even as a second-stringer, he has gone through character evolution.

The same is true for the main cast of characters, of course. Daniel Jackson died—ascended, sorry—and was replaced by Jonas Quinn. The team remembered Jackson while they thought he was dead, though, and they missed him. Jonas felt awkward taking his place. When Daniel came back—descended?—and Jonas went back to his own home world, the team didn't forget about Jonas either. In fact, he was back in another episode. So, Daniel came back and Jonas came back and Jack came back . . . maybe we needed them all back. I don't think that was the plan, but there's definitely a pattern here.

And it's okay.

If a character is needed back because of the internal logic of the story—or if an actor who looks like James Spader wants to come back to the series and the writers are good enough to make it work in the context of the story—that's not a bad thing at all. It's when we revert to that child-inspired concept from days of old that we get into trouble.

Star Trek is the poster child for this kind of shallow thinking. The guys in the red shirts never say, "Hey, Bill, what happened to Eugene?" or anything like that. It never dawns on them that if they're not Scotty, they're dead meat. It's like they don't even watch the show, let alone live it.

It's also as if many *Star Trek* fans are so accepting of what they're fed that they might actually believe there was only one Darren on *Bewitched*. And for the folks guarding the gates at Paramount, sadly, it's gone way beyond the "red shirt" problems of the original series and the "same crew" problems of the early films.

There's an entire series of *Trek* novels based on the "We need you back" concept. Seriously. Think about it. A United Federation of freakin' PLANETS to choose from and they still needed this single, solitary, individual guy back.

Not exactly proponents of paradigm shifting or thinking outside the box, I guess. Didn't Carl Sagan tell them Space is Vast? (It is; this has been verified.)

For a couple years I was a pitching writer for UPN's *Star Trek: Voyager* (I know, I'm sorry, too) when Sagan's son, Nick, was on staff. *He* certainly knew space was vast. So, he worked for *Star Trek* and he knew, but somebody at Pocket Books read the proposal for the series in question, and said, "Brilliant! We'll make it an entire series of books!"

Just so we're being candid, it sold like hotcakes, which apparently sell pretty well. And with a Milburn Drysdale-like concern for the future of the franchise and the intellectual well-being of the show's remaining fan, the folks now behind *Star Trek* continue turning out "A to A" plots (you know, something happens but at the end of the show everything's back to normal) and monologues that are supposed to pass for character development.

While this has been going on, Jack and Daniel have argued over the morality of decisions, overreacted, made mistakes, loved, lived, lost and won in the shadow of a larger, loftier issue like the survival of Earth.

Yeah, they needed Jack O'Neill back. They still do. Get used to it.

J.C. Vaughn is an expatriate adopted Texan living near Baltimore, Maryland. He is the co-writer of the comic books 24, *based on the hit Fox TV series, and* Shi. *He is the creator of* McCandless & Company, *and is also the creator of S.F.P.D., which first appeared in 2002's acclaimed Comic Book Legal Defense Fund benefit book,* More Fund Comics. *His short story "The Flight" was selected for the 2001* Breaking Boundaries *anthology, and he made his film acting debut in the award winning short* Some Trouble of a SeRRious Nature *in 2002. Vaughn is the author of more than 500 articles and columns in the collectibles field and serves as Executive Editor of Gemstone Publishing, where he works on such projects as* The Overstreet Comic Book Price Guide, Hake's Price Guide To Character Toys, Overstreet's Comic Price Review *and the weekly* Scoop *e-mail newsletter.*

Ann Wortham

SPIN THE GATE

DANIEL JACKSON: What did you see in him?
MAJ. SAMANTHA CARTER: I don't know. I guess I've always had a
   soft spot for the lunatic fringe. . . .

–"The First Commandment"

EVERYONE KNOWS that *Stargate* is all about sex. After all, the star of the show is that big, round thing that, in the words of series star Michael Shanks (Dr. Daniel Jackson), "has to get wet to work . . . ." Add to that long staff weapons. Phallic shaped zat guns. The villainous Goa'uld symbiotes who look like snakes. The most sexual of all episodes in the seventh season, "Fallout," where there was a big honkin' drill penetrating the core of Kelowna. And on and on and on. The show is filled with sexual innuendo and imagery. And for a show about military characters, there's no denying that there's a whole lot of snogging going on. Although I'm not a big fan of romantic scenarios cluttering up my science fiction shows, I thought it might be fun to look at our heroes' track records and see how they stack up. Weigh up the romantic pros and cons, as it were, based on the canonical empirical evidence we've been shown over the last seven years (or more, if you count the movie). Because frankly, although Sam Carter was talking about herself in the quote above when Daniel asked her what she saw in her ex-fiancé Jonas Hansen, I think that all the members of the SG-1 team could be said to have a bit of the lunatic fringe about them.

> JACK O'NEILL: I'm thinking they got history . . . there was some serious sparkage when she arrived.
>
> — "Crossroads"

Let's start with the big, dark and mysterious alien guy, Teal'c. Tall. Muscular. Easy on the eyes. Exotic, funky golden tattoo on the forehead. There's no denying he's one gorgeous hunk of a Jaffa. And if you're into those kinds of alien love things, you get two for the price of one in the days when he still had his symbiote. I have to admit that ranks right up there on my own personal "yuck" scale, but to each his, her or its own. For those that it bothers, the Goa'uld symbiote is now a thing of the past; unfortunately, it's been replaced by a drug dependency.

There's no denying Teal'c's got a lot of things stacked in his favor. He's strong and handsome and stalwart. He's over one hundred years old—which means he has *lots* of experience *and* he's already eligible for Social Security, even though he's fit and healthy! He's loyal to the SGC and especially SG-1 . . . and yet, there's that whole *shol'vah* thing to consider, where he betrayed Apophis. Okay, maybe *not* so loyal, then. And he wasn't quite so loyal to his wife, Drey'auc, was he? He abandoned her and his young son without a backward glance and never even mentioned their existence until several episodes into the first season when he finally admitted to O'Neill that he had a family back on Chulak. Oops. Forgot to mention that little fact.

Then we learned in "Crossroads" that he'd apparently been carrying a torch for a beautiful temple priestess, Shau'nac, for quite a long time. Even Jack noted the "sparkage" when Shau'nac arrived at the SGC. Drey'auc was still alive then, too. Of course, the fans of the show notice these things. The writers maintained, after the fact, that Teal'c and Drey'auc were "divorced" so I suppose that Teal'c technically *wasn't* a philanderer when he and Shau'nac did the wild thing in "Crossroads." That still doesn't explain the long history they seemed to share. Interestingly enough, when Teal'c dreamed about a "normal" human life in "Changeling," it was Shau'nac who played the part of his human wife, not Drey'auc.

Of course, now that Drey'auc is dead and Shau'nac is dead, it's a moot point. Teal'c is footloose and fancy free—and available, as was amply demonstrated in the seventh season episode, "Birthright," when Teal'c met up with the warrior Ishta, and it was Jaffa lust at first sight. She even survived the encounter and the romance and left through the Stargate, free to return another day (or in another episode!) for more of that wild Jaffa love thang.

> REYNARD: I thought it was obvious how much I wanted to kiss
> you since we first met.
>
> — "Forsaken"

Jonas Quinn is sort of the odd man out when it comes to the SG-1 team. He was only there for one season (the sixth) and a few episodes in the seventh, so he's a bit harder to get a handle on. But he did possess a few little quirks that helped to define him. Even though, compared to the other members of SG-1, he wasn't in as many episodes, he still managed to have his fair share of women giving him the eye. There was the thawed out Ancient woman in "Frozen," Aiyana, who seemed to catch his fancy, and he managed to sweet-talk one of the alien scientists, Zenna Volk, in "Cure." He even had the Goa'uld Nirrti playing a Mrs. Robinson routine with him in "Metamorphosis" when he wakes up among scattered cushions with one long, bare, feminine leg being waved enticingly in front of him. She apparently gave him some renovations with her DNA scrambling machine that had later repercussions on his already considerable brainpower. Who knows what other little modifications she might have made to Jonas Quinn, given the fact that she was obviously trying to seduce him? Ahem.

So what do we really know about Jonas the Kelownan? He smiles a lot—some would say way too much, but at least we know he's got good teeth. He eats incessantly and seems to have a fascination for Earth foods and The Weather Channel. He reads really fast and has a good memory. He's cute and eager to please, kind of like a puppy. He appears to be impervious to radiation since he survived exposure in "Meridian," whereas Daniel didn't, and he also appears to be resistant to exposure to naquadria, even though the other scientists working with it eventually went insane ("Shadowplay"). Throughout the sixth season, in fact, we were told that he was somehow "special" in the physical and mental sense, although we never learned exactly how and why he was so different and special. In "Descent" we found out that he can hold his breath for a really long time. (Think about it, girls.) We never saw him with an Earth girlfriend, although we did witness him flirting with a nurse . . . at which point he promptly told Sam it was a Kelownan custom for a *friend* to ask her out on his behalf. Hmm. Not really a point in his favor.

He did seem rather oblivious in "Forsaken" when Reynard gave him the come-hither treatment, and awkward to the point of dropping artifacts all over the place when she kissed him.

In the seventh season, we finally saw Jonas with a Kelownan girlfriend, Kianna. Or so we thought. It turned out she was a Goa'uld all along and he'd never really known the "real" Kianna. Ouch. Little bit of a parallel to poor Goa'uld-challenged Daniel Jackson there (more on that later), not to mention the fact that Jonas was rather tongue-tied when he realized the truth. First Nirrti, now this. In fact, it appears that if you join SG-1, you become irresistible to the Goa'uld—every single member of the team has had a relationship of some sort with either a Goa'uld, a Tok'ra or a Jaffa (who carry the infant larval form of the Goa'uld).

> JACK O'NEILL: She tried to seduce me.
> DANIEL JACKSON: Oh. You—you poor man.
>
> — "The Broca Divide"

Col. Jack O'Neill, the leader of SG-1. Ruggedly handsome. Brave. Loyal. The quintessential military hero type. Square-jawed and straight shooting. He's often made it clear that one of his overriding mantras in life is "nobody gets left behind."

O'Neill's sense of humor is somewhat of a double-edged sword. Although it might serve to diffuse tension in bad situations, it also seems to rear its head at inappropriate times, and it's often *bad* humor to boot. The fact that O'Neill quotes *The Simpsons* as his favorite show might have something to do with that.

O'Neill has been married before and seems to be carrying a bit of a torch for his ex-wife Sara in early seasons of the show, although Sara O'Neill hasn't been mentioned in more recent episodes. Her photo with their dead son Charlie can just be glimpsed by the side of his bed in the seventh season's "Fragile Balance." He definitely tells Daniel early on, in season one, that Sara left *him*, and in "Cold Lazarus" and other episodes it is obvious that O'Neill blames himself for both his son's death and his wife's departure.

O'Neill is disrespectful of authority and rules, and perfectly willing to take advantage of a situation. In "Window of Opportunity," when he realizes there are no consequences to his actions while stuck in an infinite time loop, he takes the opportunity to kiss Samantha Carter, knowing full well that while he will remember it, she won't.

He's rather dense when it comes to women sometimes, much like the other male members of SG-1. Anise, the sexy Tok'ra in "Divide & Conquer," has to spell things out for him when she wants to have sex with him. Laira in "100 Days" finds herself in basically the same situation, as does the alternate universe Sam Carter in "Point of View," who has to pointedly tell him that she was married to his counterpart in her reality before he buys a clue. Clearly, he's thinking of fishing above all. Or hockey. Or Mary Steenburgen. Or maybe Marge Simpson.

His encounters with Kynthia in "Brief Candle" and Laira in "100 Days" prove that once he gets the idea, he's easily seduced and that he can be had for food or, at the most, room and board. So, overall, a cheap date.

> JACK O'NEILL: Daniel, you dog. You keep this up, you'll have a
> girl on every planet . . . .
> —"The Broca Divide"

Dr. Daniel Jackson, the resident archeologist, linguist and supposed geek of the team. Now here is a guy who *should* have had it all. He's smart; brilliant, in fact. He's an intuitive thinker. He figured out how to make the Stargate work when no one else could. He's got multiple PhDs. He's good-looking, with or without the glasses, with piercing blue eyes. He does tend to have a bad fashion sense until later seasons, but hey, nobody's perfect, and even in oversized BDUs he manages to look quite nice. He's loyal to his friends, and brave . . . sometimes to the point of stupidity.

The drawback to it all is that Daniel Jackson is also incredibly eccentric. He can't tell anyone he was right about all of his crackpot theories involving the pyramids and aliens, therefore he isn't going to receive any credit or accolades. He talks a mile a minute. He's so distracted that he's oblivious even when a woman is undressing right in front of him. I mean, come on—in the original movie, Sha'uri was given to him as his wife and he didn't even figure it out for how long? And that's another thing. His wife's name *changed* between the movie and the series from Sha'uri to Sha're and he didn't notice? Talk about oblivious!

And let's look at the Sha're situation for a moment. Daniel was *given* a woman as a gift and he *kept her*? It's true that he did try to return her, briefly, but he didn't try too hard. For someone who seems on the surface so gentle and sweet and perfect, so vocal about moral choices, who knew there lurked the heart of a primitive chauvinist? Most guys try to impress their girls by giving them chocolate; Dr. Daniel Jackson managed to get a girl by *buying* her with chocolate!

Daniel's admitted himself that he's incredibly forgetful in love, as well. In "Chimera," he tells Sam and Teal'c that he forgot an anniversary dinner with then-girlfriend Sarah Gardner because he was so engrossed in his work, and she walked out on him. Obliviousness is not a charming attribute.

Then there's the little issue that his women seem to be very attractive to the Goa'uld as potential hosts. First Sha're is taken by Apophis and turned into a host for his queen, Amonet, and then later Daniel's ex-girlfriend Sarah Gardner becomes a host for the Goa'uld Osiris.

He also seems to have a real attraction for alien women, especially very powerful ones: Hathor, a Goa'uld, who wanted to make him her "beloved"; Shyla, an alien princess, who tried to make him her consort; Ke'ra, the Destroyer of Worlds, who tried to seduce him. Oma Desala, a powerful ascended Ancient, ascended him for who knows what purpose, but she obviously took quite a personal interest in Dr. Daniel Jackson—and let's not forget that she sent him back buck naked. Even the Goa'uld Osiris seemed rather taken with Daniel, and fixated on him while inhabiting the body of Daniel's former girlfriend.

Another *little* problem with Dr. Jackson—he tends to die. A lot. Oh, he's always come back from the dead (or ascension) so far. But who knows how long that will continue? Even assuming that *you* don't get kidnapped and turned into a Goa'uld, there's no telling how long he'll stick around before he decides to do something incredibly brave again and either dies or ascends. Jackson's track record indicates he's a risky proposition for love.

SAMANTHA CARTER: I feel compelled to warn you: most of the
    guys I've dated recently have died.

—"Chimera"

Maj. Samantha Carter, the brilliant astrophysicist of the team who
helped to write the dialing protocols that keep the Stargate running.
I've left Sam Carter until last because, well, she's had more admirers
and boyfriends and romantic entanglements and alternate universe
husbands and fiancés than any other character on the show. She really
isn't the "Black Widow" that she's sometimes made out to be, but the
evidence shows that she *can* be dangerous to know, and I do mean
in more than just the she-can-kick-your-butt-and-she-carries-a-P90
sense.

Let's just run down a list.

Jack O'Neill. In "The Broca Divide" she threw her commanding
officer onto a bench and tried to have her way with him while she
was under the influence of an alien virus. Jack looked a little worse
for wear afterwards, although he at least survived. In an alternate
universe, they were engaged, and they both ended up dead at the
hands of the Goa'uld (Jack died first, of course). In another alternate
universe, they were married and just Jack ended up dead at the hands
of the Goa'uld.

Jonas Hansen. She was engaged to him. He went nuts and
developed a God complex. He ended up dead on an alien planet.

Narim. A technologically advanced alien who made even Carter
look stupid. He fell in love with her in spite of the primitive nature
of the Tauri and although she seemed to have some feelings for him,
she couldn't commit to him, especially after the whole Jolinar incident
where she got temporarily snaked and turned into a Tok'ra herself.
After that she claimed that the shared memories of Jolinar made her
unsure of what she was feeling. Poor Narim. Narim is missing and
presumed dead after the Goa'uld attacked Tollana in "Between Two
Fires."

Felger. A geeky scientist at the SGC, he apparently has wild
fantasies about her, but they obviously aren't reciprocated. Luckily for
him, he's still alive and apparently well. Although he almost got shot
on an alien planet recently in "Avenger 2.0," when Carter took him on

a mission with her. Alone. Hmm. He'd better be careful. Who knows what the future holds?

Lt. Graham Simmons. Another character with a crush on Carter. He almost died from an alien infestation in "Message in a Bottle" after Daniel noticed that he had a "thing" for Carter and pointed it out to her. Oops. Lt. Simmons has only been seen once around the SGC since, I believe. Maybe he got smart and has been laying low.

Martouf. A Tok'ra who was mated to Jolinar but who developed feelings for Carter as herself, as well. Of course, he ended up dead. Shot by Carter when he'd been programmed by the Goa'uld to kill the President of the United States.

Orlin. Another alien. This one gave up immortality as an ascended being to come to Earth because he liked Carter's looks. He then sacrificed himself to save her. We don't know if he just ascended again or if he died permanently this time.

Joe Faxon. We first met Joe in an alternate universe of "2010," where he and Carter were married. He sort of survived but the timeline was changed. In the current timeline of "2001," he was left behind on the planet of the Aschen. We don't know what happened to the poor man after that.

Fifth. An upgraded replicator who trusted Carter and like so many others became besotted with her. She betrayed him and left him frozen in time.

Rodney McKay. A brilliant scientist and an expert on the Stargate. His expertise when it comes to the gate system probably comes the closest to rivaling Carter's own. Like every male in the universe, he is, of course, smitten with Sam Carter (apparently in spite of himself). His fatal flaw is his outrageously obnoxious personality. He managed to hold his own against Carter, though, but he was doomed. One kiss from her and he was banished to Russia. Apparently he survived the food in Russia, so they packed him off to Antarctica. And then to the Pegasus Galaxy where he's currently residing in the "lost city" of Atlantis. At least he's still alive . . . for the moment.

Agent Barrett of the NID. He's recently asked her out on a date. She turned him down, however, because she's dating someone now . . . and that would be Pete.

Pete Shanahan, whom we met in "Chimera." He's alive. So far. But he almost got killed by Osiris (what a coincidence, another one of

Daniel Jackson's possessed girlfriends). I think Pete had better watch his back.

So, what is it about Sam Carter that has all of these men risking their very lives for her? She's smart. Beautiful. She's got all the right moves, knows martial arts and can shoot a P90 with deadly accuracy. She likes motorcycles and classic cars. She comes with a great memory, including someone else's (Jolinar's), and a built-in Goa'uld detector. She's compassionate and loyal. I suppose the fact that she babbles technospeak a lot, tends to have hair that looks radioactive and dating her could be the death of you can be overlooked.

So, let's do a quick recap of the dating potential of SG-1. Teal'c: not really so loyal and not very faithful, although he's certainly nice to look at. Jonas: cute like a puppy but really rather clueless, and who knows what little time bombs Nirrti left him with. Jack: ruggedly handsome and a cheap date, but not very respectful—and he has a really bad sense of humor. Daniel: good-looking and brilliant but easily distracted. He tends to die a lot and his girlfriends have a bad habit of being abducted. Sam: brilliant and beautiful, but her technobabble can get really boring and her dating track record shows that she's a calculated risk. You know, I'm thinking maybe Sergeant Siler is a better bet. Everyone counts on him to keep things running, he's solid and dependable, he's just as muscular and handsome as the rest of them, and he's got that big wrench and all. . . .

Ann Wortham is a native Texan who currently resides in the humidity of central Florida, land of tourists, Mickey Mouse ears and inadequate roads. She has been a fan of Stargate *since the original movie and a devotee of all things science fiction since childhood. She worked for twenty-two years in the computer industry for AT&T, Lucent Technologies and IBM while spending her free time traveling and dabbling in nature and celebrity photography. She has a passion for reading, writing and publishing, and regularly writes online articles and conducts celebrity interviews for the Web.*

Daniel C. Dennett

WHERE AM I?

Daniel C. Dennett is one of the foremost experts on various aspects of the mind and the nature of human intelligence. So it seemed entirely logical to consult him on the subject of what makes a human being human . . . especially in light of the questions raised so eloquently by Stargate SG-1*'s episodes "Tin Man" and its sequel, "Double Jeopardy." This excerpt from his book* Brainstorms: Philosophical Essays on Mind and Psychology *(MIT Press, 1981) seemed eerily appropriate to the issue, and we thank him for making it available to the fans of* Stargate SG-1. . . .

REAL O'NEILL: So, um, what the hell happened here?

CLONE O'NEILL: Somebody stole my life. That's what happened.

REAL O'NEILL: You talking about my life?

CLONE O'NEILL: Hey! I've got every right to it that you do. I was kinda hoping I could figure out a way to undo all this, get myself back in my body . . . where I belong.

REAL O'NEILL: Well, it's occupied.

CLONE O'NEILL: I noticed that. What does that make me?

NOW THAT I'VE WON MY SUIT under the Freedom of Information Act, I am at liberty to reveal for the first time a curious episode in my life that may be of interest not only to those engaged in research in the philosophy of mind, artificial intelligence and neuroscience but also to the general public.

Several years ago I was approached by Pentagon officials who asked me to volunteer for a highly dangerous and secret mission. In collaboration with NASA and Howard Hughes, the Department of Defense was spending billions to develop a Supersonic Tunneling Underground Device, or STUD. It was supposed to tunnel through the earth's core at great speed and deliver a specially designed atomic warhead "right up the Red's missile silos," as one of the Pentagon brass put it.

The problem was that in an early test they had succeeded in lodging a warhead about a mile deep under Tulsa, Oklahoma, and they wanted me to retrieve it for them. "Why me?" I asked. Well, the mission involved some pioneering applications of current brain research, and they had heard of my interest in brains and, of course, my Faustian curiosity and great courage and so forth. Well, how could I refuse? The difficulty that brought the Pentagon to my door was that the device I'd been asked to recover was fiercely radioactive, in a new way. According to monitoring instruments, something about the nature of the device and its complex interactions with pockets of material deep in the earth had produced radiation that could cause severe abnormalities in certain tissues of the brain. No way had been found to shield the brain from these deadly rays, which were apparently harmless to other tissues and organs of the body. So it had been decided that the person sent to recover the device should *leave his brain behind*. It would be kept in a safe place where it could execute its normal control functions by elaborate radio links. Would I submit to a surgical procedure that would completely remove my brain, which would then be placed on a life-support system at the Manned Spacecraft Center in Houston? Each input and output pathway, as it was severed, would be restored by a pair of microminiaturized radio transceivers, one attached precisely to the brain, the other to the nerve stumps in the empty cranium. No information would be lost, all the connectivity would be preserved. At first I was a bit reluctant. Would it really work? The Houston brain surgeons encouraged me. "Think of it," they said, "as a mere *stretching* of the nerves. If your brain were just moved over an *inch* in your skull, that would not alter or impair your mind. We're simply going to make the nerves indefinitely elastic by splicing radio links into them."

I was shown around the life-support lab in Houston and saw the sparkling new vat in which my brain would be placed, were I to agree. I met the large and brilliant support team of neurologists, hematologists, biophysicists and electrical engineers, and after several days of discussions and demonstrations, I agreed to give it a try. I was subjected to an enormous array of blood tests, brain scans, experiments, interviews and the like. They took down my autobiography at great length, recorded tedious lists of my beliefs, hopes, fears and tastes. They even listed my favorite stereo recordings and gave me a crash session of psychoanalysis.

The day for surgery arrived at last and, of course, I was anesthetized and remember nothing of the operation itself. When I came out of anesthesia, I opened my eyes, looked around, and asked the inevitable, the traditional, the lamentably hackneyed post-operative question: "Where am I?" The nurse smiled down at me. "You're in Houston," she said, and I reflected that this still had a good chance of being the truth one way or another. She handed me a mirror. Sure enough, there were the tiny antennae poking up through their titanium ports cemented into my skull.

"I gather the operation was a success," I said. "I want to go see my brain." They led me (I was a bit dizzy and unsteady) down a long corridor and into the life-support lab. A cheer went up from the assembled support team, and I responded with what I hoped was a jaunty salute. Still feeling lightheaded, I was helped over to the life-support vat. I peered through the glass. There, floating in what looked like ginger ale, was undeniably a human brain, though it was almost covered with printed circuit chips, plastic tubules, electrodes and other paraphernalia. "Is that mine?" I asked. "Hit the output transmitter switch there on the side of the vat and see for yourself," the project director replied. I moved the switch to OFF, and immediately slumped, groggy and nauseated, into the arms of the technicians, one of whom kindly restored the switch to its ON position. While I recovered my equilibrium and composure, I thought to myself: "Well, here I am, sitting on a folding chair, staring through a piece of plate glass at my own brain. But wait," I said to myself. "Shouldn't I have thought, 'Here I am, suspended in a bubbling fluid, being stared at by my own eyes'?" I tried to think this latter thought. I tried to project it into the tank, offering it hopefully to my brain, but I failed to carry off the exercise with any conviction. I tried again. "Here am I, Daniel

Dennett, suspended in a bubbling fluid, being stared at by my own eyes." No, it just didn't work. Most puzzling and confusing. Being a philosopher of firm physicalist conviction, I believed unswervingly that the tokening of my thoughts was occurring somewhere in my brain. Yet, when I thought, "Here I am," where the thought occurred to me was *here*, outside the vat, where I, Dennett, was standing staring at my brain.

I tried and tried to think myself into the vat, but to no avail. I tried to build up to the task by doing mental exercises. I thought to myself, "The sun is shining *over there*," five times in rapid succession, each time mentally ostending a different place: in order, the sun-lit corner of the lab, the visible front lawn of the hospital, Houston, Mars and Jupiter. I found I had little difficulty in getting my "theres" to hop all over the celestial map with their proper references. I could loft a "there" in an instant through the farthest reaches of space, and then aim the next "there" with pinpoint accuracy at the upper left quadrant of a freckle on my arm. Why was I having such trouble with "here"? "Here in Houston" worked well enough, and so did "here in the lab," and even "here in this part of the lab," but "here in the vat" always seemed merely an unmeant mental mouthing. I tried closing my eyes while thinking it. This seemed to help, but still I couldn't manage to pull it off, except perhaps for a fleeting instant. I couldn't be sure. The discovery that I couldn't be sure was also unsettling. How did I know *where* I meant by "here" when I thought "here"? Could I *think* I meant one place when in fact I meant another? I didn't see how that could be admitted without untying the few bonds of intimacy between a person and his own mental life that had survived the onslaught of the brain scientists and philosophers, the physicalists and behaviorists. Perhaps I was incorrigible about where I *meant* when I said "here." But in my present circumstances it seemed that either I was doomed by sheer force of mental habit to thinking systematically false indexical thoughts, or where a person is (and hence where his thoughts are tokened for purposes of semantic analysis), is not necessarily where his brain, the physical seat of his soul, resides. Nagged by confusion, I attempted to orient myself by falling back on a favorite philosopher's ploy. I began naming things.

"Yorick," I said aloud to my brain, "you are my brain. The rest of my body, seated in this chair, I dub 'Hamlet.'" So here we all are: Yorick's my brain, Hamlet's my body and I am Dennett. *Now*, where am

I? And when I think "where am I?" where's that thought tokened? Is it tokened in my brain, lounging about in the vat, or right here between my ears where it *seems* to be tokened? Or nowhere? Its *temporal* coordinates give me no trouble; must it not have spatial coordinates as well? I began making a list of the alternatives.

1. *Where Hamlet goes, there goes Dennett.* This principle was easily refuted by appeal to the familiar brain transplant thought experiments so enjoyed by philosophers. If Tom and Dick switch brains, Tom is the fellow with Dick's former body—just ask him; he'll claim to be Tom, and tell you the most intimate details of Tom's autobiography. It was clear enough, then, that my current body and I could part company, but not likely that I could be separated from my brain. The rule of thumb that emerged so plainly from the thought experiments was that in a brain-transplant operation, one wanted to be the *donor*, not the recipient. Better to call such an operation a *body*-transplant, in fact. So perhaps the truth was,

2. *Where Yorick goes, there goes Dennett.* This was not at all appealing, however. How could I be in the vat and not about to go anywhere, when I was so obviously outside the vat looking in and beginning to make guilty plans to return to my room for a substantial lunch? This begged the question, I realized, but it still seemed to be getting at something important. Casting about for some support for my intuition, I hit upon a legalistic sort of argument that might have appealed to Locke.

    Suppose, I argued to myself, I were now to fly to California, rob a bank and be apprehended. In which state would I be tried: In California, where the robbery took place, or in Texas, where the brains of the outfit were located? Would I be a California felon with an out-of-state brain, or a Texas felon remotely controlling an accomplice of sorts in California? It seemed possible that I might beat such a rap just on the undecidability of that jurisdictional question, though perhaps it would be deemed an inter-state, and hence Federal, offense. In any event, suppose I were convicted. Was it likely that California would be satisfied to throw Hamlet into the brig, knowing that Yorick was living the good life and luxuriously taking the waters in Texas? Would Texas incarcerate Yorick, leaving Hamlet free to take the next boat to Rio? This alternative appealed to me. Barring capital punishment or other cruel and unusual punishment, the state would be obliged to maintain the life-support system for Yorick though they might move him from Houston to Leavenworth, and aside from the unpleasantness of the opprobrium, I, for one, would not mind at all and would consider myself a free man under those circumstances. If the state has an interest in forcibly relocating persons in institutions, it would fail to relocate me in any institution by locating Yorick there. If this were true, it suggested a third alternative.

3. *Dennett is wherever he thinks he is.* Generalized, the claim was as follows: At any given time a person has a *point of view*, and the location of the point of view (which is determined internally by the content of the point of view) is also the location of the person.

Such a proposition is not without its perplexities, but to me it seemed a step in the right direction. The only trouble was that it seemed to place one in a heads-I-win/tails-you-lose situation of unlikely infallibility as regards location. Hadn't I myself often been wrong about where I was, and at least as often uncertain? Couldn't one get lost? Of course, but getting lost *geographically* is not the only way one might get lost. If one were lost in the woods one could attempt to reassure oneself with the consolation that at least one knew where one was: one was right *here* in the familiar surroundings of one's own body. Perhaps in this case one would not have drawn one's attention to much to be thankful for. Still, there were worse plights imaginable, and I wasn't sure I wasn't in such a plight right now.

Point of view clearly had something to do with personal location, but it was itself an unclear notion. It was obvious that the content of one's point of view was not the same as, or determined by, the content of one's beliefs or thoughts. For example, what should we say about the point of view of the Cinerama viewer who shrieks and twists in his seat as the roller-coaster footage overcomes his psychic distancing? Has he forgotten that he is safely seated in the theater? Here I was inclined to say that the person is experiencing an illusory shift in point of view. In other cases, my inclination to call such shifts illusory was less strong. The workers in laboratories and plants who handle dangerous materials by operating feedback-controlled mechanical arms and hands undergo a shift in point of view that is crisper and more pronounced than anything Cinerama can provoke. They can feel the heft and slipperiness of the containers they manipulate with their metal fingers. They know perfectly well where they are and are not fooled into false beliefs by the experience, yet it is as if they were inside the isolation chamber they are peering into. With mental effort, they can manage to shift their point of view back and forth, rather like making a transparent Neckar cube or an Escher drawing change orientation before one's eyes. It does seem extravagant to suppose that in performing this bit of mental gymnastics they are transporting *themselves* back and forth.

Still their example gave me hope. If I was in fact in the vat in spite of my intuitions, I might be able to train myself to adopt that point of view even as a matter of habit. I should dwell on images of myself comfortably floating in my vat, beaming volitions to that familiar body *out there*. I reflected that the ease or difficulty of this task was presumably independent of the truth about the location of one's brain. Had I been practicing before the operation, I might now be finding it second nature. You might now yourself try such a *tromp l'oeil*. Imagine you have written an inflammatory letter that has been published in the *Times*, the result of which is that the Government has chosen to impound your brain for a probationary period of three years in its Dangerous Brain Clinic in Bethesda, Maryland. Your body of course is allowed freedom to earn a salary and thus to continue its function of laying up income to be taxed. At this moment, however, your body is seated in an auditorium listening to a peculiar account by Daniel Dennett of his own similar experience. Try it. Think yourself to Bethesda, and then hark back longingly to your body, far away, and yet *seeming* so near. It is only with long-distance restraint (yours? the government's?) that you can control your impulse to get those hands clapping in polite applause before navigating the old body to the rest room and a well-deserved glass of evening sherry in the lounge. The task of imagination is certainly difficult, but if you achieve your goal the results might be consoling.

Anyway, there I was in Houston, lost in thought as one might say, but not for long. My speculations were soon interrupted by the Houston doctors, who wished to test out my new prosthetic nervous system before sending me off on my hazardous mission. As I mentioned before, I was a bit dizzy at first, and not surprisingly, although I soon habituated myself to my new circumstances (which were, after all, well nigh indistinguishable from my old circumstances). My accommodation was not perfect, however, and to this day I continue to be plagued by minor coordination difficulties. The speed of light is fast, but finite, and as my brain and body move farther and farther apart, the delicate interaction of my feedback systems is thrown into disarray by the time lags. Just as one is rendered close to speechless by a delayed or echoic hearing of one's speaking voice so, for instance, I am virtually unable to track a moving object with my eyes whenever my brain and my body are more than a few miles apart. In most matters my impairment is scarcely detectable, though I can no longer hit a slow curve ball with the authority of yore. There are some compensations, of course. Though liquor tastes as good as ever, and warms my gullet while corroding my liver, I can drink it in any quantity I please, without becoming the slightest bit inebriated, a curiosity some of my close friends may have noticed (though I occasionally have *feigned* inebriation, so as not to draw attention to unusual circumstances). For similar reasons, I take aspirin orally for a sprained wrist, but if the pain persists I ask Houston to administer codeine to me *in vitro*. In times of illness the phone bill can be staggering.

But to return to my adventure: At length, both the doctors and I were satisfied that I was ready to undertake my subterranean mission. And so I left my brain in Houston and headed by helicopter for Tulsa. Well, in any case, that's the way it seemed to me. That's how I would put it, just off the top of my head, as it were. On the trip I reflected further about my earlier anxieties and decided that my first post-operative speculations had been tinged with panic. The matter was not nearly as strange or metaphysical as I had been supposing. Where was I? In two places, clearly: both inside the vat and outside it. Just as one can stand with one foot in Connecticut and the other in Rhode Island, I was in two places at once. I had become one of those scattered individuals we used to hear so much about. The more I considered this answer, the more obviously true it appeared. But, strange to say, the more true it appeared, the less important the question to which it could be the true answer seemed. A sad, but not unprecedented, fate for a philosophical question to suffer. This answer did not completely satisfy me, of course. There lingered some question to which I should have liked an answer, which was neither "Where are all my various and sundry parts?" nor "What is my current point of view?" Or at least there seemed to be such a question. For it did seem undeniable that in some sense I and not merely *most of me* was descending into the earth under Tulsa in search of an atomic warhead.

When I found the warhead, I was certainly glad I had left my brain behind, for the pointer on the specially built Geiger counter I had brought with me was off the dial. I called Houston on my ordinary radio and told the operations control center of my position and my progress. In return, they gave me instructions for dismantling the vehicle, based upon my on-site observations. I had set to work with my cutting torch when all of a sudden a terrible thing happened. I went stone deaf. At first I thought it was only my radio earphones that had broken, but when I tapped my helmet, I heard nothing. Apparently the auditory transceivers had gone on the fritz. I could no longer hear Houston or my own voice, but I could speak, so I started telling them what had happened. In mid-sentence, I knew something else had gone wrong. My vocal apparatus had become paralyzed. Then my right hand went limp—another transceiver had gone. I was truly in deep trouble. But worse was to follow. After a few more minutes, I went blind. I cursed my luck, and then I cursed the scientists who had led me into this grave peril. There I was, deaf, dumb and blind, in a radioactive hole more than a mile under Tulsa. Then the last of my cerebral radio links broke, and suddenly I was faced with a new and even more shocking problem: whereas an instant before I had been buried alive in Oklahoma, now I was disembodied in Houston. My recognition of my new status was not immediate. It took me several very anxious minutes before it dawned on me that my poor body lay several hundred miles away, with heart pulsing and lungs respirating, but otherwise as dead as the body of any heart transplant donor, its skull packed with useless, broken electronic gear. The shift in perspective I had earlier found well nigh impossible now seemed quite natural. Though I could think myself back into my body in the tunnel under Tulsa, it took some effort to sustain the illusion. For surely it was an illusion to suppose I was still in Oklahoma: I had lost all contact with that body.

It occurred to me then, with one of those rushes of revelation of which we should be suspicious, that I had stumbled upon an impressive demonstration of the immateriality of the souls based upon physicalist principles and premises. For as the last radio signal between Tulsa and Houston died away, had I not changed location from Tulsa to Houston at the speed of light? And had I not accomplished this without any increase in mass? What moved from A to B at such speed was surely myself, or at any rate my soul or mind—the massless center of my being and home of my consciousness. My *point of view* had lagged somewhat behind, but I had already noted the indirect bearing of point of view on personal location. I could not see how a physicalist philosopher could quarrel with this, except by taking the dire and counter-intuitive route of banishing all talk of persons. Yet the notion of personhood was so well entrenched in everyone's world view, or so it seemed to me, that any denial would be as curiously unconvincing, as systematically disingenuous, as the Cartesian negation, "non sum."[1]

The joy of philosophic discovery thus tided me over some very bad minutes or perhaps hours as the helplessness and hopelessness of my situation became more apparent to me. Waves of panic and even nausea swept over me, made all the more horrible by the absence of their normal body-dependent phenomenology. No adrenaline rush of tingles in the arms, no pounding heart, no premonitory salivation. I did feel a dread sinking feeling in my bowels at one point, and this tricked me momentarily into the false hope that I was undergoing a reversal of the process that landed me in this fix—a gradual undisembodiment. But the isolation and uniqueness of that twinge soon convinced me that it was simply the first of a plague of phantom body hallucinations that I, like any other amputee, would be all too likely to suffer.

My mood then was chaotic. On the one hand, I was fired up with elation at my philosophic discovery and was wracking my brain (one of the few familiar things I could still do), trying to figure out how to communicate my discovery to the journals; while on the other, I was bitter, lonely and filled with dread and uncertainty. Fortunately, this did not last long, for my technical support team sedated me into a dreamless sleep from which I awoke, hearing with magnificent fidelity the familiar opening strains of my favorite Brahms piano trio. So that was why they had wanted a list of my favorite recordings! It did not take me long to realize that I was hearing the music without ears. The output from the stereo stylus was being fed through some fancy rectification circuitry directly into my auditory nerve. I was mainlining Brahms, an unforgettable experience for any stereo buff.

---

[1]C.f., Jaakko Hintikka, "Cogito ergo sum: Inference or Performance?" *The Philosophical Review*, LXXI, 1962, pp. 3-32.

At the end of the record it did not surprise me to hear the reassuring voice of the project director speaking into a microphone that was now my prosthetic ear. He confirmed my analysis of what had gone wrong and assured me that steps were being taken to re-embody me. He did not elaborate, and after a few more recordings, I found myself drifting off to sleep. My sleep lasted, I later learned, for the better part of a year, and when I awoke, it was to find myself fully restored to my senses. When I looked into the mirror, though, I was a bit startled to see an unfamiliar face. Bearded and a bit heavier, bearing no doubt a family resemblance to my former face, and with the same look of spritely intelligence and resolute character, but definitely a new face. Further self-explorations of an intimate nature left me in no doubt that this was a new body, and the project director confirmed my conclusions. He did not volunteer any information on the past history of my new body and I decided (wisely, I think in retrospect) not to pry. As many philosophers unfamiliar with my ordeal have more recently speculated, the acquisition of a new body leaves one's *person* intact. And after a period of adjustment to a new voice, new muscular strengths and weaknesses and so forth, one's *personality* is by and large also preserved. More dramatic changes in personality have been routinely observed in people who have undergone extensive plastic surgery, to say nothing of sex change operations, and I think no one contests the survival of the person in such cases. In any event I soon accommodated to my new body, to the point of being unable to recover any of its novelties to my consciousness or even memory. The view in the mirror soon became utterly familiar. That view, by the way, still revealed antennae, and so I was not surprised to learn that my brain had not been moved from its haven in the life-support lab.

I decided that good old Yorick deserved a visit. I and my new body, whom we might as well call Fortinbras, strode into the familiar lab to another round of applause from the technicians, who were of course congratulating themselves, not me. Once more I stood before the vat and contemplated poor Yorick, and on a whim I once again cavalierly flicked off the output transmitter switch. Imagine my surprise when nothing happened. No fainting spell, no nausea, no noticeable change. A technician hurried to restore the switch to ON, but still I felt nothing. I demanded an explanation, which the project director hastened to provide. It seems that before they had even operated on the first occasion, they had constructed a computer duplicate of my brain, reproducing both the complete information processing structure and the computational speed of my brain in a giant computer program. After the operation, but before they had dared to send me off on my mission to Oklahoma, they had run this computer system and Yorick side by side. The incoming signals from Hamlet were sent simultaneously to Yorick's transceivers and to the computer's array of inputs. And the outputs from Yorick were not only beamed back to Hamlet, my body, but they were also recorded and checked against the simultaneous output of the computer program, which was called "Hubert" for reasons obscure to me. Over days and even weeks, the outputs were identical and synchronous, which of course did not *prove* that they had succeeded in copying the brain's functional structure, but the empirical support was greatly encouraging.

Hubert's input, and hence activity, had been kept parallel with Yorick's during my disembodied days. And now, to demonstrate this, they had actually thrown the master switch that put Hubert for the first time in on-line control of my body—not Hamlet, of course, but Fortinbras. (Hamlet, I learned, had never been recovered from its underground tomb and could be assumed by this time to have largely returned to the dust. At the head of my grave still lay the magnificent bulk of the abandoned device, with the word STUD emblazoned on its side in large letters—a circumstance which may provide archeologists of the next century with a curious insight into the burial rites of their ancestors.)

The laboratory technicians now showed me the master switch, which had two positions, labeled *B*, for Brain (they didn't know my brain's name was Yorick) and *H*, for Hubert. The switch did indeed point to *H*, and they explained to me that if I wished, I could switch it back to *B*. With my heart in my mouth (and my brain in its vat), I did this. Nothing happened. A click, that was all. To test their claim, and with the master switch now set at *B*, I hit Yorick's output transmitter switch on the vat and sure enough, I began to faint. Once the output switch was turned back on and I had recovered my wits, so to speak, I continued to play with the master switch, flipping it back and forth. I found that with the exception of the transitional click, I could detect no trace of a difference. I could switch in mid-utterance, and the sentence I had begun speaking under the control of Yorick was finished without a pause or hitch of any kind under the control of

Hubert. I had a spare brain, a prosthetic device that might some day stand me in very good stead, were some mishap to befall Yorick. Or alternatively, I could keep Yorick as a spare and use Hubert. It didn't seem to make any difference which one I chose, for the wear and tear and fatigue on my body did not have any debilitating effect on either brain, whether or not it was actually causing the motions of my body, or merely spilling its output into thin air.

The one truly unsettling aspect of this new development was the prospect, which was not long in dawning on me, of someone detaching the spare—Hubert or Yorick, as the case might be—from Fortinbras and hitching it to yet another body—some Johnny-come-lately Rosencrantz or Guildenstern. Then (if not before) there would be *two* people, that much was clear. One would be me, and the other would be a sort of super-twin brother. If there were two bodies, one under the control of Hubert and the other being controlled by Yorick, then which would the world recognize as the true Dennett? And whatever the rest of the world decided, which one would be *me*? Would I be the Yorick-brained one, in virtue of Yorick's causal priority and former intimate relationship with the original Dennett body, Hamlet? That seemed a bit legalistic, a bit too redolent of the arbitrariness of consanguinity and legal possession, to be convincing at the metaphysical level. For, suppose that before the arrival of the second body on the scene, I had been keeping Yorick as the spare for years, and letting Hubert's output drive my body—that is, Fortinbras—all that time. The Hubert-Fortinbras couple would seem then by squatter's rights (to combat one legal intuition with another) to be the true Dennett and the lawful inheritor of everything that was Dennett's. This was an interesting question, certainly, but not nearly so pressing as another question that bothered me. My strongest intuition was that in such an eventuality *I* would survive so long as *either* brain-body couple remained intact, but I had mixed emotions about whether I should want both to survive.

I discussed my worries with the technicians and the project director. The prospect of two Dennetts was abhorrent to me, I explained, largely for social reasons. I didn't want to be my own rival for the affections of my wife, nor did I like the prospect of the two Dennetts sharing my modest professor's salary. Still more vertiginous and distasteful, though, was the idea of knowing *that much* about another person, while he had the very same goods on me. How could we ever face each other? My colleagues in the lab argued that I was ignoring the bright side of the matter. Weren't there many things I wanted to do but, being only one person, had been unable to do? Now one Dennett could stay at home and be the professor and family man, while the other could strike out on a life of travel and adventure missing the family of course, but happy in the knowledge that the other Dennett was keeping the home fires burning. I could be faithful and adulterous at the same time. I could even cuckold myself—to say nothing of other more lurid possibilities my colleagues were all to ready to force upon my overtaxed imagination. But my ordeal in Oklahoma (or was it Houston?) had made me less adventurous, and I shrank from this opportunity that was being offered (though of course I was never quite sure it was being offered to *me* in the first place).

There was another prospect even more disagreeable—that the spare, Hubert or Yorick as the case might be, would be detached from any input from Fortinbras and just left detached. Then, as in the other case, there would be two Dennetts, or at least two claimants to my name and possessions, one embodied in Fortinbras and the other sadly, miserably disembodied. Both selfishness and altruism bade me take steps to prevent this from happening. So I asked that measures be taken to ensure that no one could ever tamper with the transceiver connections or the master switch without my (our? no, *my*) knowledge and consent. Since I had no desire to spend my life guarding the equipment in Houston, it was mutually decided that all the electronic connections in the lab would be carefully locked: both those that controlled the life-support system for Yorick and those that controlled the power supply for Hubert would be guarded with fail-safe devices, and I would take the only master switch, outfitted for radio remote control, with me wherever I went. I carry it strapped around my waist and—wait a moment—*here it is*. Every few months I reconnoiter the situation by switching channels. I do this only in the presence of friends of course, for if the other channel were, heaven forbid, either dead or otherwise occupied, there would have to be somebody who had my interest at heart to switch it back, to bring me back from the void. For while I could feel, see, hear and otherwise sense whatever befell my body, subsequent to such a switch, I'd be unable to control it. By the way, the two positions on the switch are intentionally unmarked, so I never have the faintest idea whether I am switching from Hubert to Yorick or vice versa. (Some of you may think that in this case I really don't know *who* I am. If it is true that in one sense I don't know who I am then that's another one of your philosophical truths of underwhelming significance.)

In any case, every time I've flipped the switch so far, nothing has happened. *So let's give it a try . . . .*

"THANK GOD! I THOUGHT YOU'D NEVER FLIP THAT SWITCH! You can't imagine how horrible it's been these last two weeks—but now you know, it's your turn in purgatory. How I've longed for this moment! You see, about two weeks ago—excuse me, ladies and gentlemen, but I've got to explain this to my . . . um, brother, I guess you could say, but he's just told you the facts, so you'll understand—about two weeks ago our two brains drifted just a bit out of synch. I don't know whether *my* brain is now Hubert or Yorick, any more than you do, but in any case, the two brains drifted apart, and of course once the process started, it snowballed, for I was in a slightly different receptive state for the input we both received, a difference that was soon magnified. In no time at all the illusion that I was in control of my body—our body—was completely dissipated. There was nothing I could do—no way to call you. YOU DIDN'T EVEN KNOW I EXISTED! It's been like being carried around in a cage, or better, like being possessed—hearing my own voice say things I didn't mean to say, watching in frustration as my own hands performed deeds I hadn't intended. You'd scratch our itches, but not the way I would have, and you kept me awake, with your tossing and turning. I've been totally exhausted, on the verge of a nervous breakdown, carried around helplessly by your frantic round of activities, sustained only by the knowledge that some day you'd throw the switch.

"Now it's your turn, but at least you'll have the comfort of knowing *I* know you're in there. Like an expectant mother, I'm eating—or at any rate tasting, smelling, seeing—for *two* now, and I'll try to make it easy for you. Don't worry. Just as soon as this colloquium is over, you and I will fly to Houston, and we'll see what can be done to get one of us another body. You can have a female body—your body could be any color you like. But let's think it over. I tell you what—to be fair, if we both want this body, I promise I'll let the project director flip a coin to settle which of us gets to keep it and which then gets to choose a new body. That should guarantee justice, shouldn't it? In any case, I'll take care of you, I promise. These people are my witnesses.

"Ladies and gentleman, this talk we have just heard is not exactly the talk *I* would have given, but I assure you that everything he said was perfectly true. And now if you'll excuse me, I think I'd—we'd—better sit down."[7]

Daniel C. Dennett, the author of Freedom Evolves *(Viking Penguin, 2003) and* Darwin's Dangerous Idea *(Simon & Schuster, 1995), is University Professor and Austin B. Fletcher Professor of Philosophy, and Director of the Center for Cognitive Studies at Tufts University. His first book,* Content and Consciousness, *appeared in 1969, followed by* Brainstorms *(1978),* Elbow Room *(1984),* The Intentional Stance *(1987),* Consciousness Explained *(1991),* Kinds of Minds *(1996) and* Brainchildren: A Collection of Essays 1984-1996 *(MIT Press and Penguin, 1998). He co-edited* The Mind's I *with Douglas Hofstadter in 1981. He is the author of over two hundred scholarly articles on various aspects on the mind, published in journals ranging from* Artificial Intelligence *and* Behavioral and Brain Sciences *to* Poetics Today *and the* Journal of Aesthetics and Art Criticism.

---

[2]Anyone familiar with the literature on this topic will recognize that my remarks owe a great deal to the explorations of Sydney Shoemaker, John Perry, David Lewis and Derek Parfit, and in particular to their papers in Amelie Rorty, ed., *The Identities of Persons*, 1976.

Susan Sizemore

I THINK HE'S
CALLED HOMER

T HE TRUTH IS, I'M A FAIRLY LATE CONVERT to *Stargate SG-1*. My love
for the show started in August 2003, seven years into the run
of the series. I loved the movie, thought I'd like the television
series based on it, but we being basic cable sort of people, and the
show initially being on Showtime, my housemate and I didn't watch
it. Now, we have this friend who was a fan from the first, and was
dying to talk to us about what had become her favorite television
series. So, when the DVDs became available, she bought the first four
seasons, insistently loaned them to us and ordered us to watch them.
Being under "Or else . . . " orders, we did.

How well I remember that first evening, when we thought only
to play the pilot and . . . I think we went through the first two disks
of season one that evening. For the next several weeks we watched a
minimum of a disk a night. The Monday night Sci Fi Channel's *Stargate
SG-1* three-hour blocks became known as "Pizza Night." In a frenzy
to catch up, we watched the show every time we found it listed on
Sci Fi or on network syndication, we bought and read the Illustrated
Companions books, checked out fan and official websites and read
magazine articles. It was fun to be so enthusiastically immersed in an

119

exceedingly well-wrought science fiction action adventure world once again. Oh, and we talked about *SG-1* incessantly with the now happily smug friend who'd known we'd get hooked if we ever just got around to watching the show. In fact, the fanaticism reached such a pitch that we were almost reluctant to interrupt this *SG-1* feeding frenzy to take a trip to England. Of course, the friend we were hooking up with in London is also an *SG-1* fan. In fact, we declared ourselves to be team SG-3 for our exploration of the country, and she met us at London's Paddington Station carrying a sign to that effect.

I mention my conversion to *SG-1* for a reason. I didn't watch the show in a weekly episode by episode, year after year way. No, I took it in in great gulps, and in doing so quickly became aware of certain patterns and themes. I fell in love with the show's attention to continuity. In fact there's only one major continuity glitch I can think of, that being Klorel/Skaara not really being picked as Apophis' son in the first episode, but showing up as his son later—which is how it should have been done in the first place, so I'm not complaining that they shamelessly ignored continuity that time to do something cool and dramatic.

But I'm not going to discuss continuity; rather I'm going to talk about something else *Stargate SG-1* does that is very dear to my heart, something I might not have had such a strong reaction to if I'd watched the show as it aired over many seasons. And that is the pop cultural references that permeate the show. I'm a writer who likes to put bits of pop culture into my own work—say, references to *Buffy the Vampire Slayer*, or *Star Wars*—and I'm forever having to fight off the ravages of copy editors who try to cut them out without any realization that those references are *important* to the story. While I delighted in all the references by *SG-1* characters to the same things I delight in, I soon came to realize that *SG-1*'s writers' penchant for the referential was not done just to be cool and funny, but there were other, serious, important reasons afoot for bringing up Homer Simpson and *The Wizard of Oz*. At least most of the time.

The people who work for the Stargate project live in, and repeatedly save, our world, and they let us know it immediately. It starts in the very first episode. One of the first things *Stargate SG-1* does is get the *MacGyver* comment up front and out of the way early in the first episode "Children of the Gods," while doing it in a way that is not silly, or seemingly self-referential. Carter uses "MacGyver" as another way of saying jury-rigged while talking about the Stargate's dialing device, and no one but we, the audience, reacts to the real reference to Richard Dean Anderson's best known role up to that time. It's a bold move, funny, and sets us down squarely not in a science fiction universe, but in our own. It says that the Goa'uld are out to get us, and SG-1 is there to stop them.

This use of popular cultural references sets a theme that runs through the whole series and grounds it in "our" reality. There are examples relating to the team's preferences in television, movies and their general awareness of the world "they" and "we" live in, in almost every episode. The show uses pop culture media references not just overtly, but covertly, slyly and pervasively. I find it charming and "real" to hear Jack complain about having to miss *The Simpsons* to go save the world, or wonder why a starship can't be called *Enterprise*.

Among the examples that come immediately to mind is O'Neill's love of *The Simpsons*, with references in many, many episodes. A non-*Simpsons* favorite of mine is a seventh season episode that opens with Carter's complaining about the plot holes in the Mel Gibson movie, *Signs*. (Though the title of the movie is never mentioned, it is wonderfully obvious what movie the scientist is complaining about—and I wanted to argue with her that she hadn't gotten the point of the film.) There's Daniel and Jack's frequent references to *The Wizard of Oz*, and Teal'c's fondness for *Star Wars* (he's seen it five times, as he states in "Ascension"). Then there's Jack's almost casual mention of the television series *ER* in the episode "Bane" (known as the icky bug episode in my household) that turns out to be the catalyst for Dr. Fraiser and Sam's figuring out how to save Teal'c's dying symbiote while the infected Teal'c is off turning into a big, nasty, flesh-eating alien dragonfly

These references serve to help make the show's premise more believable. They help foster the viewer's sense of belief in the world of *Stargate SG-1*. This helps Jack, Sam, Daniel, Teal'c, Hammond and the rest to become Everyman characters. They are *us*, but us with higher security clearances and knowing the secrets of Area 51. (There are no aliens at Area 51 . . . except when Teal'c visits.) They are us traveling to distant worlds, us saving *our* world—the world of *Star Trek* and *The Simpsons*.

The title of this essay comes from one of my favorite episodes, "Beneath the Surface." In this episode, the team have had their identities and memories stripped from them and false identities implanted. They are set to work as slave labor, maintaining the power of a city on an ice-covered world. But the *SG-1* gang can't be kept dazed and confused, or docile, for long. Soon flashes of reality begin to replace the imprinted false memories. As he begins to recover, it is Jack's respect for Gen. Hammond and his fondness for Homer Simpson that help anchor him to his world. As the bewildered O'Neill puts it, "There's a man who's very important to me. He's bald and he wears a short-sleeved shirt. I think his name is Homer." I think this is one of the most brilliant bits of dialogue ever written for the show.

Besides the overt references to "fictional" media, *SG-1* also uses more sly and subtle twists on a pop cultural phenomenon—that being *Stargate SG-1* itself. They show their awareness of their connection to the original movie when the television version of Colonel O'Neill refers to the movie version of O'Neil—the one that spells his name with one "L" and doesn't have a sense of humor—in the second season episode "Secrets." They then do a very amusing and fond parody of themselves, cable television and fandom in the fifth season episode "Wormhole X-Treme!", which takes place on the set of a show not-so-loosely based on the adventures of the "real" SG-1.

Pop culture references are used not only as anchor, but also to emphasize Teal'c's alienness, as well as Teal'c beginning to understand and appreciate the culture he now lives in. These references show character growth and are insights into the stoic warrior's personality, especially in first and second season episodes. After watching a lot of television in "Cold Lazarus," Teal'c comments to Daniel that, "Your world is strange." To which Daniel fires back, "So's yours." In "The Broca Divide," a pop culture reference of Jack's ("Lucy, I'm home.") to the justifiably clueless Teal'c does nothing to help Teal'c believe that Jack has recovered from having devolved into a primitive state. In "Message in a Bottle," when Teal'c tells the injured O'Neill that "undomesticated equines" could not force him to leave O'Neill's side, it's an indication of his beginning to understand his new home, and that the serious warrior also has a sense of humor. He uses this humor to attempt to comfort a friend, and the friend recognizes and appreciates it.

Some of the most fun I've had with my quest to pry out pop cultural nuggets has been the sly, sometimes silly, in-joke sort of things the writers have put in the episodes. Such as the sarong clad Princess

LaMoor in "Touchstone," referencing the characters frequently played by Dorothy Lamour in the old Crosby and Hope Road movies. (In "Touchstone" we also get references to The Weather Channel and ESPN.) Or, in the brilliant fourth season episode "2010," when Sam is working on a project to transform Jupiter into a star. When I first viewed the episode and a character commented that this had never been tried before, I said, "Wrong, Arthur C. Clarke in *2010*." Then I laughed, realizing that, of course, the title of the episode was "2010." Of course the writers *knew* it had been done before! This homage to Clarke was reiterated in the related episode "2001" the next season. "2001" also has yet another almost ubiquitous Oz reference—when O'Neill looks around the bucolic setting of the planet they're on and says, "Just when you think you're not in Kansas, you are."

Another of my favorite episodes is "Upgrades," where the Tok'ra give the members of SG-1 alien devices that enhance their innate abilities. These bracelets literally turn the team into superheroes, and in an homage to comic books, Daniel translates the engraved writing on his bracelet to read, "With great power comes great responsibility"—a la Spiderman. Does Stan Lee know about this?

Then there's "1969." This is an episode that needs an article all of its own. "1969" is a delight. The whole episode is referential, taking the SG-1 team time traveling back to the era of hippies, war protesters, magic buses, granny glasses and Woodstock. O'Neill calls upon references to both *Star Trek* and *Star Wars* in his answers to interrogators' questions about who he is and where he comes from, using fiction from his time to mask the reality of it. I can't think of anything more amusing than the sight of Teal'c in the Jimi Hendrix hairdo and headband. Of course, when I first saw this episode I enjoyed it immensely, but was also a bit disappointed in it. It was a time travel episode where nothing seemed to happen (I've written eight time travel novels, so I'm a bit picky on the subject.) All they needed to do was to get back home—and they did. Why travel to the past of your own world when you don't have to save the world while being there? Little did I know how pivotal this episode was to the entire *SG-1* universe. Without the events of "1969," we would not have the heroic tragedy of "2010" or the bitter sweetness of "2001."

There is also the setting and background, and premise, of the entire show, which takes another popular cultural theme—that being the Dream of Egypt—and uses this as a basis for so much of the culture of the main villains, and secret history of our world. Rewriting Egyptian and other ancient civilizations' history and myths and incorporating them into popular fiction has been going on for a long time and is especially prevalent in the visual media of movies and television. *Stargate SG-1* follows in that tradition, and throws in its own twists on mythologies from all over the world—themes that might seem exotic or esoteric, but are really the underlying foundation of our culture, popular and otherwise. *Stargate SG-1* has mined the myths, cultures, architecture and costumes of just about every ancient Earth civilization. The character of Dr. Daniel Jackson, the half-mad absentminded genius archaeologist fount of esoteric wisdom, is himself a pop culture B-movie cliché (sorry, Dan darlin', you know I love you, and don't mean that as an insult!) following in the footsteps of 1930s movie serials, Hammer horror films, mummy movies from every era and the likes of Indiana Jones.

The evil Goa'uld have taken on the personas of many ancient gods, mostly from the pantheon of Egypt, but we also encounter 'gods' from many other ancient belief systems. Even the good guy version of the Goa'uld, the Tok'ra, are descended from a Goa'uld queen that took on the persona of a Roman goddess. Those snakes, both good and evil, certainly think well of themselves, and very much seem to believe their own PR about *really* being gods.

And one group of good guys hasn't hesitated to adopt personas of Earth gods, either. In *Stargate SG-1*, the gods of the Vikings have been turned into the Asgard, alien protectors who look like little green, or in this case, gray, men but project images of themselves as looking like Viking hunks to the peoples under their protection. And one of them, Loki, even carries out alien abductions.

As I write this, season eight has just begun. Or possibly it's season seven and a half. It's kind of hard to tell with the abrupt starts and stops and lengthy pauses between episodes; that is the way things are scheduled on cable networks. At any rate, new episodes are now being shown on the Sci Fi Channel, and I am happy to say that the pop culture references just keep on coming. At the end of the first new episode shown in January, 2004, a character refers to a bad guy who'd been zombied out by a prototype of the Goa'uld sarcophagus as something from the *Evil Dead* movies. This brought a laugh that punctuated a very tense moment, and continued the show's pop cultural referential traditions. Keep it up, guys! I'll be taking notes.

And be inspired by your efforts to blend our culture with fiction in fighting off attempts of copy editors to delete references to *Stargate SG-1* from my own stuff.

Media junkie Susan Sizemore is the author of numerous novels and short stories, ranging from historical romance to epic fantasy. She has an affinity for vampire fiction, basketball, coffee, canines and movies with explosions. Her love for Stargate SG-1 *is fairly recent, but intense. She did not find any evidence of the Goa'uld on a recent trip to Egypt, but then the guides only take tourists to the official ancient sites. For more information, Susan's website address is http://susansizemore.com.*

Dr. Sten Odenwald

STARGATE: THE FINAL FRONTIER?

A S A CHILD IN SUBURBAN Oakland, California, I was spellbound by ancient Egypt. I spent hours at the Melrose Library on Foothill Boulevard reading about this fascinating civilization. Sitting at one of the massive oak reading tables with stacks of books, I sketched hieroglyphs in a notebook with the same enthusiasm that my friends collected baseball cards. I discovered astronomy as a teenager, falling in love with the mystery of space and the wonders it might hide. I learned the constellations and built telescopes, all the while reading science fiction novels by the score. Von Daniken's books intrigued me during my high school years, with his bizarre ideas about alien influences in our ancient monuments. So, it is with considerable excitement that I write this article, because the threads that weave themselves through the *Stargate SG-1* saga are in many ways the same threads that have bound much of my own curiosity about the world since childhood.

A cleverly written SF story is a seduction in which real science concepts are craftily extended into the fantasy realm so that the reader, at least for the duration of the story, believes in the plausibility of the extended science. Scientists are often put into the role of the Grinch when it comes to SF. I personally dislike this role because as an avid SF reader I seldom dwell on the technical minutia of a story. I realize full well that we are forced to make a Devil's Bargain. We violate a few laws of physics here and there and are abundantly rewarded with unimaginable vistas and adventures both dramatic and sublime. Whether we will ever create furniture from curved space (Asimov's *End of Eternity*), partake of a multidimensional reality (Moorcock's *The Sundered Worlds*) or step through a doorway onto another planet (Sagan's *Contact*), isn't really the point. The ability to fuel the imagination with these exciting possibilities, however, is the goal. After all, a properly stimulated imagination is an awesome instrument of exploration. Are you, for instance, curious at all about the scientific accuracy of *Alice in Wonderland* or the *Wizard of Oz*? I wasn't when I first encountered them either, and I am still not interested in that type of needless dissection. But there is a hidden problem, which many scientists worry about.

In today's world, the chief source of contact between astronomy and the general public is through TV and movies. Few of us have the time to get the facts straight. Competing with the voice of clarity and reason are the misconceptions we learn about the physical world through the needlessly inaccurate science we experience at the University of Hollywood. I can read SF and easily discriminate between fact and fantasy. Based on the thousands of questions I have answered from the general public and students at my Web resource *The Astronomy Cafe* (www.astronomycafe.net), the book by the same name issued in 1998 and in my latest question-and-answer book *Back to the Astronomy Cafe* (2003), the message is clear that for some readers, science fiction and fact have been fused together. You need only recall the recent flap over the Apollo moon landing "hoax" to appreciate that we have a serious problem. As the most popular SF series on cable TV, *Stargate SG-1* has proved very convincingly that not getting any of the science right is a profitable approach to 21st century SF writing—so long as you have entertaining characters and lots of drama to divert your attention.

THE BACK STORY

The single largest idea that any astronomer has to confront in the SF universe is interstellar travel (see Odenwald, 1994). For decades, pulp

SF favored an increasing evolution of V2-style rocket engines and sleek spaceships to house them. This *Buck Rogers* approach to space travel ended by the 1950s, with the adoption of hyperdrive and warp drive. One of the earliest space travel stories to adopt non-rocket travel is Gerald Grogan's "A Drop in Infinity," published in 1915. The story describes an electrified cabinet like a phone booth that a traveler steps into and is transported to an Earth in a parallel universe. You will see a similar idea of alternate worlds in *Stargate*'s episode "Point of View." Donald Wandrei's 1934 story "The Blinding Shadows" describes an inventor who connects with another dimension using a machine with lenses made of an element called Rhillium. In *Stargate*, naquadah plays the role of this mysterious element so important to Stargate physics. In 1941, Oliver Saari's "The Door" tells the story of how a gateway was found among the ruins of an ancient city in the Sahara desert. Stepping through, the traveler is transported to the surface of a planet in a distant star system. An actual space transportation system based on a human-sized doorway was mentioned in Poul Anderson's 1966 short story "Door to Anywhere," though the operating principles do not involve wormholes. Only in the 1990s has the evolution of space travel changed once again, with the increasing use of "jumpgates" and less reliance on the slow pace of warpdrive. In Robert Sawyer's 1996 book *Starplex* we read about a transit system, containing over four billion gateways built by a super-race from the future. The basic story behind the *Stargate* adventure was written in 1994 just before Sawyer's book, and similarly has a system designed by super-intelligent aliens (the Ancients), with billions of possible destinations across the galaxy. By the time of the premier episode of the TV series in 1997 (just after Sawyer's book), all of the messy technical details of operating a Stargate had been filled-in. We can expect to hear even more about this technology as future authors adopt it as an even more elegant way to get about the universe.

What I enjoy most about the *Stargate* back-story as an astronomer is that we are presented with a cosmos containing non-human races in many stages of development. The Ancients hover above the entire story as the mysterious creators of the Stargate network. This is the same theme we see played out in the 1994 series *Babylon 5*, where jumpgate technology and the First Ones predate human civilization by millions of years. *Star Trek: The Next Generation*'s 1993 episode "The Chase" includes the billion-year-old ancestor race to humans,

Klingons and Romulans. This representation of intelligent races in the Milky Way is very plausible—that is, assuming we are not alone in the cosmos.

There is an ongoing debate in some sectors of the astronomical community about how common intelligent life might be. Depending on what assumptions you make, you can estimate anywhere from one such civilization (our own!) to millions of them living in our Milky Way at any given time. So, where are they? Perhaps they have placed Earth and its immediate interstellar neighborhood under quarantine to avoid contaminating our development as in Thomas McDonough's 1987 novel *Architects of Hyperspace*. It is also possible they exist and have visited our solar system many times as we read in the engrossing 2001 novel *Manifold Space* by Stephen Baxter. But perhaps the most troubling possibility of all is that we may have missed the emergence of the last race by a few million years or more, as suggested in Lester del Rey's 1952 short story "The Years Draw Nigh" or in *Star Trek: The Next Generation*'s "The Chase." So the *Stargate* universe reflects one of several scientific possibilities we may hope to find ourselves exposed to in the distant future, and perhaps the most welcoming scenario of all: an exciting pastiche of old and young races living a few dozen light years apart, each trying to co-exist or avoid each other. It is indeed a very big galaxy to have as a backyard for such races!

Planets are now confirmed to orbit many of the nearest stars. We have discovered over 100 of them already. Various estimates suggest that 10% of the trillion-odd stars in the Milky Way probably have planets of some kind—an inevitable byproduct of the messy star forming process. So the 137 billion addresses the Stargate accesses with seven chevrons is a good ballpark from which to launch stories. Because of the relative motion between these address destinations and Earth, Carter notes in "Children of a Lesser God" that her supercomputer can only recalculate correct addresses at the rate of two every month. The reason for this, however, has nothing to do with the expansion of the universe as Carter states. This system is firmly identified as a galactic system, not an extragalactic one. By the way, the computer image of the Milky Way on the data screen Carter used in "Window of Opportunity" was badly in error. It was certainly not as visually interesting as, for instance, an actual Hubble Space Telescope photo of a real galaxy would have been.

While we are on the subject of Stargate technology, its very existence poses something of an intriguing back-story in itself. I have yet to hear of a compelling reason for a transportation system of this scale. Overpopulation? Exploration? Exploitation? Only the Asgard use it, not the Nox or the mysterious Furlings. Is it simply the creation of mindless automation and duplication by the Ancients in the style of Replicator technology? There are no hints as towhy the Ancients invested so much of their resources in creating a system this vast, when their traces are found in only a few worlds (e.g., "Window of Opportunity"). *Stargate SG-1* should be more aggressive in pursuing this storyline, which would be a captivating archeological mystery story to tell.

Stargate technology is the ultimate stage of space transportation envisioned in the SF universe. No longer do we have to waste precious story time getting to places of interest—we arrive in an instant. We can concentrate on telling intriguing and mysterious stories about alien civilizations and artifacts. We can even explore distant galaxies with no more effort than adding an eighth or ninth chevron to our addressing. *Stargate* is, in many ways, the end of the line in science fiction writing. The new "final frontier" is no longer space and our laborious travels through it in clumsy spaceships. We can now contemplate new worlds in distant galaxies or even other universes. And when we are done, the question of who built the system remains enigmatic.

A last big issue: Where are all the lethal germs? A trip to Asia or South America can often bring back a flu or stomach virus or bacterium as an unwanted hitchhiker. An off-world trip to an Earth-like planet on the TV series rarely poses a similar problem. Of course, we can't have our heroes walking around in isolation suits, but this is a very important technical issue you should always keep in mind. Our own journeys to Mars and beyond in search of life are heavily screened by NASA for contamination in both directions.

A WALK ON THE WILD SIDE OF ASTROPHYSICS

Many *Stargate* episodes feature alien skies with oversized planets or moons (e.g., "Into the Fire," "A Hundred Days," "Demon," "Fire and Water," "Prodigy"). This always enchants me and fills me with awe, even though I fully realize the gravitational tidal forces of such an arrangement would rip them asunder. Still, I am drawn to the beauty of the scenery, which as an astronomer forces me to ask, wistfully, "Darn! Why couldn't our own moon be huge and impressive in the sky?" But this awe-inspiring scenery plays on a widespread misconception that millions of students have about the scale of the solar system and planetary sizes. This misconception is reinforced every time they see these kinds of portrayals in the cinema or on TV: namely, that planets can come arbitrarily close together with no physical harm. The solution? A little more science in our fiction wouldn't hurt, but so far as my emotions are concerned, please keep on super-sizing those moons!

Sometimes a single wrong word can utterly ruin the mood and sense of escapism for an episode. There is no harm done to the story by getting the terminology correct, so it remains a mystery why such errors continue to be made. For instance, when O'Neill is golfing with Teal'c on the Stargate ramp ("Window of Opportunity") and remarks "How far is Alaris anyway?" Teal'c replies "Several billion miles." Hmmm . . . .That places Alaris just inside the orbit of Uranus. Frankly, I didn't catch this blooper when I first heard it because I was too busy laughing at the sight of golfers teeing-off at the Stargate! So much for my scientific attention to detail. In the same episode, Carter uses the term "coronal mass emission" instead of the correct term "coronal mass ejection," which you will find correctly used in the *New York Times* and other national newspapers. The result is like an off-key note played in a symphony, but even after showing this episode as a lunchtime treat to my astronomer colleagues at NASA, we all had a good laugh at this very well done episode!

Science fiction stories often revolve around basic problems in celestial mechanics. If you want to travel to a planet, just take a beeline trajectory to it (e.g., "Tangent") rather than the graceful arc demanded by Newton's laws of motion. Planets can indeed have a perpetual day and night-side as in "The Broca Divide," which means rotation and revolution times must be identical. It sounds odd, but this is not a problem. Venus comes very close to this arrangement, with a rotation period of 243 days and an orbit of 224.7 days. Planets can also be pelted by asteroids much more frequently than Earth has been, if they are in a Mars-like orbit close to an indigenous asteroid belt ("A Hundred Days"), although in our solar system the typical distance between asteroids is millions of miles and you would never have an intense asteroid shower. It's also rather implausible that a several-mile long asteroid could escape telescopic detection on Earth ("Fail Safe"). Currently, these kinds of objects are detected weeks in advance. For example, the asteroid 2002 NY40 discovered on June 14, 2002, is only 800 yards across. Its closest approach to Earth was 318,000 miles on August 17, 2002. Smaller bodies between ten and a hundred yards across often avoid early detection, such as the object 2003 SQ222 detected on September 28, 2003 only one day *after* it had already made a close approach to Earth, coming within 33,000 miles; that's inside the orbits of our geosynchronous communication satellites! A direct hit by a relatively common fifty to a hundred-yard body would produce a shock wave equal to the Tunguska Impactor, which came down over Siberia in 1909 and leveled trees twenty miles away. A mile-sized body would take out an entire continental region in a devastating firestorm, shock wave and hailstorm of incendiary rock—literally setting the atmosphere on fire. Over the ocean, a mile-sized impact would unleash a tidal wave over 1,000 feet tall. The Goa'uld would be very happy indeed, but we would be toast.

As for major planetary upheavals and rearrangements, these things really do happen. The Jupiter-sized planet orbiting the nearby star HD209458 is being evaporated by its star, and its atmosphere rains droplets of iron. But sometimes the rearrangements depicted on *Stargate* are a little farfetched. In the episode "Prodigy," M4C-862 was pulled into a polar orbit around its planet—a Jupiter-like gas giant. This kind of two-body capture is strictly forbidden unless it involves severe tidal effects to dissipate some of the kinetic energy of the encounter. It would ultimately have pulverized M4C-862. The moon was formed from just such a close encounter between Earth and a planetoid.

Some of the most violent cosmic events we hear about on the evening news have to do with solar activity. The great storms and flares of October-November 2003 illustrate how dramatic solar storms can be and what they can do. This makes for an exciting theme in science fiction ("Window of Opportunity," "2010"). The sun often ejects flares and coronal mass ejections that litter the solar system with an eleven-year cycle of increasing and decreasing storminess. Many stars are far worse in their intermittent violence than the sun. Some stars produce deadly superflares that rival the entire output of their star, and would scour the atmospheres of nearby planets. Carter plausibly describes what happens when a coronal mass ejection hits a planet with a geomagnetic field. We know that aurora on Earth can generate over 900 billion watts during a severe solar storm. As I point out in my book *The 23rd Cycle* (2000), these storms have cost us billions of dollars and dozens of failed satellites, plus electrical blackouts and the near-deaths of Apollo astronauts. But when you consider that these storms at Earth's surface are spread out over several million square miles, the amount of power delivered is only a few hundred thousand watts per square mile—far less than the energy you, or the Ancients, could collect from sunlight.

In the episode "1969," a solar flare sends the team back to the year 1969. Hammond has looked up the 1969 dates and times of two solar flares to facilitate their return to the future: one flare on the Earth-facing side, and one flare on the opposite side of the sun. In 1969, NASA was scrupulously monitoring the Sun for flares that could endanger Apollo astronauts, but there was no way to record backside flares in 1969. By the way, the story has O'Neill visiting the Gordan MacMillian Southam Observatory near Yonkers, New York, though it is actually located in Vancouver. The eruptive prominence that O'Neill sees through the eyepiece from the observatory is actually shown speeded up by a factor of about 100. This same prominence is used in the briefing room in the episode "Window of Opportunity," when Carter is describing the coronal mass ejection of a different star. Carter reminds O'Neill to "remember to use the hydrogen-alpha solar filter," which is technically correct and a nice touch to the dialogue. O'Neill is an amateur astronomer, with a private stash of equipment that rivals anything I ever owned. It is fun to watch him stand up to Carter on issues of black holes and basic astronomy, but from the informal view of an amateur astronomer. Can you imagine any experience more thrilling than Stargate travel to make you an avid astrophile? The episode was very engrossing and entertaining, and it raises an interesting question: This is such a gosh-darn simple way to time travel, why didn't the Ancients use it on P4X-639 ("Window of Opportunity") to save their colony instead of building that nasty little six-hour time loop machine? Finally, have you noticed that August-October 1969 seems to be a popular time travel destination? (See the 2000 movie *Frequency*.)

Perhaps one of the biggest errors in understanding the scope of solar physics appeared in the episode "Red Sky." The Stargate's wormhole passes into a star *en route* to its terminus gate on an Asgard-protected world. This pollutes the star that the planet orbits, causing the star's spectrum to shift into the infrared. Carter says that the only way to prevent this spectral shift from destroying the civilization is to seed the star with a few hundred kilos of a new element called Maclarium (HU-2340) to render the foreign matter inert. In the outer atmosphere of a star, a hundred kilos of impurity atoms would be outnumbered by more than a trillion trillion trillion to one. The likelihood that the PB2-908 scenario would work is even lower than the possibility that the peculiar ideas that form the basis of homeopathic medicine would: diluting a liquid so no atoms of the cure remain still leaves you with a potent medication! But there are in fact stars so rich in heavy elements that their ultraviolet light is dimmed by absorption lines and their light is dramatically reddened. The episode had the right idea, but insufficient mass to really make it happen.

According to Carter ("Exodus"), the star Vorash orbits is a blue giant "Main Sequence" star with a core temperature of fifteen million degrees and a remaining lifespan of five billion years. A "blue giant" star is not a Main Sequence star, and blue giants are typically more than ten times the mass of our sun. These kinds of massive stars actually have a lifespan less than 100 million years from birth to death, with core temperatures upwards of fifty million degrees. On the fly-out from Vorash, the star is shown to be nearly the same size as Vorash as seen from a vantage point close to Vorash. This is definitely not the size of a Main Sequence star, or even a blue giant star, as claimed. Still, I loved the imagery of exploding stars and spacecraft whooshing through stellar photospheres with leaping prominences.

No science fiction story in the modern age is complete without black holes. Virtually all such stories get the basic physics very wrong, and keep promoting a serious misconception to the general public: namely, that black holes "suck." In fact, they do no such thing. Were the sun to quietly become a black hole tomorrow, planets would still orbit as they do today, with no tendency to slowly slide into the dark maw of this gravitational pit. But since Disney's *The Black Hole* hit the theaters back in 1979, no story has avoided this "sucking" trap. Plus, it is cinematically just too darn exciting to omit. Heck, I enjoy the drama of the story, too! By the way, for you worriers, if the sun was swapped with an equal-mass black hole, there would be no effect on the orbits of any of the planets—not even Mercury. The gravitational field of this black hole would look identical to that of our sun, so there would be no dynamical reason for the orbits to change rapidly. I could add some interesting caveats to this statement, but they are unimportant over the life of our planet, and for that matter the entire Milky Way galaxy!

Stargate's entry into this black hole genre is the thrilling episode "A Matter of Time," but you also find black holes mentioned in the episodes "Singularity" and "Exodus." In "A Matter of Time," planet P3X-451 orbits a black hole, and Earth will be sucked into it stone by stone unless the gateway can be closed. The time dilation effects were qualitatively right on the money, as was the issue of proper time. Everyone claimed their own time was progressing normally, but when they compared their passage of time with people located far from them, there were major differences. I don't think people could freely travel from one time zone to the other in the easy way Hammond and Carter did.

P3X-451 also appears in the episode "Exodus," where it is used to remove matter from the Vorash star. According to Carter, once the Stargate to P3X-451 is opened and the black hole begins extracting matter, the Vorash star's pressure and gravity balance will be destabilized and the star will explode within an hour. Actually this would never happen. If you removed matter from the surface of a star, the star's core would decompress in a few hours. This causes the core's fusion reactions to become less efficient and so the core cools. A star would not explode unless you *added* matter to it, which would compress its core, causing the fusion reactions to suddenly burn hotter and produce more pressure. Yet the star would still not detonate. Instead, its outer layers would move outwards to establish a new equilibrium size. We know of many binary star systems where a companion star is the beneficiary of matter expelled by the primary star (e.g., Cygnus X-1). This does not cause the primary star to supernova. In fact, the companion star itself (neutron star, white dwarf or black hole) actually becomes the site of a nova-like explosion. So, Vorash's star would have remained intact. Also, the Stargate is put in the coronosphere (not a proper astronomical term, but I like it!), where the density of the gas is so low a Stargate-sized event horizon could not intercept enough matter to change the mass of the star appreciably in an hour, even flowing at light-speed. By the way, star-tinkering seems to be the next frontier in modern SF. In the 1995 *Star Trek* movie *Generations*, the evil Dr. Soran used an element called Trilithium to create a quantum implosion (I love that term!) in a star, causing it to detonate within minutes. Still, I really enjoy the audacity of these stories, and I don't worry too much about the technical details. The visual impact of the explosions is never a disappointment!

I hope you didn't miss it! One of the rare moments in SF history appeared in the episode "Prodigy," where Carter gives an advanced lecture on theoretical physics at the U.S Air Force Academy. What was exciting for me was the use of equations on a blackboard to provide the "wow" for the background story. You can fudge words and mix up dialog without causing a major problem for the flow of a story, but equations are not the same thing. They just sit there with their appropriateness and errors on full, lingering display for all to see using freeze-framing. The swapped variables pointed out by Cadet Hailey are actually the least of the mathematical problems. Carter makes several mistakes that most graduate students in astronomy would have caught immediately. On the right-hand board, her first equation is the famous formula for the Schwarschild metric of a non-rotating black hole, but instead of the first term having a negative sign, it has an incorrect positive sign. The next equation defines dt/dr, which is supposed to represent the rate of change of proper time (or coordinate time—I can't really tell from the letter shape) with respect to distance from the black hole (not sure what this would have to do with any lecture on higher-dimensional space-times!). It seems to be missing an exponent in the second quantity inside the square bracket. The third equation has both unbalanced parenthesis and square brackets, which at the very minimum would have made it logically impossible to evaluate. (This is the same mistake she makes on the blackboard in the episode "A Matter of Time.") As for the concluding sentence that "3 dimensions vs. string theory of 26 dimensions or 10 dimensional spacetime where N=10," which is exactly what is written on the blackboard, this summation does not follow from anything on the right-hand board. The equations on the left-hand board, meanwhile, could relate to some aspect of string theory, but it is not obvious what the logical interconnections might be. The audio narration for this episode by director Peter DeLuise and writer Paul Mullie says that the equations were copied out of a textbook on "higher dimensions" and copied to the blackboard by someone from the Props Department. The good news, however, is that the use of a blackboard filled with roughly appropriate equations is intriguing to the non-physicist. They look appropriately mysterious and serve their role very well. As with all the other science in SF, they are caricatures of the real things. The venue, however, is another matter. So far as the story is concerned, I think the bottom line is that what appears on either blackboard is way beyond the grasp of any undergraduate in physics and is badly out of place at an undergraduate institution such as the U.S. Air Force Academy. But it works incredibly well in expressing the elegant mathematics that astrophysicists use in describing black holes. By the way, my other favorite mathematics scene is in "A Matter of Time," when Carter turns to Teal'c and asks, "You know anything about quantum gravity? . . . Apparently, neither do I." This is exactly what a real astronomer would have said when confronted with this problem!

Scattered here and there among the episodes are other minor lapses that had little impact on the story. The episode "Tangent" boasts a short trip into the solar system in an Earth-hybrid Death Glider, at a speed of "a million miles an hour." It would take a whopping twenty-three days to reach Jupiter on a direct flight, and the radio time delay would be closer to ninety minutes, not merely "several minutes." Later on, Teal'c and O'Neill do a fifteen-second space walk with no space suit. It sounds bizarre, but it might be possible to do this for a few seconds (remember *2001: A Space Odyssey*?). However, the pain would be agonizing as your skin is quickly freeze-dried, and your capillaries begin to rupture underneath this dried, nerve-rich membrane. I didn't hear any screams in this episode (remember *Total Recall*?), or signs of skin distress on their faces after rescue—not even a blemish.

Another fun topic is alternate universes. In "There But For The Grace Of God," Daniel Jackson is shifted into an alternate reality by a quantum mirror device (what a lovely name!). Since the 1950s, physicists have considered a number of scenarios where there could be alternate "parallel" universes out there around the corner in some other dimension or distant location within our space-time continuum. Since the 1980s, cosmologists such as Andre Linde have proposed that other universes with different physical laws could exist out there, far beyond the horizon to our visible universe. Even string theory has a version of this kind of "multiverse" cosmology in the form of M-Theory, with three-dimensional universes floating like pieces of paper in some eleven-dimensional void. Carter does a great technical job describing the possibilities, but logically, these universes would look nothing like ours in terms of histories we could recognize as minor variants of our own. Still, this episode presents an intriguing theme, and executes it with great skill. By the way, the term "multiverse" was invented by SF author Michael Moorcock in what was for me at age 16 an influential book, *The Sundered Worlds*.

ALL THE WORLD'S A STAGE

Stargate has the most engaging characters I have encountered in a TV science fiction series, with the possible exception of *Babylon 5*. Not surprisingly for a series set in 1999, the characters look and act like people I might know, and they live in neighborhoods like the ones I have visited. The characters are compelling, make human mistakes, use humor appropriately and are not as full of themselves or self-conscious of what they are saying as the SF characters in other series. In fact, I find myself watching many episodes, not because I am involved with the stories, but because I am involved with the characters and how they interact! Only in *Babylon 5* did I feel similarly spellbound and emotionally involved.

As an astronomer, I feel a particular bond with Carter, played by actress Amanda Tapping, though the bond would be greater if she had come from an academic rather than military milieu. The only other woman astronomer of note in recent movies is Dr. Jane Arroway in *Contact*, intensely played by actress Jodi Foster, and executed with great skill and breathtaking technical accuracy. The story was, of course, written by a professional astronomer—Carl Sagan. I consider her character the high-water mark for all actors and actresses who want to portray the true essence of what an astronomer is like. Unlike Arroway, Carter is forced to approach astronomy from within the excruciating formality of a military background. Carter is brilliant, a bit reserved and as an officer works very hard to maintain purely professional relationships with her colleagues, even in situations that demanded a far more human response. For instance, she wakes up after being dead and says "Hi!" ("Entity") instead of dissolving into an emotional pile of rubble as I would have. But there is a logic to Carter that truly escapes me. In fact, it presents such a paradox that it begs an episode to work out, rather than the intriguing fragments we are treated to in "Prodigy" and "The Devil You Know."

We know why O'Neill and Daniel got involved with the Air Force: O'Neill is career-military, and Jackson got drafted but remains a civilian consultant. Their backgrounds and personalities make perfect logical sense in the series. But what explains Samantha Carter? Based on what she is able to innovate in such very short order, Major Carter is the most brilliant scientist that humanity has ever produced. I know of no card-carrying astrophysicists that can create their own working particle accelerators ("A Hundred Days"), psyche-out exotic alien crystal technology and deal with the subtleties of general relativity ("A Matter of Time") in the short time required of Carter (typically less than a day). Even as a physicist, this combination of theoretical insight and practical hands-on engineering ability is completely foreign. Incredibly, she has no civilian pedigree as a theoretical astrophysicist. Contrary to popular "can-do" myths, Carter's mastery of theoretical physics cannot come from being self-taught. There is also no logical reason for how she ended up in a late-1990s military academy setting with mastery in astrophysics, rather than at a major civilian astrophysical research institution such as Harvard or Caltech. As a leading world authority on relativistic astrophysics ("Prodigy," "Children of a Lesser God"), her reputation has to derive from some civilian lineage, certainly not from a military academy! In fact, the alternate Dr. Carter from the parallel universe in "Point of View" is a much more believable astrophysicist, even down to her outward appearance and temperament. Her personality and conversational style are exactly interchangeable with Dr. Arroway (a Ph.D. from MIT). I think the Dr. Carter from the parallel universe, with Boot Camp training, could easily have handled munitions as well as Major Carter and the civilian Daniel Jackson. Then again, you would have had a different chemistry between Carter and O'Neill with substantial repercussions to the series. Oh well. Perhaps as in the real world, it's best not to tinker with a working relationship.

So how does a grumpy astronomer like me feel about the *Stargate SG-1* experience? I may have just performed a needless dissection of the series, but this is not my state of mind when I am watching the episodes. The bottom line is that *Stargate SG-1* artfully and seductively modifies those scientific principles it needs in order to entertain us each week! In the season one DVD featurette, actress Amanda Tapping says, "This should be a show that entertains and allows people to think beyond what they normally think about.

Maybe take you to a different place and make you ask questions. Is that possible? Yeah, it is!" I think Ms. Tapping strikes the only chord that really makes any sense in SF. A good, compelling story never succeeds on the basis of its technical and scientific accuracy. SF is an art form very close to painting and music. Its elements are chosen to emotionally bring us somewhere else for a few moments in our busy lives, not to technically explain how we got there. This place is based on the universe we wistfully wish we could inhabit, rather than the all-too-restrictive one we find ourselves in 24/7/365. SF is not supposed to be docu-drama! By holding *Stargate SG-1* up to the mirror of exacting scientific accuracy, we are not playing fair with the whole artistic point of the story-telling. We walk through an art museum and criticize the Old Masters for their lack of photographic realism and never really get the point of it all. But if we chose to make the journey in a different way and simply enjoy the moments of pleasant and sometimes thought-provoking escape, we end up where Ms. Tapping would prefer us to be. In the grand scheme of things, what is the harm in that?

REFERENCES

Anderson, Poul. "Door to Anywhere" in *Galaxy Science Fiction*, New York: The Guinn Co., December 1966.

Asimov, I. *The End of Eternity*, Greenwich: Fawcett Publications, 1971.

Baxter, Stephen. *Manifold Space*. New York: Ballantine Books, 2001.

del Rey, Lester. "The Years Draw Nigh" in *Beachheads in Space*, August Derleth, ed. New York: Berkeley Publishing, 1952.

Grogan, Gerald. *A Drop in Infinity*, London: John Lane, 1915.

McDonough, Thomas. *Architects of Hyperspace*, New York: Avon Books, 1987.

Moorcock, M. *The Sundered Worlds*, New York: Paperback Library, Inc., 1965.

Sagan, Carl. *Contact*, New York: Simon and Schuster, 1985.

Stargate Tech Center (http://www.stargate-tech.net/esy/gate.htm)

Stargate SG-1 Episode Archive (http://www.sg1archive.com/)

Gateworld Omnipedia (http://www/gateworld.net/omnipedia/index.shtml)

Episode Scripts (http://www.stargatefan.com/scripts/s4/window.htm)

Odenwald, S.F. "Faster Than Light" (http://www.astronomycafe.net/qadir/astravel.html)

Odenwald, S.F. Astronomy Cafe (http://www.astronomycafe.net)

Odenwald, S.F. *The Astronomy Cafe*, New York. W.H. Freeman, 1998.

Odenwald, S.F. *The 23rd Cycle*, New York: Columbia University Press, 2000.

Odenwald, S.F. *Back to the Astronomy Cafe*, Bolder: Westview Press, 2003.

Saari, Oliver. "The Door" in *Astounding Science Fiction*, November 1941.

Sawyer, Robert. *Starplex*, New York: Ace Books, 1996.

Wandrei, Donald. "The Blinding Shadows" in *Astounding Science Fiction*, May 1934.

Sten Odenwald received his Ph.D. in astronomy from Harvard University in 1982, and has since been employed by the Space Sciences Division of the Naval Research Laboratory (1982-1990), BDM International (1991-1992), the Applied Research Corporation (1993-1996) and most recently Raytheon (1996-2000+), all located in the greater Washington, D.C. area. He has turned his creative energies toward public education, writing for magazines such as Astronomy *and* Sky and Telescope. *He has won a number of awards from NASA, Raytheon and the American Astronomical Society for his education work. He is the author of four books,* The Astronomy Cafe *(1998),* The 23rd Cycle: Learning to Live with a Stormy Star *(2000),* Patterns in the Void: Why Nothing is Important *(2002) and* Back to the Astronomy Cafe *(2003). His award-winning website* The Astronomy Cafe *(www.astronomycafe.com) is a great place to visit for information on space and astronomy from A to Z. Dr. Odenwald currently works with NASA as Education and Public Outreach Manager for the IMAGE satellite project, and is involved with the NASA Office of Space Science's "Sun-Earth Connection Education Form," where he develops new NASA resources in solar-terrestrial science education, and works with teachers at national conventions and workshops across the country. He received NASA's "Excellence in Outreach" award in 1999 from the Goddard Space Flight Center.*

Roxanne Conrad

WHEN IN ROME, DON'T WEAR THAT

The Fashion Police Interrogate Stargate SG-1

FASHION. Dame Edith Sitwell, one of my favorite poets, said, "Good taste is the worst vice ever invented," and she wasn't wrong; fashion has claimed more victims—especially these days—than even the most popularly-quoted disease. (Not Ebola, please. Ebola's so last week.)

What does fashion have to do with our favorite show, *Stargate SG-1*? The same as it has to do with everyday life. It either creates a note of reality that separates clothing from costume, or it dooms the audience to struggle constantly to suspend disbelief—to fit into an off-the-rack universe. Creating a style is all about owning the style, setting the trend and looking natural doing it.

So how successful is *Stargate SG-1* in achieving that goal? I give it mixed results, but with one very important great big honkin' check mark in the plus column: it owns its style.

So join me as we do a fast, merciless review of fashion, substance and sanity in the worlds beyond our own. . . .

THE THEORY:
A BLURRY FAST-FORWARD STYLE GUIDE

Stargate SG-1 has a challenge. It's bigger than that faced by, say, *Star Trek*, that has largely solved theirs by applying bumps to foreheads and reverting to the ever-popular Spandex jumpsuit for curvy females. (This from a show that pioneered the whole idea of Miniskirts in Space! How far we've come. . . .) *Stargate's* problem is larger than that faced by another of my ultimate fave SF shows, the way-ahead-of-its-time *Blake's 7*, which still preferred late 70s-chic leather, lamé and stacked heels for their fearless (and mostly ruthless) adventurers. It's even more daunting than the problem of how to dress diverse alien races on *Babylon 5*, which went with the daring idea of actually going back to classical influences for their inspiration.

Stargate's challenge is to create alien civilizations, nearly every week, that remind us that Earth really is, in a weird sort of way, the center of the universe. What we experienced here is echoed out there . . . and warped. Egyptians become Goa'uld and Jaffa. Crete gives birth to the Land of Light. Nazi Germany is echoed on Euronda, and the Wild West comes to life when Daniel and Jack take up arms against settlers in "Beast of Burden."

In other words, we rarely meet a truly alien race. Fashion in the *Stargate*verse is all about reminding us of ourselves, and seeing ourselves in those we meet, for good or bad.

Even, um, our heroes.

JACK O'NEILL
I base my fashion taste on what doesn't itch. —Gilda Radner

Leaving aside that Jack's favorite outfit probably consists of standard-issue Battle Dress Uniform, Jack's a comfort-driven kind of guy. Utilitarian. Fashion for him mostly exists as something other people care about. His closet must contain rows of faded jeans, faded flannel shirts and faded t-shirts worn soft with years of acquaintance. That's his true self, and boy, does he own that style.

But there's a dark side to Jack O'Neill. It comes out in "Window of Opportunity" with a hilarious scream. The egg-yolk-yellow snowboarder shirt? The goofy cap? No wonder Sam looked so astonished when he kissed her; she was blinded by the fashion disaster. And only a true sadist could torture a golf outfit to such twisted extremes. I call Jack's homage to the PGA "Payne Stewart On Acid."

His best outfit: Jack cleans up just fine in a neatly tailored dress blue uniform. He carries it with dignity, grace and charm . . . and it never looks like something he put on for the day. It looks like something he is, through and through.

His worst outfit: Dear God. I'm still having flashbacks to the golfing thing. And Jack, really, could we talk about the layering problem? Long-sleeved long underwear under oversized shirts really isn't for you. Trust me on this.

However, it's so lovely to see Richard Dean Anderson refuse to Just-For-Men his hair back to its 1997 color! It gives me hope for mankind and the final demise of the comb-over . . . not to mention how easy it makes it to date episodes by the amount of gray in his hair.

SAMANTHA CARTER

If the shoe fits, it's too expensive. –Adrienne Gusof

Sam, you are a goddess among TV women. You're tall, you're strong, you're totally credible as a fighter—when you stand up with the team, you look like one of them, and yet you carry it off with a flair and femininity all your own.

But what's with the hair, Sam? I'm feeling much better about season seven's 'do, but let's face it, the artfully disarranged look of seasons four, five and six had more to do with stylists than sensibility. Packing the hair gel and blow dryer might be feasible, although I don't know where you pick up that *truly* universal power converter—are you hooking up to a portable naquadah generator? Lord knows many of the races you run into could use a good conditioner (hello, Nox? pick up the clue phone!), but keeping that look fabulous must require a lot of intensive mirror time. I like your short, kicky, dry-on-the-go styles better. So do the guys of SG-1, who no doubt used to stand around grumbling as you fluffed the layers into a halo before a firefight.

You have the additional burden of makeup. (Well, I know, everyone on the team does, but it's the job of guys to not *look* like they do.) Yours is totally believable, most of the time. Natural, not overdone, and when you've been beaten and wounded, you actually *look* like you've been beaten and wounded. Kudos for knowing (and showing) the beauty inside, Major.

Though most often you toe the base party line, we've seen you in an interesting variety of outfits: fluffy spring colors, ruffles, leather motorcycle duds, severe pantsuits *a la X-Files*, cleavage and fabulous shoes. Like most women, you're an enigma. I recently said to a guy that all women have five basic sections in their closet: work clothes, comfy clothes, party clothes, formal wear and clothes you don't show your mother. You've displayed all of them, which, to my mind, just makes you even more real as a character.

Her best outfit: It would have been a tough call until season seven's "Chimera," but now there's no doubt. The black party dress with the killer shoes. Take *that*, Buffy.

Her worst outfit: It may just be me, but I'm going with the motorcycle leathers. I'm all for growing as a person, but there's a reason Sam got double-takes from others when she breezed in. It looked like a costume, not comfort.

DANIEL JACKSON
A fashion is nothing but an induced epidemic.
–George Bernard Shaw

Who knew Dr. Danny was such a hunk? When you first saw him on Abydos, wrapped in all those beige layers, he had a romantic charm, and let's face it, *everything* goes with those eyes. But over time, Daniel's displayed both an endearingly awkward fashion sense and a fearsome ability to simply overcome it by the force of his, er, presence.

Leaving aside the robes, Daniel's style was originally something like Jack's, only quite a few degrees less cool; he clearly preferred shopping at the Wal-Mart bargain racks, which genericized him to undistinguished cuts and fabrics. The very picture of an academic, with not so much a contempt for fashion as a blissful ignorance of it, he rarely looked comfortable in anything . . . even BDUs.

And then something changed. Around the time that Daniel's boyish mop of hair was shorn (probably by Hathor, that wench) he developed a personal sense of style. Whether the Hathor hair triggered it, or he just woke up and smelled the catalogs, he began to look both more comfortable and more overtly sexy . . . and by the time he bared his glistening biceps in "Beneath The Surface," any trace of his former academic awkwardness was gone. These days, it's hip to be square, especially when Dr. Danny is the poster child.

His best outfit: oatmeal sweater. Just say those two words to any well-confessed Daniel 'ho, and you'd better have a drool cup ready.

His worst outfit: I'm torn on this one, but I'll have to go with Slave Boy Danny in "Summit." Though the arms were definitely on display, the strange little Pillsbury Doughboy armbands should have been left in the closet.

TEAL'C
People think I have an interesting walk. Hell, I'm just trying to hold in my gut. –Robert Mitchum[1]

For a guy from an alien culture more reminiscent of Abydos than Armani, Teal'c picked up the fashion clue early in the game. Granted, some of his early choices were probably dictated by either Jack or Daniel, but even by the wonderful "Fire and Water" we saw Teal'c beginning to understand the strange customs of this world, and the relationship of dark suits to funerals. He has a fashion challenge much like Spock's: hats are definitely advised when roaming around in public at home. It's a little ironic that Teal'c can flash his Apophis badge to anybody beyond the Stargate, but passing it off as a fashion statement at home is too risky.

Teal'c, interestingly, always wears clothing as costumes; his body is still remembering the weight of armor and a serpent head. That's not only consistent with character, it gives him an interesting sense of otherness reminiscent of *Star Trek*'s Seven of Nine and the ever-popular Data.

His best outfit: I'm going to go with his fabulous "1969" Jimi Hendrix homage. Close runner up: his Lunch Lady 'do rag and unbelievably pink outfit in "Wormhole X-Treme!"

His worst outfit: Even though it's his home planet, he just doesn't look at home in Chulak's robes. And dude, what's up with the bleached-blond chin in season five? Eeep!

I could take some potshots at Colonel Maybourne's fashion evolution, from sinister-but-classy military to stubbled-and-goofy civilian (although

---

[1] Apologies, Chris, but it was too apropos.

I loved the nod to Hannibal Lecter) . . . but we should probably move on to the really juicy stuff.

The aliens.

There's so much to choose from that it's an embarrassment of riches, so I'll just have to stick with the most interesting and obvious offenders—or examples—of fashion dos and don'ts at the galactic level.

HATHOR
It pains me physically to see a woman victimized, rendered pathetic, by fashion. –Yves Saint-Laurent

Hathor is, to me, the most blatant example of Egyptian Hooker Chic in the *Stargate* universe. From her henna-red Cleopatra bob to her over-gilded corset, she is just plain wrong, and Goa'uld to the bone. Trust a snake to reinterpret ancient fashions according to their most gaudy elements.

Egyptian royalty, in real-world terms, had a lot in common with modern-day women. They bathed often, shaved and waxed (all over, generally), wore makeup and were concerned about finding remedies for wrinkles and stretch marks. Their fashions were based on environment: hot climate, light fabrics, frequent bathing. In fact, if Hathor had *really* wanted to make an over-the-top fashion statement, she could have worn a royal robe open in front to the navel with no underwear. That was quite the fad, back in the day.

Interestingly, Hathor's man-enslaving pheromones also have a historical parallel, in a less sinister sense. Egyptian women loved perfumes and oils. High-born ladies used expensive frankincense and myrrh (sometimes in the form of scented cones on their heads, er, wigs), but even poor women were provided with scented oils as part of their wages. Perfume was, literally, money. (And we think free coffee is a perk.)

Hathor had it right in the broadest strokes: Egyptian clothing was definitely form-fitting, made to flatter a woman's figure, and if you had it, you completely flaunted it.

But—Hathor?—word to the wise: go flaunt it somewhere else. Whoops . . . too late.

BAAL
Luxury must be comfortable, otherwise it is not luxury.
—Coco Chanel

The best dressed of the Goa'uld (albeit narrowly beating out the classy Lord Yu for the title), Baal evokes the sinister elegance of a black mamba. His style origins don't owe much to the ancient land of Canaan from which he sprang. Though information on their clothing is scarce, they were probably very similar to the Assyrian fashions, which ran to robes and an abundance of tassels (although, interestingly, the Canaanites seemed to have a Goa'uld-like affinity for silk and finer cloth). His style is probably closer to the Medes and Persians, but then Baal was a very popular god. He got around.

Our Baal is all about the lines. Long black coats with shadowy nuanced patterns, an abundance of buttons—sleek, fast, deadly, complicated. But his Goa'uld origins betray themselves in fabrics: gorgeous brocades, lush dark velvets. And heck, even his personal Lo'tar dresses better than Hathor. (That's gotta sting, for a major goddess.)

In the evolution of the Goa'uld from over-the-top gilded dandies to the cruel and elegant debut of Baal—wasn't Jack's torture in "Abyss" effectively augmented by the gorgeous, tailored appearance of his nemesis?—he represents what we should *really* fear.

The Goa'uld *not* being fashion victims.

THE TOLLAN/ASCHEN/EURONDANS
When people are free to do as they please, they usually imitate each other. —Eric Hoffer

I have a corollary to the Jack O'Neill truism of "Never trust people without a sense of humor": Don't rely on those without fashion sense, either. Not that the Tollan were bad, per se . . . they were just, well, boring. Nice architecture, but their color sense ran the gamut from dove gray to smoke gray, with the occasional dramatic departure to black. (Silver was a shock.) How can you fall in love with a people whose boldest interior design statement is pastel? Sure, they had technology. I'd still rather find out who supplied the Goa'uld.

And, as a corollary to the corollary, there's the Aschen. Bland. And check out "2010" to see the devastatingly chilling effect they had on Earth fashion. That's reason enough to lock their planet out of the dialing computer, forget about their essential slimy evil nature. Not to mention those Euronda folks, who gave boring a bad name in "The Other Side." (I still maintain that they accidentally switched the names of episodes. *This* one should have been entitled "Shades of Gray.")

THE LAND OF LIGHT
Fashion is made to become unfashionable. –Coco Chanel

I'm torn about the Land of Light. They're genuinely nice (though somewhat dim) folks; they even tried to offer the hand of friendship to the Tollan. (There was a marriage made in hell, if ever there was one. I shudder to think what that blend of fashion sensibilities might have spawned. Ditto for Jonas's people had they not been dicking around being picky refugees.) And hey, the Land of Light also had some of the coolest buildings and meeting rooms of any place SG-1 has placed its booted feet.

Interestingly, the inhabitants of the Land of Light have stuck close to their cultural roots. Their clothing has all of the color and shape of traditional Cretan *haute couture*, with one important R-rated exception: traditional women's bodices covered the arms and shoulders, angled in to connect to the skirts at the waist, and left the breasts completely bare. Think a corset, in reverse. (Even their jackets made the same, ah, dramatic open-air statement.) Their skirts were bell-shaped, evoking later French and Spanish fashions of the fourteenth and fifteenth centuries. (The bodices on the gentlemen of "Broca Divide" are a stretch, sartorially speaking; men in Crete were garbed more like the guards Teal'c smacks down. Draped linen loincloths, a fashion probably borrowed from Egypt, were quite the done thing.)

I love people who stick to tradition . . . but can adapt to family hour ratings systems.

THE TOK'RA
Fashion is a form of ugliness so intolerable that we have to alter it every six months. –Oscar Wilde

The Tok'ra like to say they're nothing like the Goa'uld, and the truth is, they aren't. Goa'uld are all about color, comfort, flash and fashion;

the Tok'ra are more or less the sourpuss Roundheads to the Goa'uld's flamboyant Restoration. The Goa'uld never met a fun fur they didn't like; the Tok'ra apparently don't like anything fun, much less furry. Those crystal tunnels just don't look comfy . . . and let's face it, who wants to sit on a Tok'ra chair for long? Jacob Carter, bless him, carries off the Tok'ra faux-reptile-skin uniform with aplomb and style, making it every bit his own just as he did the USAF dress blues . . . but others aren't so lucky. (Thankfully—unlike Apophis—the Tok'ra do not go in for the bare knees look.)

Take Tok'ra Spice. Excuse me, Anise/Freya. It's not her fault that she was born with a "take me, take me now!" body; but it IS her fault that she's the exception to the demure Tok'ra conservative movement, with her Spandex, peek-a-boo bras and pouty lips. I strongly suspect Anise/Freya of being a Goa'uld plant. Any day now, she's going to take over the resistance and turn them to churning out gaudy jewelry and push-up bras for the masses. (Do we really *know* who owns Victoria's Secret, anyway?)

THE ASGARD
You should try to be an individual. Just like everybody else.
–Anonymous

You wouldn't think that the Asgard would enter into a fashion discussion, but here's the weird thing: they have fashion. Oh, not in the sense of wearing something . . . but they're one of only two races that we've seen who literally wear nothing. (And the second race, the plant guys in "One False Step," were wearing bodysuits and paint, we all know that.) Going naked, now *that's* a fashion statement. It's bold. It's unique. And clearly, it says a lot about their environment and climate.

But mostly, it just says, "I'm a little gray guy, just like those pictures in Mulder's office." And that's just . . . cool. Not to mention reminding us, once again, of our own myths and histories.

THE AMAZONS

All women's dresses, in every age and country, are
merely variations on the eternal struggle between
the admitted desire to dress and the unadmitted
desire to undress. Lin Yutang

OK, I had to include the ladies from "Birthright" in season seven, because (a) I loved their history, and (b) where else would you get a good look at what was on offer from Frederick's of Jaffa? These ladies were just plain interesting. Universally attractive—which, okay, they're Jaffa, and that does seem to happen. And dressed in standard-issue fantasy armor for the female form. That is, impractical but highly decorative armor that both lifts *and* separates.

They were refugees from the Goa'uld System Lord Moloch—a very bad dude indeed, especially back in the Canaanite origins of his mythology. The episode might have ignored the costuming aspects of historical record, but they certainly understood Moloch; he was, indeed, a consumer of babies, the genuine evil article. Sacrificing a child to Moloch's fires was an act of great ritual significance.

And if the Amazons had been true to their Amazonian roots, they would have been lighter by one breast each, probably, to facilitate firing their bows. And the Amazons were traditionally portrayed as big on animal skins, mostly fastened over one shoulder a la cavewoman chic. Not especially fetching, as pinup girls, so it's logical that they might have picked up a fashion tip or two along the millennia.

I personally think Anise is supplying them on the q.t.

THE ASCENDED

Wise people, after they have listened to the laws, become
serene, like a deep, smooth still lake. –Dhammapada, V. 82

They glow. Lots. (Except when Daniel doesn't, leaving aside the fabulous gleam of his oatmeal sweater.) They also seem to tend toward robes, which blow in unfelt winds (even Daniel, in "Full Circle," though he was cheating by wearing his Abydonian garb instead of the standard-issue Ascended White). Jack O'Neill's description of them as "glowing jellyfish" isn't far from the truth, from a fashionista point of view.

Angels, anyone?

And Anubis, dude, I know you're stuck halfway back from Enlightenment (half-lightenment?), but you ought to know by now that the whole *Star Wars* Evil Emperor Palpatine look is so *over*. You may not have a face, but nobody's scared of a sack of dirty laundry, no matter how smoothly it glides across the floor. I know, you're going for the prototypical Evil Medieval Monk look, but boy. The team's still gonna send you to that great Laundromat in the sky, where you'll be put in the perpetual fluff cycle to stick to that one, cursed, static-ridden sock.

THERE AND BACK AGAIN
Fashion is something that goes in one year and out the other.
–Denise Klahn

I have to commend the writers, the set technicians and artists, the costumers and—maybe above all—the actors, for making us believe this wide, wild *Stargate* universe.

From naked Asgard to overdressed Goa'uld, it all makes a certain kind of sense. Every race's "look" reminds us of home in some way: good, bad, scary, hilarious, indifferent. It's interesting that the color scheme reserved for the *most* frightening of *Stargate* villains . . . the ones who mirror our own very worst traits . . . is devoid of style at all. Grays evoke a colorless, empty-souled society. We traditionally associate villains with the dashing darkness of Baal or even the brooding, not-very-menacing faceless gloom of Anubis. Unrelieved grays in plain fabrics remind us of lives not fully lived, of ashes and of atrocity. It reminds us of the human race's seemingly unlimited potential for villainy.

The hard work that *Stargate* has put into creating this alien universe has paid off in a rich, varied, constantly interesting tapestry that reminds us, once again, of ourselves.

Because, as Jack O'Neill would say, it really is all about us. Honest.

The author of twelve novels and a host of short stories, Roxanne Longstreet Conrad's most recent books are Ill Wind *and* Heat Stroke *(as Rachel Caine) and* Exile, Texas *(as Roxanne Conrad). She is a professional writer, editor and business communicator, a recovering accountant, and is a dedicated (some might say rabid) fan of*

Stargate SG-1. *She has also contributed to BenBella Books's* Seven Seasons of Buffy *anthology. She resides in the Dallas, Texas, area with her husband, artist R. Cat Conrad, and their rather eclectic pets—reptiles with Latin names and sweet dispositions. Visit her websites: www.rachelcaine.com and www.artistsinresidence.com/rlc.*

Kelley Walters

I'M NOT AN ARCHETYPE BUT I PLAY ONE ON TV

Myth and Meaning in Stargate SG-1

ARCHETYPES ARE A DOORWAY into a collective dream. Walk through the door and you get a glimpse of yourself as a person. But like looking into a scrying glass, the glimpse is more than it appears. Look deeper and you'll see not only yourself, but all of humanity looking back at you.

The psychologist Carl Jung said, "The psyche is not of today. Its ancestry goes back many millions of years. Individual consciousness is only the flower and the fruit of a season, sprung from the perennial rhizome beneath the earth."[1]

The collective conscience, "the storehouse of ideas and forces shared by every human being who ever lived,"[2] responds instinctively

---

[1] *The Portable Jung*, edited by Joseph Campbell, translated by R.F.C. Hull. New York: Penguin, 1976.

[2] Johnson, Joni E., *The Complete Idiot's Guide to Psychology*, New York: Alpha Books, 2003.

to archetypes, recognizing universal truth, a lesson that has been learned or perhaps still being learned.

More than just moving us, studying archetypes encourages us to grow. Robert H. Hopcke, a marriage and family therapist and author of several books on Jung, says, "Psychological growth occurs only when one attempts to bring the content of the archetypes into conscious awareness and establish a relationship between one's conscious life and the archetypal level of human existence."[3]

Archetypes move us by accessing that storehouse of ideas and forces and triggering instinctive responses. This is what gives tales like *The Odyssey* and *Beowulf* their potency. Watching Odysseus outwit the Lotus Eater or seeing Beowulf rip the arms off Grendel appeals to the hero (and adolescent kid) in all of us. But cultures change over time, and the stories that make sense in one era don't have the same impact in others.

That's why shows such as *Alias*, *Buffy the Vampire Slayer* and *The X-Files* have such broad appeal. Shows like these have penetrated the culture-consciousness of our generation, becoming archetypes of their own.

Stargate SG-1 is another show that accesses archetypes. Through its plots and characters it blends the heart with intellect, and it shows the positive impact of both friendship and work on our lives. It also reminds us that, no matter how far from the cave we've come, stories still play an important role in our lives.

Along with books, movies and opera, television transmits myths. Archetypes, those "universally recognizable symbols . . . associated with an instinctive tendency to feel and think in a special way"[4] bring those myths to life.

When looking for the themes and patterns in the lives of the *Stargate* characters, I found they, too, lent themselves to certain, universal motifs. In my mind, Teal'c became the Warrior, Sam the Scientist, Daniel the Hero and Jack the Pragmatist.

Caroline Myss, medical intuitive and author of *Sacred Contracts*, says, "The Warrior archetype represents physical strength and the ability to protect, defend and fight for one's rights . . . .The warrior

---

[3] Hopcke, Robert H. *A Guided Tour of the Collected Works of C.G. Jung*, Boston: Shambala Publications Inc., 1999.
[4] Johnson. (See footnote number two.)

archetype is just as connected to the female psyche as the male. Women have long been defenders of their families and the Amazon tribe of Warrior Women has become legendary because of their ability to engage in fierce battle. . . . "[5] I make this point because archetypes transcend gender. Women can be Warriors and men can be Mothers.

I chose these archetypes because they seem to be the primary archetype for each character, but they are not the only ones. You might watch *Stargate SG-1* and see an entirely different set. This is the true power of archetypes: Through their collective message they speak to each of us individually, giving us the opportunity to reshape our lives or our world.

TEAL'C – THE WARRIOR

A Warrior possesses self-discipline, noble self-sacrifice, loyalty and courage. He does not kill for the sake of killing, but will kill—or die—in the name of his beliefs. From courage to loyalty, to the optimism of the Divine Fool that he must display when facing impossible challenges, Teal'c personifies the Warrior.

One facet of the Warrior's shadow is the Traitor. Like Benedict Arnold, Teal'c can be seen as either hero or traitor. No longer served by his position as Apophis's First Prime, he defects to become a member of SG-1, Apophis's enemy, and begins fighting on behalf of the Tau'ri, people from Earth. We think he's a hero because he is no longer working for evil, and yet the title he carries throughout his own culture is "shol'va," or traitor. Yet, as evidenced in season seven's episode, "Death Knell," it is Teal'c's courage to live the life he chooses that gives all Jaffa a choice.

The shadow side of the Warrior also shows itself when war stops being about honor and turns men into cogs in a military machine. In *Fire in the Belly*, philosopher Sam Keen says, "Warfare, which began as a heroic way for an individual to make a name for himself, gradually metamorphosed into conflict without individuality or honor."[6]

This becomes apparent in books like *All Quiet on the Western Front* or the more recent *Flanders,* by Patricia Anthony. The boys in these

[5] Myss, Caroline, *Sacred Contracts, Awakening Your Divine Potential*, New York: Random House, 2002.
[6] Keen, Sam, *Fire in the Belly*, New York: Bantam, 1991.

stories, on fire with a desire to serve, take to the front lines believing that war is a heroic and honorable way of becoming men. Yet they find themselves fighting a war that sees them as nothing more than cannon fodder, a task that puts them at risk, not just for physical death but for spiritual decimation. The only way these young men are able to keep their spirits alive is to find their own code of values and fight according to it, regardless of what is happening around them.

Teal'c's decision to leave the service of Apophis came as a result of his dissatisfaction with the negative way in which Apophis used his power. Apophis saw both humans and Jaffa as tools, or cogs in the wheel, useful only for his pleasure and the Goa'uld race's gain. Believing that the honor of the warrior is in the individual's fight for autonomy, Teal'c left his old life behind, allowing himself to be stripped of his command and his family, and began using his energy to fight for freedom.

In "A Hundred Days," Teal'c displays noble self-sacrifice, loyalty, divine foolishness and courage when he attempts to rescue Jack from Edora. He must dig through several feet of hardened rock to get to the surface. He has four hours of oxygen, only what he can carry, and his strength and determination to fuel him; he can't escape through the Stargate, either. (And if that doesn't signify divine foolishness, what does?)

Like all Warriors, he also has luck. Without luck, the great Warrior of classic literature, Beowulf, would not have found the sword he needed to strike against Grendel's mother. Without the sword, he would have perished in the cave, torn apart by her violent rage.

When Laira hears Sam's voice on the walkie-talkie and gives it to Jack, Teal'c also escapes death. His luck depends, literally, on the kindness of a stranger.

There is another aspect of the Warrior's shadow side that Teal'c must face, and that is integrating his emotions with his duties. As First Prime, Teal'c's job was to serve Apophis, regardless of his feelings. It took many years of friendship with the Tau'ri before he was comfortable expressing emotions.

In the Hindu epic, the *Mahabharata*, the great Warrior Arunja is about to lead his troops in battle. He sees his great-uncle and his teacher in the ranks of the opposing troops and refuses to fight, not wanting to kill the people he loves.

Krishna, disguised as his chariot driver, eventually convinces him to fight, and Arunja leads his troops into action. By acknowledging and working through his fear, sadness and grief, Arunja was able to fight with both strength and courage, and ultimately to win the war.

Part of Arunja's journey was also to experience self-doubt. He wondered whether he was made to be a Warrior, since he was willing to lay down his sword rather than kill the men he loved. Like Arunja, Teal'c has had his own battle with self-doubt.

In the episode "The Changeling," Teal'c and his mentor Bra'tac are ambushed. Due to the stress, Teal'c's symbiote eventually dies, and he is forced to take tretonin, a drug derived from symbiotes, to keep his body functioning.

Without his symbiote, Teal'c's invulnerability is compromised. Like Samson's hair, Teal'c's symbiote symbolizes his strength. And like Samson pulling down the pillars in the temple, it takes an extraordinary situation to teach him that a real Warrior's strength lies not in his body, but in his heart.

In "Orpheus," Teal'c must rescue Bra'tac and his own son, Rya'c, from a Jaffa death camp. Faced with his own weakness, or "kek," which in his language is a synonym for death, Teal'c refuses to fight, letting himself be beaten senseless and later taking Rya'c's place in front of the firing squad.

Believing he is no longer of use, Teal'c is willing to give up his life for his son's. But his comrades pull him back into the fight by reminding him what it means to be a real Warrior, and by giving him the chance to work his "mojo" again.

Compare this man to the Teal'c we met in "Children of the Gods," and you can see his evolution from a soldier who choked down his feelings to a man who now acknowledges them and uses them to make positive change for himself and his people.

Teal'c's true power came in determining his own code of ethics and living accordingly, even when it meant giving up his home and his position as Apophis's First Prime. In these ways, he shows the positive side of the Warrior archetype and becomes a symbol of courage and hope.

SAMANTHA CARTER – THE SCIENTIST

Albert Einstein once said, "The important thing is not to stop questioning." If it is the Scientist's job to question, then Sam Carter is truly a Scientist at heart. With every trip through the Stargate, she finds questions that need answers, and often her answers are the difference between life and death.

Courage, struggle and a willingness to defy convention are also hallmarks of the Scientist archetype. But these very traits often put them in conflict with society or authority.

Newton, for instance, wasn't just thinking outside the box when he proposed his theories on gravity and motion—he built an entirely *new* box. And Einstein wouldn't have needed to apologize to Newton if *he* hadn't proposed the Theory of Relativity.

Scientists must be willing to set themselves apart from what is known and search for that which is not, even when it means breaking tradition or flying in the face of convention. In other words, part of the Scientist's job description includes a rebellious nature.

If the Scientist archetype has a dark side, this is certainly part of it. Why else would the words "Mad Scientist" provoke such a visceral response?

If anyone embodied the Mad Scientist it was Dr. Frankenstein, whose love for science became a need to control life. You could also say the Tok'ra Anise exhibits this side of the Scientist in "Upgrades," when she tells SG-1 she wants them to test a set of armbands that give them superhuman power. Even her host, Freya, is in on the lie, asking them to "forgive the scientist in Anise," when it is the Scientist in Anise who is putting them at risk.

But taken in healthy doses, that wild, rebellious streak is what makes Scientists pursue a line of questioning that most other people would never consider.

Luckily for Sam she's found a job that supports her wild streak—both as a Scientist and as a soldier. It's no secret that Sam (like the rest of the crew) is an adrenaline junkie who thrives on adventure. In her case, this comes out by piloting planes in the Gulf War, going on dangerous missions through the Gate and joyriding on her motorcycle.

But it also comes out in her personal life. In "The First Commandment," she admits she was once engaged to Hansen, because she "had a soft spot for the lunatic fringe." In "Prodigy," she takes the precocious (and rebellious) cadet Jennifer Hailey under her wing because she reminds her of herself.

As an astrophysicist, it's her job to look at the universe in new ways, and as a member of SG-1, it's also her job to *experience* it. The Stargate program is built on the backbone of science and it's Sam's mission (along with SG-1 and the other teams) to gather information and technology to protect Earth from the Goa'uld.

One of the things that I find most fascinating about Samantha Carter is her tendency to be a Scientist wherever she is. Check her out in "There But for the Grace of God" and "Point of View." On two separate occasions, alternate-universe Sam chose not to be a soldier—but remained a scientist, one who was pivotal in the creation and running of the Stargate program in both realities. And, in these episodes, Dr. Carter was able to apply her knowledge of the Stargate to bring a positive result for our planet—if not her own.

And in "Beneath the Surface," she, Daniel, Jack and Teal'c are brainwashed and have false memories implanted so that they can be used as slaves. They labor underground to supply energy to a city, believing that they are helping their people survive an ice age. Though Sam does not remember anything about her former life, the nature of her archetype shows in the way she continues to seek answers and use them for the good of society. She offers to improve the efficiency of the equipment that she and the other slaves use. While her offer is not accepted by her superiors, her knowledge of the equipment allows her to make a life-saving choice at a critical moment.

Sam exemplifies other positive aspects of the Scientist, especially when motivated by concern for others. In "A Hundred Days," when Jack is trapped on Edora, Sam builds a particle beam generator to rescue him. And, in "Small Victories," she finds a way to save Thor's home world, something even the super-intelligent Asgard weren't able to do.

Sam also saves the day in "Jolinar's Memories" when she breaks the team out of their prison cell by using physics as the key; she has the team pack a steaming fissure with debris, so when the steam erupts, it blows the debris into the cover that's trapping them in their cell, ripping it off and giving them a way to freedom.

But what happens when a Scientist's knowledge is used against them? Look at the scientists of the Holocaust. Some supported Hitler's regime, but others were forced to harm people in the name of science, under fear of death or personal ruin. Another example of this plays out in the Val Kilmer movie *The Saint*, when the dictator, Ivan Tretiak, forces the Russian scientist to solve the mystery of cold fusion.

In Sam's case, the examples are a little closer to home. In one instance, Jack ordered her to create the planet-destroying naquadah bomb in "Chain Reaction," even though it would destroy the people who lived there. She was also instructed to set the reactor to explode in "Scorched Earth" to destroy the terraforming ship (and all that was left of an intelligent species with it). Because Sam was under orders, she put her own beliefs aside and did as she was told. Fortunately the situations resolved satisfactorily, but I think this says something about the friction that often exists between the Scientist and rest of the world.

Science is power, and like any power it can be used for good or evil. Fortunately, Sam uses her powers for good. She has taken an inherently rebellious nature and questing mind and honed them into a life of strength and purpose.

DANIEL – THE HERO

The Hero's journey has gotten a lot of press over the last twenty years, since Joseph Campbell's seminal book, *Hero with a Thousand Faces*, became the topic of the PBS special, *The Power of Myth*. This journey serves as a metaphor for the emotional journey that men take in breaking from their families and forming their own lives. (The Heroine's journey can be different, more about going within and forming a deep connection with ourselves and the universe, rather than passing outward tests and achieving separation.)

In broad terms, the journey can be broken down into three phases. The first is the *separation* from one's previous state of being. The second is the *initiation* phase, during which one dwells between two worlds (not-here and not-there). The third is the *return* to some new role or status in the society.[7]

It is important to note that the phases of the Hero's path aren't always taken in order. The Hero can jump from step to step, the steps

[7] The Hero's Journey, Maricopa Center for Learning & Instruction (MCLI) and the South Mountain Community College Storytelling Institute, August 15, 2002, http://www.mcli.distmaricopa.edu/smc/journey

might overlap, or some might be left out entirely. The issue of the Hero's journey isn't the stages themselves, but the process of transformation. These merely act as guides.

Separation

Separation is the first stage, in which a series of events happen that allow the Hero to be propelled headlong into his journey. In "Children of the Gods," Daniel begins the Separation phase when he accepts Jack's Kleenex-box invitation and returns to Earth. Then Sha're is taken from him and he begins his Initiation.

Initiation

Initiation starts with a series of trials that test the Hero's strength, determination and heart. Think of Odysseus, fighting his way home to Ithaca and facing creatures like the Lotus Eaters, Cyclops and Circe.

Daniel's first Trial begins in "Children of the Gods," when Sha're is taken as a host for the Goa'uld Amonet. At that moment, the focus of Daniel's life shifts. No longer a happy, satisfied family man, he is now a man driven and haunted by his wife's disappearance.

In the episode "Secrets," Daniel meets his second test. It has been a year since Sha're was abducted to serve the Goa'uld, and Daniel returns to Abydos to tell her father, Kasuf, that his search for her will likely continue "for many seasons." Ironically, he finds that Sha're is already there, with her father, on Abydos.

The challenge, then, isn't to find her, but to *lose* her a second time. Yet Daniel is not defeated; instead he allows the reunion to fuel his determination to find her.

The third Trial comes in "Forever In A Day," when Daniel must finally let go of Sha're for good. In this episode, Daniel again meets Sha're on Abydos, where her symbiote, Amonet, has enslaved the Abydonian people.

Amonet fires her hand device at Daniel, and Teal'c kills her. Yet Sha're continues to appear to Daniel in dreams, begging him to forgive Teal'c for killing her and to work with him to find Amonet's son.

Daniel doesn't realize that Sha're is not yet dead—that she is, in fact, using the Goa'uld hand device to communicate with him. At the moment Daniel fully grasps her wishes, reality rewinds and once again, Daniel finds himself face-to-face with Amonet.

Teal'c kills her—for real, this time—but instead of being rendered impotent by rage and grief, Daniel is able to immediately forgive Teal'c and charge himself with the task of finding his wife's child.

And so his path shifts. He is still on the Hero's journey, but like all Heroes, he has been molded and changed by his Trials.

In "Maternal Instinct," Daniel moves to the next phase of Initiation, called Meeting the Goddess, in which the Hero "experiences a love that has the power and significance of the all-powerful, all encompassing, unconditional love that a fortunate infant may experience with his or her mother."[8]

Through the course of the episode, Daniel undergoes a transformation in which his mind is awakened to higher realms. When they find the baby, Daniel chooses to give him to Oma Desala for safekeeping, knowing that she will care for and protect him.

Having fulfilled Sha're's wishes, his quest shifts again (although he is not yet conscious of it), from his wife, to her son, to his own inner journey.

In "Meridian," Daniel takes two large steps in which he confronts the authority figure in his old life *and* dies to that life. Often the authority that the Hero must confront is his father, but since Daniel's real father is dead, the authority becomes Oma Desala, one of the only beings whose power he truly reveres.

The Hero's Journey, a website devoted to exploring the classic mythical story structure, says, "For the transformation to take place, the person he or she has been must be 'killed' so that the new self can come into being. Sometimes this killing is literal, and the earthly journey for that character is either over or moves into a different realm."[9]

Exposed to a lethal dose of radiation, Daniel is offered the choice between death and ascension by Oma Desala. But first, he must answer a question: whether his life has been a success or a failure. This is a question he first started considering during the events of "Maternal Instinct." Here is their conversation from "Meridian":

> DANIEL: You said I was the only one qualified to judge myself?
> So however much I want to achieve enlightenment or

[8] MCLI
[9] See footnote number seven.

whatever you want to call it, what happens if I look at my life and I don't honestly believe I deserve it?

OMA: The success or failure of your deeds does not add up to the sum of your life. Your spirit cannot be weighed. Judge yourself by the intention of your actions and by the strength with which you faced the challenges that have stood in your way.

DANIEL: What if I can't?

OMA: The people closest to you have been trying to tell you, you have made a difference. That you did change things for the better.

DANIEL: Not enough.

OMA: The universe is vast and we are so small. There is only one thing we can truly control.

DANIEL: What's that?

OMA: Whether we are good or evil.

Believing that he is acting on the side of the good, Daniel takes the final step of Initiation, *Apotheosis*. As Hero's Journey says, "to apotheosize is to deify. When someone dies a physical death, or dies to the self to live in spirit, he or she moves beyond the pairs of opposites to a state of divine knowledge, love, compassion and bliss. This is a god-like state; the person is in heaven and beyond all strife."[10]

Return

During "Abyss," Daniel begins the final stage of his journey, the Return. Ironically, the first step of this phase is the Refusal to Return, which Daniel lives out by refusing to help Jack break free of Baal's grasp. He knows from experience that the Ancients will banish anyone who inappropriately advances a lower being's evolution.

But in "Full Circle," Daniel realizes that living by the Ancients' rules isn't enough for him. He must take back his own power. Thus, he deliberately attempts to stop Anubis from destroying Abydos, even though he knows it will result in banishment, or worse. This phase of the journey is called Magic Flight, and it leads us right into the next phase, Rescue from Without.

---

[10] See footnote number seven.

Daniel requires some serious rescuing in "Fallen," when he shows up in an alien world stripped of his memory (and his clothes!). Now he is the master of no world, not even his own. He must depend on the people of his new planet to save him, and eventually, when SG-1 arrives, they complete the rescue and take him back to Earth.

By the middle of season seven, Daniel is nearing the end of his Hero's Journey. He has returned to Earth and rejoined SG-1. But he is not yet the Master of Two Worlds. The transition from Ascended Being to human has left him restless, dissatisfied.

He still must achieve the balance between his time in the higher realms and the man he has become. This final step, Freedom to Live, means the Hero has fully integrated his experiences, has let go of his fear of death and is available to experience each moment. He has no regrets, feels no anticipation about the future . . . he simply *is*.

As with all archetypes, there is a shadow side. For the Hero, the shadow could mean getting stuck on any one step, or failing to complete a task. It can also mean abusing the power that comes with all the knowledge the Hero's journey brings.

In "Absolute Power," for instance, Shifu gave Daniel all the knowledge of the Goa'uld in order to protect the earth and Daniel used it to control the world. Of course, it was a dream, but still, the possibility for corruption exists in Daniel, as it does in each of us.

The bottom line, though, is that Daniel, like the other members of SG-1, exhibits the Hero's positive qualities more often than the negative, using them to improve his life and the lives of the people around him.

· JACK O'NEILL – THE PRAGMATIST

The Pragmatist focuses on performing the task at hand, and on doing what must be done to succeed or survive. At his or her best, a Pragmatist exhibits loyalty, presence in the moment and a refusal to give up. They don't rely on faith or on what-ifs, but on taking what the situation gives them and spinning it to benefit themselves, the people they love or society at large.

Jack O'Neill is a Pragmatist. He likes his toys, his sarcasm and fulfilling a mission—not necessarily in that order. He doesn't want to hear Sam's scientific explanations. He wants the bottom line, spelled out in easy-to-understand-and-implement instructions. And he's not interested in Daniel's diplomacy or philosophy, either. He doesn't want to waste time talking; he wants to get the job done.

Pragmatism might be overlooked as an archetype, or even looked down on as being too "of the world" to be truly spiritual. And yet it's just this ability to do "what comes next" that is at the heart of many meditative practices and spiritual disciplines.

Buddhists spend years learning to live in the moment. Sufis make themselves completely available to go where God's breath blows them. When philosopher Gunilla Norris writes about baking bread as a meditation, she's living the archetype of pragmatism by doing what needs to be done. Her awareness of each crystalline moment brings her fully to life.

Pragmatists make lemonade of life's sourest lemons. They keep moving even when they want to stop, believing that good planning, sheer will or just plain luck will get them out alive. Emotions don't slow them down either. Take, for example, Jack's decision to explode the bomb in "Scorched Earth," even though he knows it means Daniel's death.

As a military commander, Jack understands that circumstances might force him to sacrifice one person for the good of the whole. It's not a decision he takes lightly—he mourns Daniel's impending death—but the bottom line is, he is willing to sacrifice anyone, even a friend, for the greater good if the situation allows him no other choice.

A great example of moving on, and of being in the moment, occurs in "A Hundred Days." Trapped on the planet Edora when a Goa'uld attack buries the Stargate, Jack begins to believe he's never going home, and over the next three months slowly integrates into Edora's slower pace and simpler life.

Finally, he settles so fully into his new life that he is willing to face not only his future but also his past. When Laira, the widow he has been staying with, asks him to help her conceive a child, he agrees. Although the show doesn't touch on this directly, his decision to face parenthood again after the loss of his son, Charlie, seems like a signal that his grief had finally eased.

We never know for certain if Laira did conceive, but I found Jack's agreement to be an act of hope, born from pragmatism. If he can't go home, then he is willing to commit himself wholly to his new place, even to the point of starting another family.

Even so, he can't quite leave the old world behind. Jack tells Laira that there will always be part of him that can't let go of his former life, and Laira, also a Pragmatist, tells him, "That's not the part I want." Her acknowledgement of his past, and the fact that she obviously cares for him, seem to give him the freedom to take that step.

Like all archetypes, this one has a shadow side. You can become too practical and forget that there's more to life than work. (If I were applying the Pragmatist to anyone else, I'd have to point the finger at Major Carter for this one!)

You can also turn your pragmatism into oppressive power that you use for personal gain. Check out Colonel Maybourne, a Pragmatist without a conscience. He wants something, so he takes it, with no concern for the rules. He might try to paint it as being for the good of everyone, as in "Shades of Gray," when he is leading a group of renegades to steal alien technology "for the good of the country." But that doesn't change the fact that he's taking by force what isn't his, and what hasn't been offered.

Even Jack seems to live out the shadow side of the Pragmatist in the same episode, when he infiltrates Maybourne's operation in order to flush out the traitors. Daniel, Teal'c and Sam, unaware of his involvement, are shocked by his actions when he steals alien technology, but there is a ring of truth in his speech about preferring to be a living thief than dead and honest.

When it comes to life and death, Jack will always choose life. He tries to leave no soldier behind, even in situations where escape seems impossible. In "Abyss," Baal kills Jack and revives him in the sarcophagus so many times that Daniel, frightened for his friend's soul, comes out of the higher realms to help him ascend.

Jack refuses, claiming that he'd do whatever it took to get Daniel back if the situation were reversed. Here's a transcript from that scene to illustrate.

JACK: Okay, put yourself in my shoes and me in yours.
DANIEL: You'd be here for me.
JACK: Damn straight! I'd have busted you out—blown this rat hole to hell and made sure that son-of-a-bitch suffered!
DANIEL: The others would have stopped you.

JACK: They'd have a hell of a fight on their hands.
DANIEL: You wouldn't do that.
JACK: Baal would be dead—
DANIEL: Jack—
JACK: —And don't think I'd stop there!
DANIEL: You're a better man than that.
JACK: That's where you're wrong!

For Jack, being what Daniel calls a "better man" actually means giving up, wimping out, which is what he thinks Daniel has done. He wouldn't just save Daniel, he'd avenge his death by destroying everything in his path. It's a dangerous side of pragmatism, getting so focused on one outcome that you can't see the entire picture clearly.

In this moment, Jack and Daniel are like a precariously balanced fulcrum, with Daniel seeing the entire scope of this situation and beyond, and Jack stuck in a moment from which he cannot escape.

Despite these occasional lapses into the shadow, Jack tends to exhibit the archetype's more positive aspects. Pragmatism isn't about being the smartest, the strongest or even the most compassionate. It's simply about being willing to get the job done, no matter what it takes, regardless of the weighty toll the responsibility inflicts on one's own soul.

CONCLUSION

Carl Jung once said, "the archetypal images decide the fate of man."[11] While I'm not quite convinced they decide our fates, I do know that they offer a view into our most instinctive selves, and are an excellent tool for learning more about who we are and how we live.

Each of the characters on *Stargate SG-1* offers valuable insights into our own lives, especially when seen through an archetypal lens. This is the true power of storytelling, the kind brought forth in the ancient stories of *The Odyssey* and *Beowulf*, and breathed to life as modern myths through art forms like television, movies and opera.

Archetypes give us a chance to take a step back and see ourselves from a big-picture perspective. They speak to something deeply subconscious in each of us, holding up a mirror to the traits we all

---

[11] Jung, C.G., *C.G. Jung Psychological Reflections: An Anthology of His Writings, 1905-1961*, translated by Jolande Jacobi and R.F.C. Hull, New Jersey: Princeton Univ. Press, 1973, 39.

share, as well as the trials we all face. If we listen, they have much to tell us.

Even when it's our favorite TV character doing the talking.

Kelley Walters has a Masters in Spirituality from Holy Names College, where she studied with groundbreaking teachers like Matthew Fox, Thomas Berry and Brian Swimme. She is the food editor and a regular columnist for the Chattanooga Pulse, *and has written for* Veggie Life *and* SageWoman. *She lives at home in Chattanooga with her husband and their animal companions, Coco and Clare.*

Bradley H. Sinor

FEAR AND LOATHING ON CIMMERIA

W HEN I FIRST REALIZED that the members of SG-1 were going off in search of the Norse Gods in the episode "Thor's Hammer," the initial images that came to mind were the Marvel Comics' interpretations of Thor and the other residents of Asgard. Would the team encounter heroically proportioned beings in nifty costumes? (Call me a victim of popular culture.) Or would they find something far different awaiting them on Cimmeria?

The answer to both questions is yes.

As he does many times, it's our intrepid friend Daniel Jackson who sets things in motion. Stargate Command needs intel about what goes on out there, and our favorite expert on matters arcane has been busy with his books, backtracking the gods. He's highly motivated, what with his lovely wife having been kidnapped and turned into a host for a Goa'uld, but there are larger matters at stake. His research indicates that the snakeheads may not be the only players in the divinity game.

For a little planet way the heck out in the boonies of the Milky Way galaxy, Earth seems to attract a lot of attention from other species. Perhaps it's the climate, but maybe Zed in *Men In Black* was more right than he knew and word has gotten around that this little blue marble of a planet is a good place to hold an "intergalactic kegger."

Since Goa'uld domination of earthly worshipers seems to have been the inspiration for the Egyptian myth cycle, Daniel speculates that there may have been other alien visitors, whom he dubs the Teachers, beings of great power and knowledge that helped mankind. When General Hammond asks where these Teachers might be found, the reply is that they need to look to the Vikings.

(Yes, we all know by now that "viking" is really more of a verb than a noun, but it's TV writing, and I'm willing to cut some slack if there's a good payoff at the end.)

The slide show Daniel gives to make his sale is certainly reminiscent of the action-packed pages of the comics, and it serves to jog Teal'c's memory when he recognizes the Hammer of Thor symbol. He says it represents a planet called Cimmeria, a place that the Goa'uld go out of their way to avoid. Apparently something very nasty happened to them there a long time ago, and they are not in the market for a repeat experience.

O'Neill suggests that if these Teachers are still around, it might not hurt to look them up. His casual tone makes a trip to a place that has put a number one scare into the Goa'uld sound like nothing more than a walk in the park. (What a guy!)

Historically, Cimmeria was the name of a bleak and fog-bound country in the west, visited by Odysseus in Homer's *Odyssey*. Readers of sword and sorcery fantasy will readily recognize the name as the homeland of Conan the Barbarian, created by Texan Robert E. Howard in the pulp pages of *Weird Tales* magazine in the 1930s. Perhaps the name also conjures memories of a crashing soundtrack music and bold cinematic images of a certain muscular film star turned California governor who is not Ronald Reagan. Was Carl Orff's *O Fortuna* playing in the minds of the team as they geared up?

Howard's own poem "Cimmeria" provides a good description of his fictional world and consequently the planet—not to mention some of the more scenic parts of the Vancouver area.

The dark woods, masking slopes of somber hills;
The gray clouds' leaden everlasting arch;

The dusky streams that flowed without a sound;
And the lone winds that whispered down the passes

Brrr. Look all you want, but you won't find that spot on any AAA touring list.

The team's arrival on Cimmeria is rough as they come tumbling through the Stargate as though they'd made the passage through the wormhole at a dead run. (Someone should have tipped off the SGC engineers about installing some of those nifty "inertial dampeners" so popular with the *Star Trek* writers.) This was definitely not the most dignified moment for O'Neill, and to add insult to injury, the first reaction of the locals is to start roaring with laughter, followed by chanting Thor's name. Uh-oh, looks like some kind of home team advantage is in operation.

Ominous and confusing, it still beats being shot at by overdressed baddies. That the Cimmerians are familiar with the Stargate, what it's for and that it still works, is fairly obvious. Tales of it and a respect for what it represents must have been passed down from generation to generation. They have, no doubt, seen any number of gods—or in their view, "Ettens"—show up and get smacked by the Thor's Hammer that stands guard before the gate. The look on the Cimmerians' faces definitely says that they know what's about to happen, and it does, zapping Teal'c and O'Neill off to parts unknown. At least, we *hope* so. Glowing light shows like that frequently mean death or—for the star—a three-act case of amnesia.

This is a bad moment for Captain Carter—who is now in command. She's not happy, but up to it, ready to follow established protocol, which is contact SGC and bring help, but more locals arrive, led by an intense-looking woman on horseback. She is Gairwyn, a friendly sort but with a sword strapped across her back for easy access to the blade. Women being armed and not afraid to fight fits the traditions of many of the northern European cultures. In some cases they were even more dangerous than the men. Gairwyn looks like she knows how to use her weapon and appears comfortable about putting her knowledge to work—fans of Red Sonja and her sister-in-spirit Xena rejoice.

One thing about this episode is that they got the costumes correct for the Earth time period that the Cimmerians' ancestors came from. A notable point being the helmets, especially Thor's. One popular misconception heavily perpetuated by inaccurate but really keen-looking nineteenth century illustration, not to mention a number of

Hollywood movies, is that the North Men wore helmets with big wings or horns on them. Nope, those were just for show. (Or, as of late, comedic effect.) It would make absolutely no sense for a warrior to go into battle with something sticking out from his head that an enemy could grab to yank him off balance. If you want more on that theme, ask any member of the Society for Creative Anachronism. Ask very carefully.

"You're a little short for gods," is the first thing Gairwyn says when surveying the new arrivals. Here we could take this as the show's writers making a reference to *Star Wars, Episode 4*, it being a variation on Princess Leia's first words to her would-be rescuer, Luke Skywalker. Armed and with plenty of friends to back her up, Gairwyn is in a strong enough strategic position to express an honest opinion, as well as a good sense of humor. Apparently the Cimmerians are on friendly terms with their gods.

Those words also let what's left of the team, and the audience, infer that Gairwyn and her people may have actually *seen* those gods. Scary thought. In the *SG-1* universe this is a bit of data one does not take lightly, considering previous experience with the egomaniacal Goa'uld.

This first contact situation gathers the information that the one person who might know where to find O'Neill and Teal'c is a woman named Kendra—who was once a Goa'uld host. (But she's much better now.)

How's that again? On more than one occasion since the first episode, it's been fixed as being impossible to get the parasite out of a human body without killing the host. Once a TV series' rules are set, few are willing to make major alterations or developments in its universe, at least not this early in the run. The usual pattern has always been to leave everything intact and unchanged at the end of each episode. In the play-it-safe world of series television it takes real brass *cojones* to make permanent changes in their writer's bible and—hooray—the producers of *SG-1* seem to be well-equipped.

Now we've got Kendra, living proof of an accepted assumption being incorrect. She explains that the Goa'uld, which she describes as her "beast," was driven from her body by Thor's Hammer in an extremely painful process, "like needles in my brain."

Okay, the process hurts a little, but just take a look at the flash of hope on Daniel Jackson's face at this news. You know he's thinking long and hard about the possibility of bringing the wife to Cimmeria for a Goa'uld-ectomy.

Of course he has to check *this* out.

Kendra doesn't want to return to the labyrinth because it reminds her of what she had been, a conquering beast who killed with impunity. She loathes any memory of that time in her life and is vague about who her beast had been. I suspect that this Goa'uld made quite a reputation for herself when out and about in the galaxy. It might not have been all that safe for Kendra to leave even if she retained memories of her home world's dialing address. Why should she go back when she'd likely be put to death for the capital crime of "impudence"? Or is it "insolence" this week? The Gou'ald certainly have their issues; I suggest intensive therapy and Xanax four times a day to get over themselves.

It is interesting to see that though Kendra has been exposed to the high-tech of the Goa'uld she has fully embraced the beliefs of her adopted home world. One might speculate that after the experience of being a "god" she'd be highly allergic to spiritual matters of any kind. Perhaps her painful cleansing by Thor left her with a unique understanding of its necessity for inner healing.

Many cultural myths require their heroes to go through a terrible testing to emerge stronger for the experience. The German philosopher Fredrick Nietzsche summed it up in the phrase, "That which does not kill us, makes us stronger"—which has been the basis for countless book, film and TV plots as well as spawning a seriously twisted political strategy.

Kendra survived her testing, but her growth has been on hold for ten years because of her hatred of what she was, and she must be aware of it. The "voices" of Thor and the Valkyries in the thunder and wind convince her to move forward.

Lucky for Daniel and Sam it's the storm season in Vancouver. (On the other hand, when is it not?)

Meanwhile, in another part of the planet, O'Neill and Teal'c are deep inside the labyrinth where Kendra once wandered. They're dealing with Thor—and what an impressive fellow he is, even if he is just a fancy answering machine. Standing a good foot taller than the six-foot Jack O'Neill, dressed in helmet and a cape and holding his legendary war hammer, Thor cuts a formidable figure, just like something out of an issue of Marvel Comics. This is more like it!

But appearances are deceiving. In the second season episode "Thor's Chariot," the SG-1 team returns to Cimmeria and finds that Thor and his people, the Asgard, actually don't bear much resemblance to humans. Rather, they are near-twins to the gray aliens who supposedly crashed in Roswell, New Mexico. Where's Fox Mulder when you need him?

The small gray aliens that F.B.I. agents Mulder and Scully tracked during the nine-year run of the *X-Files* had a much more sinister agenda than the chummier Asgard of the *SG-1* universe. It's just possible that they might be a renegade branch of the Asgardian race. I would definitely prefer hanging out with Thor and his associates; they want to help people and maybe toss back some ale. The other grays are more interested in introducing humans to the business ends of probes and other, even less pleasant things. Ugh. Certainly Loki was a member of that galactic S&M club in "Fragile Balance." It goes without saying that O'Neill would have been more than pleased to do some reciprocation in kind on Loki's skinny gray ass, only with the business end of a P90.

But back to Cimmerian deductions: that the Asgard used holograms when they landed in northern Europe to impress the natives makes a lot of sense. It's a lot easier to have a positive impact on a primitive people when you look like giant idealized versions of themselves than some little gray guys with big heads and an allergy to clothing. The Asgard are no fools when it comes to successful public relations with the monkey boys. That their tech appears as magic to a younger civilization is no surprise. As Arthur C. Clarke observed, "Any sufficiently advanced technology is indistinguishable from magic." Heck, I'm still trying to figure out how clapping switches on my desk lamp.

There are small bureaucratic details to Thor's speech to indicate his message is aimed specifically for Gou'ald ears. A native Cimmerian wouldn't understand those bits, but it's clear from the "you snakeheads are a pain in the ass" tone that Goa'uld are chopped liver from any angle when they face the Hammer of Thor. Well, it's good to know the old boy is just as disgusted with the Gou'ald as we are. It gets better: the human host is free to leave. That's an open door for O'Neill but leaves no exit strategy for Teal'c, who will die and die ugly without his symbiot. No way is O'Neill going to leave his buddy behind. This is early in the series; the characters are still bonding, but what we come to know to be a key factor in O'Neill's attitude is already a given. Teal'c is clearly impressed that O'Neill will stick by him, thick and thin. The colonel will find a way out, even if he has to cut one himself with a Swiss army knife—or its USAF equivalent.

But that's a static problem to solve. We have to up the stakes, but still stick to northern European myth cycles; so how about a nice dose of Grendel? Nothing fits the bill like a giant armor-skinned humanoid with really big teeth and claws spoiling for a fight. (Or lunch.) You wouldn't want the SG-1 team to get bored, would you?

The creature has a good scary entrance, and the fact that the deadpan Teal'c reveals a flash of fear and alarm is enough to get anyone's goose flesh up. He recovers his cool—mostly—but by now we know the thing has got to be something truly formidable to shake the big guy's usually rock-solid confidence.

The thing recognizes him as a Jaffa, then proclaims itself to be Unas, the First One, and seems to expect that's enough to get Teal'c to come to heel. Legend among the Jaffa holds that the Unas race was born on the same planet as the Goa'uld, and were the parasites' first hosts and fiercest warriors. In Earth's archeological history, Unas was the last king of Egypt's Fifth Dynasty, who died in 2323 BC. Myth has it that King Unas, once he'd reached the heavens, was a touch peckish and hunted down the gods, cooking and eating them to take in their magic. His Cimmerian-trapped namesake has not been so obliging as to have kicked off yet, nor is he especially fastidious about playing the chef. Raw meat is just *fine* so far as he's concerned. Shades of Gollum chowing down on his latest cave catch!

This is definitely not what Teal'c wants to hear. The Unas have become the stuff of myth among the subjects of the System Lords, tales used to frighten Jaffa children In other words, the boogieman. Until now the only things we've seen able to put the wind up the Jaffa have been their own cruel gods. You mean there's something *worse* out there than Apophis in one of his "moods"?

Teal'c's first words to it—"You do not exist"—are really very significant both in content and delivery. He's trying to convince himself of that fact. This leads me to suspect that Teal'c was one of those children who were really frightened by the old tales. Jaffa society is a harsh and demanding one; their Goa'uld masters would not let it be anything else. Yet even the harshest societies have their tender moments, usually involving families and children; kids love to hear the most outrageous stories, even the ones that scare the dickens out of them. The image of a very young Teal'c hiding under his blankets, afraid of the monster in the closet, is something to which we can all relate.

When you face something that has terrified you on that level there are generally only two reactions: flight or fight. Teal'c chooses the latter; of course it's not like there's a whole lot of latitude in the matter for him. He has grown into a full-blown bad-ass Jaffa warrior who's stood up to a god. Beyond a good work out, what's a primitive boogieman to him? O'Neill and his MP5 for backup doesn't even come into it.

But this creature is pretty tough and creepy. In startling contrast to his fierce exterior (most expressively played by Vincent Hammond) is his deep, melodious, beautifully cultured Gou'ald voice, provided by one of the most recognizable actors in the world, James Earl Jones. Jones brings to the Unas the same hypnotic intensity that he brought to the words of Darth Vader in the *Star Wars* series. One can only wonder if the actor Hammond knew that Jones was going to dub him. Maybe upon viewing "Thor's Hammer" he got the same surprise that David Prowse had when he didn't hear his voice coming from the screen at the movie's premiere.

It's a nice touch to have James Earl Jones involved in this episode. Later in the series we learn Teal'c is a major *Star Wars* fan, having seen it at least five times. It's no huge stretch to accept him identifying with a Tatooine hayseed leaving his desert home to fight Bad Guys. Luke Skywalker, the lone hero, who proved that one man standing against tyranny can truly kick some serious butt . . . uh . . . makes a difference.

It is only after Teal'c and O'Neill have downed Unas with their primitive technology (very handy, those bullets) that Teal'c mentions they might still have a problem. According to legend, the creatures are supposed to possess great regenerative powers and may not really be dead even when they appear to be. He compares the Unas to the legend of the Earth vampire. What kind of TV has he been watching, anyway?

"Do we have to go back and pound a stake through its heart?" asks O'Neill. I have the distinct idea that Jack has also seen enough old monster flicks—or *Simpsons* Halloween episodes—that such an action would soon become standard operating procedure for future SGC teams and he won't need to ask. Personally I'd arm the lot of them with Samurai swords and provide extensive training on the best ways to lop off heads—which usually does the trick for stopping most sentient species. They could hire an antiques dealer named MacLeod to instruct them on the finer "points" of the maneuver.

This also makes me wonder how the Unas ended up on this chilly backwater in the first place. Whatever the reason, the critter is stuck there and has been for a very, very *long* time, alternating bouts of hibernation with feasting on hapless humans or really stupid Goa'ulds. No wonder he's got an attitude that would make Klingons look like peace activists.

Later in the series we encounter the creatures a number of times. Some are (almost) friendly; others prove to be as nasty as their looks. They are a race that commands instant respect, though, if not an overwhelming need to run away from them. O'Neill's description on one occasion of "a big, stinky monster" was certainly inspired by this first encounter. There obviously wasn't much in the way of getting hot bathing water in the labyrinth.

This Unas, too crazy to know when he's out-gunned, keeps coming back for more abuse and just might outlast the ammunition. On the other hand, Teal'c's pretty skilled with the old hand-to-claw combat strategy and shows himself well when it comes to whacking oversized monsters with a big stick. He makes a choice to attack this First One and force it into the archway of Thor's Hammer, knowing that in all probability he will be killed as well, possibly considering it not a bad trade off since he can't leave the labyrinth alive anyway. Not only is he protecting O'Neill with this move, but also avenging himself on the terror and fear that the tales of the Unas may have raised in him as a small boy. Teal'c is a man with issues but he is willing to deal with them, head on, complete with a dramatic soundtrack and some slick martial-arts moves.

Teal'c doesn't die, though it would have been a suitable noble sacrifice if he had. It's a tradition in TV to have actors leaving a series, be it syndicated, network or soap opera, to die heroically. Look at what happens to Daniel Jackson in the fifth season finale "Meridian," when he saved a whole planet—or at least a sizable chunk of it.

Daniel, Carter and Kendra arrive in time for the big finale: toasted Goa'uld with a side order of dead Unas and a somewhat shaken but not stirred Teal'c. By now they all know Thor's Hammer is the one hope they've found that will free the people they care about from their Goa'uld captors.

Now it comes down to the *real* climax for the *SG-1* über-fan: the character interplay. There's not a lot of dialogue, and you don't need it when you have actors who know what they're doing and enough close ups to see what's going on behind their eyes. It's painful and it's sad. Teal'c, the Jaffa who helped the bad guys for most of his life, who is all too aware of his responsibility in uncounted acts of brutality, is willing to remain in the labyrinth. (What a martyr!)

But O'Neill, though he's lost a surrogate son to the Goa'uld, doesn't even consider it. He knows there may be dire consequences in the future, but he has to deal with the here and now, and he doesn't leave his people behind.

He also has a point to make. O'Neill's not the sort to discuss things, but he's an expert at reading people. Certainly he's noticed Teal'c's subtle reactions of surprise to his style of command and attitude, and by now he's gathered a few clues as to just how big the bridge was that Teal'c burned when he threw his lot in to join the SGC. He gave up *everything* except the armor on his back and sense of personal honor in an effort to do the Right Thing. People like that are thin on the ground; you look after them and let them know they are family. Considering Teal'c's background, *family* is one hell of a powerful word with a world of connotations attached, and O'Neill didn't just pick it out of his helmet at random. By his reaction to this nicely underplayed declaration, you know that Teal'c is more willing than ever to fight, kill and die for his friends, not as a matter of duty but because that's what you do to take care of your own, and he knows O'Neill will do the same for him.

But what of the other team members? Carter's military; the concept would have been drilled into her way back in basic training and likely long before that, what with her being a life-long Air Force brat. So that leaves the "outsider."

It's no accident that O'Neill picks Daniel to do the dirty work of destroying the gizmo that can fry the Goa'uld and free the host. O'Neill could just as easily have done it himself, or thrown the staff weapon to Carter; she's the logical choice, being in the chain of command. Daniel's just a civilian consultant after all. It's not his job until O'Neill makes it so. He's got to know for himself that Daniel will also do the Right Thing by the team. There's some doubt, to judge by O'Neill's muttered, "Come on," as Daniel hesitates, hating what he knows he must do, then finally making the sacrifice that will free Teal'c. One hopes that afterwards Teal'c at least bought him a thank-you drink. Or several, considering the circumstances. They've all had a tough time of it.

Growing past your fears is something that everyone has to do at one time or another. Daniel worked past his and came through for the team even if it did tear his guts out. Kendra faced hers by returning to the Labyrinth. Teal'c faced his childhood fears of the Unas and overcame them. All three are the stronger for it. The small nod he gives Kendra before the team departs Cimmeria, and her own acknowledgement of him, another survivor of Goa'uld slavery, is proof that they have both come a long way and refuse to let their fears control them. That Daniel remembers to give Kendra a small gift from Earth for the Asgard, as a remembrance of their first contact, shows his own forgiveness and optimism toward the unknown future.

This isn't going to be the last battle with inner demons that SG-1 must face or the only moral dilemmas that have to be overcome, but they face them and learn and grow from the experience.

Not a bad example to follow, eh?

Not too long ago a friend of Brad's commented that Brad wrote family stories. "Yeah," Brad told him. "If you're related to the Addam's Family or one of Dracula's relatives." Be that as it may, Brad has seen more than his share of short stories published in the last few years in such anthologies as Warrior Fantastic, Knight Fantastic, Dracula in London, Bubbas of the Apocalypse, Merlin, Lord of the Fantastic *and others. Two collections of his short fiction have been released by Yard Dog Press:* Dark and Stormy Nights *and* In the Shadows. *He has also seen his non-fiction appear in* Dark Zones, Starlog, Personal Demons, Enterprise, California Highway Patrolman, Top Deck *and* Long Island Monthly *among many, many others. As prolific a writer as he is easy-going, Brad and his spouse Sue have been known to hang in bars with editors Conrad and Elrod discussing deep and profound topics, like why publishing doesn't pay better, and "who" bought the last round . . . ?*

James Tichenor

A SEASON OF STARGATE

We asked James Tichenor, Visual Effects Director on Stargate SG-1, *to share some of what his life was like during the insanity of a typical production season. Here is his diary chronicling some of the ups, downs and ultimate triumphs of season six.*

FEBRUARY 4, 2002

THE FIRST DAY OF SEASON SIX. One hundred plus episodes of *Stargate* are blurring into each other. You can't help but feel a little overwhelmed at having been on the same show for so long. My year on *Stargate* is eleven months long, so I don't even get the chance to work on other projects and take a break from the *Stargate* universe, as most of the production crew does. The first day of prep of a new season is a little overwhelming. But thank God I have a job, and obviously, if I've stuck around as long as I have, it must be a pretty damn fine job. I certainly can't complain.

This year, as part of my deal to come back and in lieu of a pay increase, Brad has been extremely kind and generous and supportive enough to let me pitch and write a script for the show. I used to write,

183

years and years and years ago, and have always wanted to keep writing. I just couldn't make a go of it as a professional screenwriter. It's a great perk and makes me feel as if I am still working on my first love. I hope to hell it works out . . . .

We're off on a day long survey to all our old haunts: Stokes Pit and the Studios in the old Norco bicycle factory. It's fun seeing all the old work mates, friends now after so many seasons together. We all fall back into our roles, following director Martin Wood around the gravel pit as he explains what we are going to shoot over the next month. The first two episodes have a good hundred visual effects shots: a couple virtual sets, lots of spaceships and a high atmosphere flight sequence. In other words, everything to be expected from a *Stargate* episode. I chat with our new Art Director Richardo Spinache—ten years ago, we first met on season three of a small Canadian TV series called *The Odyssey*. New and familiar faces always brighten the shock of coming back to the same show year in and year out.

FEBRUARY 5, 2002

Day two and already the novelty is wearing off. Another few hours of surveying this morning and afternoon. Long lunch, brutal drives from one end of the Lower Mainland to the other; the airport in Richmond, then out to Stokes pit in Surrey. I wonder: how many more times will we shoot Stokes pit?

It's a joke to call this a "job." How the hell is wandering around a gravel pit, arguing with a madman director about shot construction, traipsing through the brush, pretending to stand on the edge of five foot cliffs that will become hundreds of feet high through the magic of visual effects—how is this working? This is fun. It's like playing, like we're all a bunch of kids making up stories in the secret fort.

Does anyone else feel guilty about this, other than me?

FEBRUARY 6, 2002

We are in the boardroom, right next to the production office. All the department heads are present. Everyone is saying hello, talking about their time off and what fun they got up to on the break. I am noticeably silent, as I worked almost into January and had at most a month off. Nothing to report here.

Slowly, the meeting gets underway. It's been a frantic push to read the first two scripts and try to pull together all the questions that will need to be asked, to come to some sort of realistic number for our visual effects budget. The first two episodes are huge, basically one big TV movie. The show has grown accustomed to getting a lot of effects for a fairly decent price, and like every big episode, the start of the meeting is basically exec-producer Robert Cooper and Martin Wood saying, "This time, let's *really* push the boundaries." Of course, this is standard procedure: they always want more than we had last time, and inevitably this means that every subsequent episode will be judged on the latest big push. We are always trying to top ourselves. I guess this is why so many effects supervisors end up saying no, we can't do this or that or the other. I mean, in reality, VFX *can* do anything. It's just whether we can pay for it, and whether we have the time in the schedule to pull it off.

I know it's a big effects episode when I can't turn the pages in the script fast enough to keep up with Alex, our first A.D. For every non-effect stop in the meeting there are two effects pauses. Everyone looks at Shannon and me for the answers I don't have yet, and I want to scream, "I just got the script! How am I supposed to know what to do here?"

You know it's a big episode when the department heads look at you more than the director, with sympathetic terror. You know it's a big episode when you find your heart racing faster and faster and the challenge is to get out of the meeting before you have a stroke or a heart attack.

These first two episodes? They're big.

FEBRUARY 7, 2002

Same room, different day, smaller, more elite group of people. Today is the day of the brutal six-hour Visual Effects Meeting. They always come the day after the concept meeting and on a show like this, it is a long and exhausting meeting. To go along with that, my back is giving me major grief, and I had to cancel my doctor's appointment to keep plugging through the budget.

We all take the budget apart, number by number, shot by shot, and then put it back together again, usually a little lower than going in, but every once in a while, higher. We cut a bit out today and ended up putting a lot back in with the final shot, an attack run on a massive ancient weapon system, all to be built using 3-D computer graphics. The point was made that we are debuting on a new network, and we have to think of these two episodes as a sort of mini-pilot. I'm all game to spend money, what visual effects supervisor isn't? But when confronted with the reality of deadlines shorter than last year and shows that just get bigger and bigger, I'd be lying if I didn't admit to being a wee bit nervous. I kind of like the feeling, kind of get off on it, which is sick and pathetic, and am sure that this is not unusual. I'd bet there isn't a director alive who doesn't get a little turned on standing in front of a fuck-off big crew, commanding their every motion. It is a little gross to admit. Sorry. But shit, damn, it's a godawful lot of money to play with.

FEBRUARY 11, 2002

Storyboards. Endless, endless storyboards. But this is the fun part, working out the shots, dreaming up the neat ideas that will end up torturing some poor elf sitting behind their computer in just a few weeks time. What's nice about the *Stargate* machine is that we have all been here so long and are so comfortable with each other that ego is rarely an issue. Martin and I and Sam the storyboarder can sit together for eight hours and spitball ideas, and no one is right and no one is wrong. And in the end we end up with some pretty nifty boards. I am never sure who these boards help, other than us visual effectors and maybe the editors. In the end, most of the shots will change from what we have on paper, but every once in a while we will come up with an idea for a sequence of shots that just works, and that, in the end, is why we come to work. Like making a little magic.

So much of effects today are created on computers and in a way I think that has strained the magic of it all. What used to be "How did they do that?" has now become "Oh, they did that with computers." No less ingenious and no less work, but the magic is different. It's really hard for the layman to appreciate a particularly elegant particle system solution or a perfect UV fur map. And it's kind of sad how our part of the industry has opened up, become so free with the secrets. I think we need a Code of Visual Effects, where only the initiated get to know how stuff is done. Like magicians.

But then again, a lot of VFX supervisors work this way—playing everything close to their vests—and damned if they aren't despised throughout the film industry. These people use the mysterious nature of their work as a way to gain control over the whole film making process and to keep as many people in the dark as possible. This isn't what I'm talking about, this power grab using knowledge (or lack of it). What I mean is that, outside of the industry, we would be better served keeping the lid on the "how we did it" jar, not just in terms of visual effects, but everything in film production. DVD documentaries: bad. By giving away all the secrets of how movies are made, we end up stripping the magic from the medium and, in the end, that magic is what keeps the audience coming back.

FEBRUARY 15, 2002

Friday night at 7 P.M., I get a phone call. I'm summoned over to the Post Department and they drop a bombshell. We have to deliver the first two shows much sooner than we had originally thought. Shows that have two to three times the effects won't get any extra work time. It's as simple as that. Network demands.

I know that this is the way on many other shows, but that doesn't make it right. Why spend all that extra money to rush something out, if in the end it's gonna look like crap? The old rule, the old film cliché—faster, better, cheaper, pick any two—is true to a certain point, but only to a point. I can try and bring in as many vendors and as many artists as possible to work on the show, but many times, it's not the number of shots but the level of shot difficulty and the ability to complete them to an acceptable level of quality. No one will remember that we didn't have enough time or enough money. They'll only see the end result and forever after we will be judged on that.

But at the end of the day, if the network won't give us more time and the producers won't write smaller shows, something has to give. And the horrifying thing is to be the little mouse stuck between these two elephants.

Visual effects and post are the mice, if there is any confusion.

So do I say, sure, we'll deliver what you want to the compressed schedule, then try and spread the work around to as many facilities as possible and just get it done, but probably in the end have to sacrifice quality? Or do I scream bloody murder?

What is important here? What's the goal? Great effects, on time and on budget. So how do we do this? Spreading the effects all over the planet is not going to give us great effects, no matter how much money we have, especially as time is short. If I can't be with the artists for direction, then it's not going to work. I've already learned that.

So next step is—what is the chaff in the process? What screws us up? On regular shows, it's the number of revisions. Get rid of that and we might make up a day or two, maybe save ourselves from blowing the basic deadlines. But arguably, the effects won't be as great, at least in the producer's eyes, because they will never have had the chance to make the changes they want. And most of the time, the changes they request do make the effects better, sometimes radically so. Who determines whether the shots are great? I might think we have nailed it, but if I hear from the Producers, "We think this shot sucks," who's to say they are wrong and I am right?

Again, thoughts of getting out drift through my head. But come on, get real: we need the fucking money. And furthermore, this is my job, and I don't quit. I have to stay here and figure this out. And at some point I have to start working on the script Brad has given me the opportunity to write. Yikes! I feel like it's all coming crashing down around me, but I am sure, somehow, we will figure it out. We always do. We always end up in this position, up against some wall or another. But I am surrounded by such smart, talented people that sometimes it feels almost impossible for us to screw it up.

As long as the shots look good. That's all that matters. And that we don't kill ourselves in the process.

MARCH 8, 2002

I haven't written in a long time—almost two weeks. What have I been doing all this time?

Shooting. We shot the first two episodes over the course of thirteen days. The last was a second unit night shoot, the first night work we've done in over a year, I think. It was cold and I was completely unused to dealing with weather and darkness and everything that most of the rest of the film community takes for granted. Hell, I'm a digital guy. What's with the weather? At least we got to blow things up, which made things a little warmer.

I'm trying to figure out a way to deal with the main title sequence that our new network, the Sci Fi Channel, wants us to do, but I don't have the time to properly supervise. I live in horror of burning the candle at both ends, as I have done in past years, only to finish the work and then suddenly be thrust into the arrival my first child. Must sleep now! If I don't I will be doomed. But if I do, I might already be doomed.

Oh yeah, Andy called tonight and asked if we could do some effects for the Sci Fi promos being shot Tuesday. A couple Stargate shots, some holograms and a virtual world. Due in three weeks. Hello? He said he didn't want to make my head explode, but I didn't hear him, because my head had exploded.

We're prepping the next episode, "Abyss," a mixed gravity piece (science fiction is so weird). Martin and I are trying to get our heads around the idea of shooting multiple gravity planes in one set— foreground bad guy standing on the ground, O'Neill pinned to a wall, two different gravity fields. How much can we move the camera without getting into motion control, which is a no-no? How to use the big rotating set the art department is building, and how to tie O'Neill falling in one set with other characters watching in another, all made to look as if it's the same shot? And this rotating set has to fit into our Norco stage, where the ceiling sometimes seems to brush the top of my head. If my head didn't explode before . . . .

Okay, I'm going to break my "don't tell" rule of effects and describe how we're going to do a particularly interesting shot in "Abyss." But don't get mad at me if I ruin the magic. The magician who explains how the magic works risks alienating the audience.

At one point in the story, O'Neill is taken to a cell by a couple of Jaffa. He's thrown into the cell, and as he falls to the floor, one of the Jaffa pushes a button outside the door. We the audience might think: oh, he's activating the forcefield, to keep O'Neill locked up. Ah ha! First step of magic: misdirection (misdirection is key to executing a good magic trick—make the audience think one thing is going to happen, then surprise them with another). Somehow, O'Neill begins sliding to the back of the cell. How does that work? Wires? Magnets? We watch as O'Neill, at the back of the cell, magically walks on the back wall. It's as if the Jaffa have shifted the gravity in the cell from the floor to the wall. Weird. Magic. I hope.

This is a pretty fun shot, and will only work because production has committed to building one fairly expensive set piece. What Richard is actually acting in is a set that can be tipped 90 degrees. The set starts on its side and then slowly rotates onto its back. The real trick (magic) is that the camera is mounted to the outside mouth of the set, locked onto it, so that when the set tips back, relative to the camera, nothing of the set changes. If no one were in the set as you filmed the tipping, visually on film, nothing would happen. It would look as if you were filming an empty set. You kind of have to see the shot to understand.

Once we composite the hallway and the Jaffa in front of the element of O'Neill in the tipping set, we have a foreground element that looks normal (Jaffa standing on *terra firma*), to contrast against this weird shifting gravity element of O'Neill sliding to the back of his cell.

In some ways, when you watch the finished shot, it will look very simple, very subtle. There should be a moment where the audience's mind does a little twist, as they realize something is not quite right, as O'Neill begins walking on the back wall, and (hopefully) a moment similar to when your card, against all odds, is revealed at the top of the deck. This is a magical "ah-ha" moment, and I think it triggers the emotions, a sense of wonder, a sense that the universe, our existence, is full of mystery—strange and unsettling, a little shifting shock that life is not quite what you thought it was—the same sense children feel when they experience some magical moment of life that we adults already know the secret behind. This is what good magic does, what great effects do and, I hope, what this shot will do for just a moment. Create a sense of wonder, a "how is that possible" moment. Make the audience feel as they did when they were three. Bring magic back into life.

We aim high.

Of course, all good things come with pain. As we are designing the shot, we realize that to mount that camera on the rotating set at the distance it needs to be to match the foreground element of the Jaffa, we have to set the camera about eight feet from the mouth of the rotating set. We suddenly realize that the set is fourteen feet long, the camera mount adds eight feet, but the roof of the studio is only twenty feet. Uh oh.

I also want the shot to be one continuous piece—I want to see O'Neill led down the hall by the Jaffa, thrown into the (regular) cell, the Jaffa going over to the button and pushing it, O'Neill sliding down to the back of the cell and then standing up on the back wall. All one shot, no cuts. But because of the height restrictions of the set, we're not going to be able to get as far back from the rotating set, which means we have to be closer on the practical set, which means we won't be able to see the Jaffa go across the frame. Which means we'll have to cut, which means we have to compromise what we can get out of the shot. Which means it's not going to be as good a shot as the shot in my head, and it won't evoke as much of that "wonder feeling" in the audience (every piece that you design into a shot goes into maximizing that feeling). Which is the story of making television shows. Compromise.

One caveat here: Not all effects are meant to evoke the "wow" magical moment. A lot of shots, more and more, are simply about filling out the frame—making a set bigger, going into space, advancing the story. The trick is to know the difference and make the best of the magic moment when you can.

MARCH 10, 2002

I visited Image Engine, who will take the brunt of the first episode's effects. We are already hard at work on anamatics that have to be ready for editing, which is underway as we make our changes.

And must not forget "Frozen," where we are building an Antarctic research dome for a few shots. That's a simple show and it's easy to let it slip from the mind until it's too late. And my script, must write the script; shouldn't be doing this diary, should be writing the script. And Wendy just gets bigger and the inevitable baby seems to float nearer and nearer.

Now I know the season has really started.

MARCH 12, 2002

I am sitting at my desk waiting to be called to set. I've been waiting since two this afternoon. I blew off a couple of meetings with Rainmaker and GVFX, thinking that we would get to our shot right around my 4 P.M. set call, but so far nothing has happened and it's going on 5 P.M. Not that this is unusual. The film industry's number one cliché is "hurry up and wait."

We've got the director's cuts of the first two episodes. Shannon Gurney, my VFX coordinator, is madly spotting the show, transferring onscreen timecodes into our database. With deadlines as tight as they are, the quoting process, where the vendor estimates what it will cost to do a particular shot, is accelerated. We have to get these quotes in and figure out whether or not we are over budget, whether what we shot has exceeded what we budgeted, at least according to our faithful vendors. I have a bad feeling that we will have, as our schedule is accelerated, which will necessitate more overtime hours in the suites.

At the same time, I am shooting promos for the Sci Fi network. Of course I want to help as much as I can, but the preliminary storyboards were far too ambitious for what we could do in the time we had. It's always time and money, time and money, and compromise on everyone's part. I have to start passing more stuff off to Michelle Comens, who is the other supervisor on the show, and more than capable of dealing with it. I am trying to keep the main title sequence going, which has to be delivered almost at the same time as the first two episodes' effects. Keeping a smile on my face and a pleasant attitude is the trick when you really want to scream, "I can't do anymore!"

MARCH 21, 2002

Four days of madness on set. I've completely ignored everything else, including all effects that we are working on for the previous two shows. I wish I could cover it all, but . . . .The artists are screaming for direction, which I will finally give them this afternoon.

Set was phenomenally difficult and mindfucking. The multiple gravity field twists are totally surreal; can you believe that the equipment manufacturers don't design their film gear to be inverted ninety degrees? I feel for Martin Wood, our fearless director. What he had to do to keep "Abyss" in his head! Not just remembering the cuts and shots he had to get, but also the pieces, as many times a shot would be composed of elements shot on three different sets. The hardest part for all of us was just keeping up. Martin's style is amazingly fluid. He loves to be inspired by the sets and the situation, so we always have to be prepared to abandon the prep plan and make it up on the fly. Which is fun, if a little stressful. Just a little. The trick is to try and watch everything as it's being shot, including the non-effects stuff, to try and build a cut of the show in my head, to know what's leading into what and where the effect is going to sit in the sequence. The flipside of that is: Who has the time to sit on set watching the monitors all day?

I think the hardest part of my job is keeping up to five shows in varying stages of construction together in my head at any one time. Everyone else (other than the producers and post, to a certain extent) can focus on one episode, finish the work and then leave it behind. But while I am early prepping an episode, I am shooting another, waiting for post on a third and directing the effects for another two. It's not surprising that scene numbers begin to blur together. And how do you communicate on a film set if you don't know scene numbers?

MARCH 27, 2002

Finally have gotten caught up after last week's marathon visual effects shooting madness. Everyone seems pleased to have had a little attention paid to them. I can feel the crunch coming, and sometimes have to spend more time calming the artists down while inside I'm boiling over. Nothing worse than an artist strobing in his or her tiny little cubicle of digital death. But lucky me—ninety-nine percent of the people I work with are such pros that while I think I am calming them down, most of the time they are taking care of me.

APRIL 12, 2002

Poor Image Engine is in virtual world hell. They are creating the whole vista of a massive two football-field-sized atomic weapon firing hot white electric beams into the computer generated Stargate. Sounds easy but . . . .I realized last week that I should have had built a practical model, but I keep this to myself. Like so much in our jobs, hindsight is what it is.

The world plays as a massive ancient weapon on a planet the superbadguy Anubis controls. He has focused the huge beam weapon to shoot through the Stargate at SG-1, and now we are in a race against time to disable the weapon.

The world Craig Van Den Biggelaar at Image Engine has built is phenomenally massive. My first request was that we be able to move from a far vista on a hill, fly over the trees and then right into the center of the weapon. Film is about presenting contrasts—big wide shots down to extreme close-ups, the bad guy vs. the good guy, hard white light in the midst of black, black shadows. Contrast. Contrast and three dimensions. This is what seems to work best in telling visual stories.

So in the beginning, I told Craig to build his model for both the wide view and the close view, in one shot. The usual method would be to build one virtual model for the wide view that has the scope and scale but none of the fine detail. Then you would cut in close and build a separate model for close up detail.

But since I wanted to move from wide to close (contrast in one shot), Craig has to come up with a way to build the model that has all the wide and close detail and is still renderable. And that looked good from both views. Tall order.

So while all the effects houses scramble to get their shots into presentable shape, I am "encouraging" GVFX to get working on "Abyss," the sets-at-ninety-degrees show. We are shooting the episode entitled "Frozen," which is actually our break show—it has a couple establishing angles on a big, science dome in Antarctica, as well as a number of trick shots involving frostbite and such, but compared to the previous five episodes, it's a breeze. I pulled almost twenty-one hours yesterday, as I got the emergency upgrade to fill in for Andy, our second unit director, who was filling in for Martin on main unit. Of course, lucky me: shooting call for 6 P.M., and that was after a full day figuring out what exactly was wanted out on the second unit. I got the call as I was in the middle of working on the outline for my script. Why am I wasting time here—I should be working on that!

APRIL 19, 2002

I've just realized that I've been so busy, I've completely forgotten about this diary. I am feeling particularly guilty about the lack of a nice coherent through line for this piece and hope those patient enough to have made it this far will forgive me. I know I was going to answer the question as to whether this is the "dream job," but I've been too busy to think about it. Maybe another theme to watch for is "overworked expectant-father visual effect supervisors getting little sleep and complaining a lot" and that the general thrust of the plot of this article is "How the hell am I going to get everything I have to do done?"

APRIL 23, 2002

You know things are rough when you start fighting with the artists. Of all the people to yell at and be yelled at by, the artists are the last folk I need to alienate. At the same time, I work too much?! I asked one to-remain-nameless CG genius (and I honestly don't mean that facetiously) when his last day off was. He said, a month. A month! Christ, it's no wonder he freaks out when I ask for changes to his shots. I had to demand that he go home and sleep. It's been a while since I've seen someone so tired. Each year, we push the effects harder and harder, and what with the shorter deadlines, I am terrified that we may have finally pushed ourselves over the edge.

APRIL 29, 2002

One of these days I'm going to research the idea of the subjective perception of reality—a niche subject to be sure. Everything that we do in effects is based around the idea of "does it look real?" We are always asking ourselves—is this shot real? Will people believe it? What can we do to make it look real? Film and television is all about creating the perception of reality.

I am trying to get Robert Cooper to approve the big, massive virtual weapon we have been working on for the last three months. He doesn't think it looks real. Too CG. Which is understandable, to a certain extent, considering it is all CG.

There are lots of tricks of the trade, lots of little things that we do to make our effects look real. The first step is to go with the premise that one camera shot all the action in the scene, even if it's composed of elements shot at different times. Same with elements generated in a computer. You match the lens, you match the relationship of the camera to the elements, you match the light on all the elements, and you simulate all these things in the computer.

But even when you do all of this, sometimes the shots still don't look real. Sometimes you have to fake it, add stuff like smoke or fog or lens flares or glows, create natural events in the frame that trick people into thinking the shot was captured live.

But you know, even then, sometimes the shots don't always work.

My belief in the reality of the shot may not necessarily be the same as yours. You can get ten people in a room and ask them if they think a particular shot looks real. Odds are at least three out of the ten will not believe the shot. Odds are there will be something in the shot that makes people go, "I don't believe it." And as the nonbelievers make their case, they will throw the believers into doubt. People will stop believing their eyes.

And a crazier thing that happens is when people know that what they are seeing is not real, many times their minds won't let them believe in the shot, no matter how good it looks. This is the worst-case scenario. They know that the matte painted building wasn't actually filmed live but was generated in post. But these people, the nonbelievers, just cannot get over the hump of believing in what they are seeing. They will find a million things wrong with it. Show the same shot to someone who doesn't know that it contains computer generated elements, and ask them to tell you what is real and what isn't and many times they end up picking the wrong element.

Or show them a shot of a photograph of a lovely mountain vista and tell them that it is a visual effect, and they will give you a long list of reasons why the shot doesn't work. Tell them that the shot is completely real, and they'll now have a hard time believing it wasn't computer generated.

Judging what is real and what isn't real is hard, freaky, surreal work. Getting a consensus on how real something looks, and how real we can expect something to look—that is the real fundamental challenge for everyone who does visual effects.

MAY 1, 2002

It's delivered. It's done. Thank God. The first two episodes, the two-parter, is in the can and the stuff looks great. If this seems a little shocking and out of nowhere, like the climax to a story that is not properly set up, then you are right. It is. If we had another couple weeks and maybe another 1,000 words, I'd lead into the final stretch here with more of a play-by-play, but what the hell, it's done. Another Herculean effort on the part of the immensely talented group of artists who either agree or are "persuaded" to work on *Stargate*.

Now, gotta finish "Abyss" and "Frozen," gotta shoot "The Other Guys" and Brad and Robert have started talking about the mid-season two-parter, which they promise is going to be "bigger than ever"! Great. Oh yeah, gotta start writing the script, once I've revised the outline . . . .And the main titles, what's happening with those . . . .And having a baby. Having a baby. Mustn't forget about the baby . . . .How much longer until hiatus?

Yeah, it's a pretty fine job. No denying that.

MAY 17, 2002

"Little" Callum Tichenor was born this morning at 3:40 A.M. 9 lbs, 11 oz, 22 1/2" long. His father is no longer able to speak in the first person, as his mind has literally melted. But he is in love, and for a week or so, might not think about work.

If fifteen years of film work hasn't driven James out of the industry, nothing will. He's tried everything—writing, effects, directing, production assisting, editing, you name it. Sometimes he feels like he's meant to be there, and sometimes he doesn't. Years and years of Stargate, *a doomed season of* Kingdom Hospital, Warriors of Virtue *and countless TV movies and series. Who knows what the future will hold. . . .*

P.N. Elrod

THE VILLAINS I LOVE TO HATE

C HELSEA QUINN YARBRO once pointed out to me that a hero is only as good as the villain—or words to that effect. Since "the team" on *Stargate SG-1* is composed of some conspicuously heroic personalities, it makes sense that they have a surfeit of especially bad baddies to outwit, out-fight and generally have a good laugh over at the end of an episode. And don't I love them for it? Oh, yes.

SG-1 has faced more than its fair share of formidable antagonists, yet there are some in that cruel and cantankerous crowd who go above and beyond (or rather below and beneath) to command my grudging respect along with a kind of satisfying loathing. Not a few of the actors playing the roles of these transgalactic nasties have cadres of loyal followers of their own across the globe. (And you wondered where all those evil lackeys came from—the fan clubs, of course!)

MINIONS AND MASTERS:
WHO'S RUNNING WHO . . . WHOM . . . WHATEVER

The Jaffa

My first introduction to *Stargate* villainy—so far as the TV series is concerned—was the sudden, brutal and bloody entrance of the Jaffa into an otherwise backwater missile silo inside Cheyenne Mountain. (This is where old props go when they're not put up for auction on Ebay.)

The Gate-crashers make one hell of a stormy entrance to our world, their faces masked, their weapons powerful, their movements impersonal and robotic. Their body-concealing, hard-edged armor draws attention away from what's about to happen next—and then it's too late. All eyes are focused on the fire-spewing, death-dealing staffs, a most scary and effective source of terror to the primitive people they're used to subjugating.

Though surprised, our forces respond in kind—but it's a losing fight from the start. We're caught flat-footed, we lose fast and ugly and the baddies carry off one of our own to join Apophis's harem. (Good grief, the lengths some guys will go to get a date!)

The intel gathered in the aftermath of this encounter is slim, but we know the Opposition soldiers have tough hides. Certainly the teams that went through the Gate on later missions must have included armor-piercing rounds for their ordnance. I wouldn't leave the SGC with anything less than an anti-tank gun, but that's just me.

Later in the series, the Jaffa armor gets softer; maybe Apophis made cutbacks in military spending so he could build a new walk-in closet for his ankle bracelets. The Jaffa—except for Teal'c—become less accurate in their targeting, unless it's important to the plot for one of The Team—*go us!*—to be wounded in the line of duty. While some individual Jaffa will sometimes surface for a moment in the spotlight to either turn against their master or do a sneaky-Pete betrayal of our heroes, as villains they're mostly regulated to the role of MP5 (later P90) fodder. They're still pretty tough, though, and don't you just love their all-purpose word, *kree*! It's good for everything from sending thousands to their doom to announcing free cookies in the Green Room.

The Goa'uld

Okay, now *these* things have all the charm (not to mention squirmy shape) of a pissed-off mamba, combined with a high intellect, a psychotic attitude and an ego the size of—well, think of something really, really BIG, then triple it and square the result. Now, give them space travel, high-tech weapons and a few million worshipers to do their evil bidding, and that's one hell of a galactic plague strutting around in gold lamé and bad hats. The only thing worse than their temper is their fashion-sense, which is expertly covered in another essay.

The Goa'uld (or as O'Neill has been known to address them on occasion, snakeheads) are just terminally nasty to free-thinkers of any kind. They're natural bullies; it's part of their DNA to enslave other species, and so far as this fan is concerned the only good Goa'uld is a dead 'un. And I mean *really* dead, no popping into a handy sarcophagus for resuscitation in a later episode. It's been known to happen, but not if you cut their little snaky bodies out and have a barbecue. Invite over a few Unas, make a block party of it.

Apparently the Goa'uld started out being the big fish in a small pond, until they figured how to burrow into another being's head and take over its every action. This makes them the intergalactic equivalent of the advertising industry. Once the snakes acquired opposable thumbs, the rest was easy: just keep infecting higher and higher forms of life, steal some tech and become gods. All the wrigglers are doing it this millennium.

Each crop of Goa'uld stems from a "queen," who passes on her knowledge to her offspring. Since the Tok'ra—a benign offshoot—are fairly nice because their queen was a sweetie, it suggests that perhaps one truly evil queen is responsible for this pack of vicious, power-hungry, sadistic brats. Quick, someone hand me a grenade! On the other hand, as a visit to the ancient Goa'uld homeworld proved, this negativity seems to be standard equipment for all the snakes, and it's the Tok'ra who could be the mutants. Scary thought.

As an aggressive species that takes survival of the fittest (and meanest) to the utmost extreme, the Goa'uld should have died out ages ago from killing each other off, but they just keep popping up, stubborn as weeds. They do have a weakness: that Ego Thing. They like an enemy subjugated and worshipping them, which gives that enemy a chance to try, try another day. (We Tau'ri are really good at that.) Of course, if their enemies try *too* hard, the Goa'uld have no problem with destroying whole planets. Wasteful, but effective.

INDIVIDUAL GOA'ULD, A.K.A. THE SNAKEHEAD SQUAD

Apophis

We've gotten to know and hate this big-eyed cutie-pie over the course of several episodes the last seven seasons. The name Apophis—I always want to say *bless you!* whenever I hear it—took for himself was that of the Egyptian god of war and death, and he's lived down to it by trying to bump off the SGC and all their relatives at regular intervals.

He has some very serious issues about people being "insolent," and he likes them to "suffer" a lot. So lines like "You will suffer greatly for your insolence" are big with him and his many cronies. That, and showing off his knees. I firmly believe his knees have killed more enemies than all his Jaffa warriors combined. One glimpse, and you fall away shrieking, "My eyes! My *eyes!!*" Later on he got around to covering them up. Perhaps his wife had a word with him on the topic. Thank you, Amonet.

He did garner some sympathy when he surrendered to the SGC and spent some time flat on his back with the infamous knees (and the rest of his busted-up body) held immobile by restraints. His hapless host was allowed to surface, and proved to be just another victim of snaky evil.

Yeah, we felt bad for him, but when they both died, I'd have seen to it there were some seriously necessary parts missing before returning the bodies through the Gate. I figure a little brain-ectomy on the snake would do the trick. The N.I.D could have it for a Christmas prezzy.

Hathor

Hathor: beautiful and bad to the bone, she's the nasty prom queen who effortlessly charms away the cute hunk you want for yourself. When she casts her hypnotic gaze on any man, his brain turns to suet. No male can resist her—even Christopher Lowell, who would be cheerfully over-decorating her quarters, given enough leopard print fabric and gold paint.

At every viewing party I've ever attended where Hathor's episodes are run, the females in the crowd, to a woman, sneer, hiss and boo this babe with a sincere, undying loathing. The men sigh with wistful appreciation. She represents all the bombshells who ever wafted away with every stud we ever liked. Of course, the poor klutz is clueless that he's being zapped by a hard-hearted harpy who will use him, then dump him like an old pair of pantyhose.

Hathor's got an edge. It's not *enough* to have a killer body, a face that would send Helen of Troy rushing to a plastic surgeon and—oh, so *unfair!*—brains, she's also got that Pheromone Thing going. One whiff and our otherwise stalwart airmen are tripping on their tongues to do her bidding. We must rescue them from themselves!

Fortunately the women of the SGC are more than up to the task. Along with devotion to duty and saving the Earth, perhaps they are also motivated by memories of their personal nasty prom queens—that, or just out of patience with the men being pushovers for a push-up bra.

With or without the pheromones, Hathor's not shy about her sexuality. She's in absolute control of her men, and it makes her bold and flirty. Even the usually stand-offish O'Neill got a dose of her close-quarters combat style. (X sure marked the spot on *that* encounter.) And as for Daniel—just how long did it take for his new bed to arrive after he and Hathor so thoroughly broke the first one? Her sinuous touchy-feely attitude with her personal guards—all major studs from Muscle Beach, dang it!—tends to inspire blood-boiling rage in otherwise calm and sensible women.

Why? *Because she has what we ALL want for ourselves!*
The bitch.

Baal

Okay, I can understand this dude having Tau'ri fan clubs. He's dishy, dashy, deadly and looks good in black. Bad boys are hotties, and no mistake.

But he's still a freakin' mass-murdering, snakehead Goa'uld!

That means never *ever* trust him, even if the package does have a great smile and Sean Connery eyes and really white teeth and is cute and tall and hunky and moves like panther on "baal" bearings and . . . .
Never mind.

Osiris

Ahem. This guy started out as a guy, until taking over a girl for his host. He must have liked the sex-change, because Osiris was in no hurry to migrate to different digs This was his downfall, eventually, since it gave Dr. Jackson a reason to attempt a rescue of the host and hopefully break his seasons-spanning jinx with women. On the other hand, Danny-boy's knight-to-the-rescue act managed to screw up a means to rid the galaxy of the Goa'uld for good. Naughty-naughty for not following orders, but on the *other* other hand, if he had, I'd be wondering where the hell he stored his conscience that day.

Nirrti

Great, another bodacious babe in a killer bod, dominatrix duds and an attitude like Joseph Mengele crossed with Hannibal Lector. She dices and splices DNA like a sushi chef, then stands back to watch her victims squirm—or go splash. In S&M heels, yet. She's a bad scientist for method, and if there's any justice she will certainly pay for it with hammer toes and varicose veins. (Ah, but too late, her victims introduced her to their own home-cooked version of telekinetic Twist-a-Roni on her neck. Good riddance!)

Anubis

He's got all the trappings of larger-than-life villainy: ominous presence, the Voice, evil minions, black robe with hood (extra large) and lately a bunch of butt-ugly super-soldiers, but alas, he suffers from B-movie dialogue, as O'Neill has noted. *Does* anyone really talk like that? Nah. Only another Goa'uld. No doubt I-will-suffer-greatly-for-my-insolence.

Anubis is on the border between Goa'uld and the Ascended (those glowing squiddy things that float around doing nothing, kind of like one's supervisor at work), but I think he's really a second string choice from Central Casting. Everyone else was down with the flu when the call went out and he fit the costume, so the powers that be shrugged and told him where to stand. Heck, that's how I once got a part in a play.

It's hard to take this guy seriously, and I don't. It's dang near impossible to be intimidated by a pile of dirty laundry. The galaxy is full of Maytags. Sooner or later he will have a fatal encounter with washday.

From O'Neill's first snarky remark to the U.S. president laughing in Anubis's—uh—hood, I've been all set to see this one's fall from pomposity. Unfortunately, what he lacks in depth of character he makes up for in firepower, so Earth has had several close shaves. I'm rather hoping what's left of the other Goa'uld will finally gang up and zap him, or at the very least let's find a sandy-haired farm kid from a desert planet to help get the big A tossed into a bottomless techno-pit.

Oh—that's been *done.*

Dang. On to Plan B, then. Whatever it is. How do you jump this thing ahead to spin cycle . . . ?

GALAXY-A GO-GO: WHAT ELSE IS OUT TO GET US

As if the Goa'uld weren't enough, we've got to deal with *other* heavies doing their level best to steal the butter from our fritters. Why are we humans so popular for conquest or total destruction? No matter. THEY are out there—or right here at home—and when it comes to them you can't be too paranoi—

Shh! What's that? I *heard* something! Quick—where's the C-4?

The Replicators

From their first appearance they inspire freak-out. At least in me, but I have a problem with bugs; it's a Texas Thing, as General Hammond might inform you. There's gotta be at least three thousand kinds of spiders in the world and four thousand of 'em live in the Lone Star State. Replicators would be at home here, yasurefineyoubetcha.

They combine the swiftness of roaches, the icky thin legs of spiders, spew acid more accurately than a spitting cobra and multiply faster than fire ants. Merge those qualities with a hive intelligence, the relentless machine march of their background music, a resistance to bullets and self-repairing components, and you've got a batch of tough, nasty critters no insecticide can dent. The almost god-like Asgard are getting their skinny gray butts kicked by these things.

Even O'Neill appeared to be unnerved by 'em!

Now *that's* scary.

The Team's managed to buy some time for the Asgard to get their extermination act together, but put a wiggle in it, fellas. We don't want another episode requiring the use of full auto weapons being fired inside the steel guts of a submarine, 'k?

The Aschen

Quiet dressers, quiet talkers, politely friendly, if not hinting at patronization, the Aschen remind me of an under-dressed but otherwise well-trained *maitre d'* at a good restaurant. They show you what's on the menu, make a recommendation if you ask and otherwise remain invisible as you rush headlong ordering up exactly what they want you to have. They play their strong points (tech superiority and patience) against our weak ones (wanting that oh-so-cool-tech *right now*). They understand the power of greed and how to use our desires against us, offering such a *nice* piece of candy, only it's poisoned.

Their method of conquest as evidenced in "2010" is remarkably patient. Give us a shot to make us nearly ageless, but taint it with infertility. We die out in a hundred years leaving young-looking corpses and the planet intact so Aschen developers can sweep in with plans for beachfront condos.

Clever bastards. That's their more subtle approach. Their past conquests—decimating millions and seeing to it that the oblivious survivors are grateful to be growing wheat—must have been found questionable even in their emotionally hygienic society. It's possible that some of their cool-faced leaders decided this was far too messy and ugly. Riots are *so* noisy. Much better to obliterate those millions by seeing to it they're simply never born and the current population doesn't figure the problem out too quickly. Then deny everything.

For bad guys, they are possibly *the* most insidious we've ever encountered, all too ready to cut loose with the deadliest biological weapons they can custom design. O'Neill's instincts about them are all too right. Don't trust anyone without a sense of humor. Even the Goa'uld have been known to smile—nastily—but you know where you stand with *them*. The Aschen really *are* what happens when the bean counters take over.

The "Foothold" Aliens

Next time you invade, guys, leave a card.

I've a fondness for this nameless lot of big uglies; they're pretty danged efficient and organized at their job, with contingency plans out the wazoo. We're not sure why they invaded, but they were good at it, having covered their armored asses on the usual weak points of impersonating other—uh—beings and not getting caught at it. Usually when this kind of thing happens it's just a single changeling involved and that person's friends eventually figure it out because he ain't quite himself today. Not so for this bunch; they go in for wholesale copying on a scale that would impress a Xerox CEO.

I'd like to see them back again sometime, but on the other hand, they have a lot of intel on us thanks to the ones that made it through the Gate—they might just *win*.

The Re'tu

We're back to the spider thing again, only these are a lot bigger, armed with blaster weapons and a conscious intellect. And they're invisible. Yow.

Fortunately for us, most Re'tu are not rabid terrorist types, or there would be several large radioactive holes in Colorado with Cheyenne Mountain as the new Crater Lake. Thanks to "Mom" Re'tu, we escaped yet another invasion, but I don't think putting palm scanners on the dialing computers is nearly enough security to keep them out. Neither is waiting for Teal'c to get another tummy ache when one of those critters strays too close to Junior.

Oops. Teal'c is symbiot-free these days. New plan? Anybody . . . ?

Maybe Carter's picked apart the Re'tu-revealing flashlight thingy the Tok'ra gave us, and we have a searchlight version mounted in the gate room. If I were Hammond, I'd certainly see about setting something like that up. It wouldn't hurt to have those attached to every MALP sent through as well. Of course the cute kid—with those big brown eyes I suspect he might be another O'Neill clone—should be able to help the Tok'ra in locating rebel worlds to put on our dialing lockout list.

Let's hope their rebels don't figure out how to use their own 'gates or we could end up as *chutney a la Re'tu.*

WITH FRIENDS LIKE THESE . . .

Sad to say, but many of our best allies are also our worst enemies. I will resist the temptation to list real-world examples of this, but such are the facts of life on Earth. Things are no different beyond the Gate.

We've established alliances with various offshoots of humankind and with several truly alien races, but let's remember that they all have their own problems and aren't always ready or able to help solve ours. I mean, why should they? What's in it for *them?*

The Tok'ra

I know, they're supposed to be good guys, but c'mon, when it comes down to the basics, from any angle they're still *snakes*, and they have their own agenda.

The Tok'ra are usually willing to do us a good turn; after all, we have manpower and raw material and could possibly be a source for new hosts. Combine that with their really keen tech toys and we should together be able to read the Goa'uld the riot act. But the Tok'ra keep their toys to themselves for the most part, unless it's in their interest to be generous, or they can manipulate us into play-testing the new ones for them. They did not do themselves much good in the PR department treating The Team like lab rats, though, in "Upgrades," If we didn't need them to bail us out now and then, I'd say chuck the whole alliance thing altogether.

But then there's Jacob Carter, or as I have been known to refer to him, Sam's Sexy Dad. (It's the leather outfit, eye-twinkle and that whisky-husky voice, oh *my*.)

He was the first Tau'ri willing to become a host for a Tok'ra, though he did barf once the idea sank in. He blamed it on his medication, but I wasn't buying that one. Sure, having a snake jump into his head would cure his disease, lengthen his life, yadda, yadda, but he *did* have to sacrifice his inner privacy to make it happen. Blending is a big honor with the Tok'ra; it's one hell of a violation of self to a Tau'ri. I've got nothing but respect for the man for being able to make that kind of an adjustment, and no small curiosity about some of the undoubtedly interesting internal conversations he must have with his snake, whose last host was female.

The Tok'ra also have this martyr thing going, which likely accounts for their dwindling numbers. They *do* have that predilection for suicide missions. Their beloved queen lost, then found, then lost to them again—and apparently they're unable to produce a replacement, which is weird since the other snakeheads seem to have no trouble coming up with new mamas. All you need is a male donor and a hot tub. Heck, you can find those at many upscale hotels these days.

Maybe the Tok'ra should put in for a little Earthside shore leave so they can chill out and get in the mood.

Unlike the Goa'uld, the Tok'ra *are* nice about vacating when the host says to split, but on a few memorable occasions the snakes have done their own thing by taking over the host. I'm still ticked off with Kanan for hijacking O'Neill's bod and using it to fulfill his deepest, most heartfelt needs.

Why should he alone get to do that? *I* want a turn, dammit!

The N.I.D.

The N.I.D., an organization so secret even *they* don't know what the letters stand for. I'll vote for Nasty Industrious Dickheads; I'm sure O'Neill—who's been shot at by these guys—will agree, adding several choice and venerable Anglo-Saxon epithets under his breath.

Supposedly they're a kind of "civilian oversight" meant to keep an eye on the doings at SGC. Yeah, right. This bunch has a so-called "rogue unit" hell bent on acquiring alien technology, ostensibly for the defense of Mommy Earth, but ultimately it's the money and power they're jonesing for. Who is *their* oversight? Kinsey? Oh pul-lee-ze . . . .

They've substituted a fake Stargate for a spare they found in the Antarctica, swiped needed tech from harmless natives, done deals with Goa'uld, stolen from our alien allies and killed people on our side to advance their goals. Sleaze in suits, this gang, and they're so insufferably *smug* about it, too. There's nothing worse than a fanatic who knows he's right.

They missed the memo about "fooling around with alien toys can be dangerous," as The Team—*go us!*—has learned over the years. But the N.I.D. thinks they're "special." It won't happen to *them*. HA! Isn't it great when they trip on their own conceit and our guys are there to see 'em fall? Or better yet, trip them!

Senator (later V.P.) Kinsey

Oh, I dearly love to hate this guy. He's as slick and slimy as an eel in oil. He's got a pricey suit, a manly handshake, media polish and positively enjoys screwing over lesser beings when not sucking up to superior ones. While he'd be hateful enough as a mere used car salesman, he's unfortunately only a heartbeat away from the Presidency. Woe to us should that happen. The Goa'uld would be running things faster than you could say *Jaffa, kree!*

Kinsey loves his power, but he's not got the spine to hold onto it when confronted by a bully larger than himself. He may be able to order people around, but he's clueless about how to *lead*. He was more than ready to bolt when Anubis (just a hologram version at that!) appeared at the Oval Office. This big, buff politico was ready to cave before a pile of dirty laundry, fer gawd's sake! Thankfully we had a guy with real *cojones* in charge, who faced down the baddy; otherwise Kinsey would be apologizing to the Goa'uld for our naughty planet being in the way of their nice, shiny spaceships.

While I wouldn't mind if the jerk got killed in action, that just might elevate him to the level of "hero." I'd much rather he be packed off to serve as ambassador at large in some scenic spot . . . that black hole planet comes to mind.

Col. Frank Simmons

This guy is a more effective version of Kinsey, in that he makes no effort to be friendly to the people he's screwing over. Well, a morsel of honesty doesn't make up for the fact that he's a nasty bit of goods, willing to shoot a man in the back—in one case, O'Neill—to achieve his goals.

But like the other N.I.D. baddies, he suffers from the "but *I'm* special" syndrome and thinks he's got his six covered when the consequences of his actions surface to bite him—or jump into his brain and take him over. Was O'Neill as satisfied to space him as I was to watch him get spaced? I *live* for those moments!

Col. Harry Maybourne

Harry, Harry, Harry, you're a Baaaad Boy, but still likeable. Once you shucked the uniform you turned quite charming, even vulnerable. You started out as a hard ass, then came around to Our Side. Sort of. You've got your own agenda, and we should always remember that.

What a long and winding road your career has been, first as a ramrod-up-the-butt, order-following N.I.D. stooge, then a rogue player selling things you don't own to the highest bidder, then surprising us with a nature-boy kick by wanting to find paradise. Must have been your little vacation in the tropics that awakened that side of you and turned you into a romantic optimist.

You're a fast learner, I'll give you that, and among your other talents you are absolutely tops at pressing O'Neill's buttons. I love watching you two playing in the same sandbox. Talk about the Odd Couple. In a twisted way you're O'Neill's dark side, and had either of you zigged instead of zagged, might your positions have been reversed? Now *there's* a sick-puppy plot for a parallel universe story.

But in this reality you eventually found the alien sanctuary you'd been looking for, and I'm happy for you; however, you've got a weakness for being in the middle of the action, so I hope you will return.

In the meantime, during your sojourn with the Tok'ra, I wish you luck at working out how to make the perfect margarita.

Invite me over once you get it nailed.

Those are the *Stargate SG-1* villains that have made an impression on my pun'kin brain. I'm sure you have your own faves to hate, or respect, or have a sneaking admiration for, but hope never to meet in real life.

Thankfully, as of this writing, the series is going strong, with a promising spin-off on the way. I'm looking forward to seeing what future desperados are out there running amok in the galaxy (or galaxies), confident that The Team—and future ones—are up to the task of kicking their collective asses.

Go us!!!

P.N. "Pat" Elrod has written over twenty novels, at least as many short stories and co-edited two fiction collections. This non-fiction effort, though, has threatened to turn the usual come-and-go grin on her face into a permanent fixture. The indisputable fact is that she has a "thing" for Colonel O'Neill, and fervently wishes he'd shift himself to come over to pick it up. Preferably bringing along a six-pack and pizza. She's free next weekend.

James Anthony Kuhoric

STARGATE SG-1: CREATIVITY, CONTINUITY AND THE MODERN LICENSED COMIC BOOK

ONTINUITY IS DEFINED as a set story and timeline that builds interwoven details into it with each continuing installment of the tale. In the context of writing a licensed project based upon a television or theatrical program, in this case *Stargate SG-1*, one must accurately incorporate the established histories and details presented from existing stories while developing a new chapter in the property's mythos. In any licensed medium, from video games to spin-off television programs to novelizations, it is an essential part of the creation process. The end product's success pivots on the creator's ability to craft a tale that not only fits in the appropriate set of guidelines, but also adheres to the particulars set by the source show's existing episode log

All mediums present their own sets of peculiarities and idiosyncrasies in developing a new storyline for established characters and events, but one of the most highly dependent on adherence to the rules of continuity is the comic book or graphic novel. Reliant upon the use of artist-created images of live action and animation programming, the licensed comic book has to both appease the fan with the appropriate attention to continuity detail, as well as provide an artistic vision that is similar enough to the source property to establish a familiar paradigm and elicit feelings of familiarity when reading it. Everything from the art to the dialogue must ring true to form a vision that is both complementary and builds upon the continuity library of the license. Even more so than novels, the comic book has a history of developing licensed properties and expanding the adventures of entertainment's most popular programs.

In America, the comic book market is undersized compared to the exposure seen across the world. As the price and mature content of Western comics increased, the fan base shifted significantly from the once primary children's market to focus on young adults with disposable income. Today, the comic book collector has a well-defined set of priorities and biases that determine the type of books he or she seeks out. The maturing of the reading audience has worked to shape the type of books that are published, giving rise to the modern licensed line of products.

In its three years on the air, the original *Star Trek* series created the standard by which television science fiction continuity would be judged. The series developed a cast of reoccurring characters that would endure long beyond the original television run. It was the fans of the show who demanded additional adventures and products based on the crew of the Starship *Enterprise*, eventually turning the fledgling series into a merchandising giant for Paramount Pictures. A mass of merchandise and licensed books followed over the next four decades, creating an accumulation of collectibles that would surpass all other franchises. Comic books were an essential part of expanding the *Star Trek* brand, giving thousands of readers a wealth of additional adventures for the property's original characters up to and beyond the first theatrical release in 1979.

This takes us to the case in point—the *Stargate* comic book series, and the difficulty of developing stories for a beloved franchise with a rich history of continuity. There is no arguing over the fact that *Stargate SG-1* is one of the most creative and innovative science fiction programs on television. The series has earned a place of honor among the longest-running (and most revered) of its kind due to several factors that are rare in the genre. Groundbreaking special effects, innovative stories and realistic character development set it apart from the majority of syndicated cable programming of any variety. All of these features point toward *Stargate SG-1*'s greatest strength: its voluminous and intricate continuity. Over seven years of constant change and compilation of adventures through the Stargate, the program has amassed one of the most intricate and detailed libraries of continuity in television history. From obscure alien species to dire System Lords, *Stargate SG-1* has woven an elaborate web of interconnecting events and dramatic consequences that fans cherish.

To some extent, all licensed products based on television or theatrical properties have the same basic problem. If the source show has an all-embracing continuity or history, the resulting licensed product needs to find a happy medium between producing stories that fit comfortably within its existing parameters, or set themselves just outside the framework where they can develop their own continuity. When the first *Stargate* novels and comic books were published, they focused on the characters and events laid out in the motion picture. Jack O'Neil (the spelling changed to O'Neill for the release of *Stargate SG-1*) and Daniel Jackson were the focal points of the books.

The first comic books, originally published by a small company named Entity Comics, were loose adaptations of the theatrical release. While the series was a limited engagement from 1996 to 1997, the beginning development of a more far-reaching story scope was evident. After the first self-titled *Stargate* series, several short-lived mini series were produced, including *Stargate: Doomsday World, One Nation Under Ra, Rebellion, Underworld* and *The New Adventures Collection.* Before the *Stargate SG-1* pilot premiered in the summer of 1997 on Showtime, these series had taken the first steps of developing stories past the initial adaptation of the film, setting the comic book continuity groundwork for a team of military specialists who would travel through the Stargate to other worlds on regular missions. Had the series continued past the first few installments, there might have been a similar library of adventures set before the established continuity of the ongoing TV series, as in the case of the early *Star Wars* comic strips. *Stargate SG-1* fans often seek out these hard to find series in order to take a rare look at a divergent line of adventures set within the boundaries of their favorite program.

In 2003 Avatar Press developed the Pulsar Press line of licensed comics, in which *Stargate SG-1* was featured. From the beginning, the publisher focused on producing products that were designed to make the adherence to continuity a primary goal. Having learned the successful lessons of past licensed products, Avatar was set upon developing a line that was faithful to the most important facets of licensed comics—style, story and continuity. The first goal was to ensure that the license granted would include likeness rights for the actors of the show. This was a pivotal part of developing a visual story medium that appealed to readers. The early licensed comic books, including the first *Stargate* comic years earlier, were hurt by not obtaining these rights. Readers want the art in the books to look like their favorite actors. Underestimating this simple factor can lead to an extremely short engagement in the medium. Beyond the art, story is the main selling point. If the reader can be engaged with an innovative story that complies with the rules laid down by the core show, they are more likely to continue to buy the product after the novelty of a new series has worn off.

Creativity is an essential part in developing a successful book of any type, but in the case of the licensed comic book, it must coexist with a strict adherence to continuity. Nothing hurts the respectability of a product more than disregard for the histories set down by the source program. Thus, if one seeks to develop a licensed comic book that will appeal to the modern fan, there is an immediate need for the contributing creators to be equally both hired professionals and fans of the property.

It was here that Avatar began in developing their *Stargate SG-1* comic book series. Publisher William Christensen sought out creators for his new books who were experienced professionals as well as fans and supporters of each license. In the case of *Stargate SG-1*, he found an artist who had done striking work for DC Comics' *Smallville* comic book series and a writer who had extensive experience in licensed science fiction, having worked on *Battlestar Galactica* and *First Wave*. He had created a team with the experience and passion for the genre to develop the property. The new *Stargate* comic books would have all the features fans clamored for, including the look and feel of the television series.

Creating a licensed comic book series for a program with the voluminous continuity of *Stargate SG-1* requires a writer to compile significant amounts of research before jumping in. Under normal work-for-hire restrictions, writing for comic books requires a passing familiarity with the character or source material. For example, writing a story for *Batman* or *Spider-Man* requires that the writer be familiar with the characters, understand their abilities and know their general backgrounds. In the case of most licensed properties, MGM provides creators with a story bible that outlines the main characters and sets parameters for what they can or cannot do with them.

The *Stargate SG-1* story bible is a monster unto itself, consisting of over 200 pages of background and outlines of existing continuity. In the pages of the story bible, the writer can find general guidelines and notes on the characters and their existing histories through detailed episode outlines. The character notes describe the main characters' main personality traits, common preferences and quirks. Most of this information is of the basest type. For example, Samantha Carter, the team's leading astrophysicist, is described as the smartest member of the SG-1 unit and always capable of offering a scientifically based explanation of events and technologies. It doesn't tell you about the sexual tension between Sam and Jack, or explain that she would rather spend the weekend deconstructing the inner workings of an alien device than have a social life. The creators have to know and understand the characters deeper than any superficial descriptions to produce work that will feel like the source show. It is the incredible attention to detail that the *Stargate* television writers maintain that has helped to create the vast crossover of details from multiple episodes that are wrapped into an intricate web of continuity. Without a clear understanding of the matrix the television writers use, it is virtually impossible to achieve ideal scripting.

The program bible is specific about things that cannot be included in potential scripts as well. One of the areas that are restricted in *Stargate SG-1* is the use of "magic" or magical creatures like dragons or imps. The writers of the television series are very conscious of *SG-1* being a science-based show and have restricted fantasy elements from the program. That is not to say that the team couldn't encounter an alien race that seems to have magical abilities, as long as they present a logical guess at what scientific properties could be causing the effect. It is possible as well to encounter aliens that look like dragons, but they would have to be mortal, having biological features that support any abilities they have. By instituting these subtle rules the program ensures its original intent is maintained in all media with which the name is associated.

With that information, a creator can design a story featuring characters that can be fine-tuned by the editor. In most cases, crosschecking of continuity by the editor can eliminate any potential conflicts, allowing the writer to begin work almost immediately. In the case of a licensed series with extensive continuity, there are far more checks and balances involved. First, the writer must be very familiar with the property. It is a daunting task to hand a creator 150 episodes of a series and expect them to be able to view and retain the information within any amount of time. If the source show is more restricted, perhaps in the first series of its run or was limited to a few seasons, this approach is more acceptable.

In the case of *Stargate SG-1* it is a virtual impossibility to expect someone to get up to speed with the program in less than three to six months. Assuming the writer is familiar enough with the property to begin penning proposals, they can turn in general ideas for upcoming series. The accepted format for these mini-proposals is the single paragraph pitch, in which the story and all pertinent events are described for approval. In the case of a multi-issue project, the pitch often requires a detailed outline of proposed events in each issue with the summary paragraph. These pitches are reviewed for continuity and content by the resident editor, and immediate revisions are requested if there is anything that contradicts existing back stories or is in any way contradictory to the characters' established personality traits. After the editor has confirmed that the pitch is in line with their publishing plans, the plot is turned in to MGM for their continuity check and approval stage. The licensor is perhaps the most critical of potential pitches, as they have the final say on every facet of the story. Every aspect must fit in with their expectations and future plans for the upcoming season.

Once the plots are approved, the creative process begins anew at the scripting and then penciling stages. Each stage goes through a similar review process that mimics the plot approval stage. At each point, the publishing or licensor editors can either request revisions or nix the entire plot if things go in an unexpected direction. When all of the final approvals have been given, the pages are sent off for finishing and pre-production work prior to the printing of the final product.

One of the most difficult continuity problems a creator can face is the uncertainty of an official factor in the series. For example, in *Stargate SG-1*, the team fought a race of creatures from a parallel dimension that were attempting to destroy all possible hosts for the Goa'uld. The Reetou were interesting creatures that were bound to be revisited in the future and are featured in the upcoming series, *Stargate SG-1: Bug Hunt*. The official spelling of the race is in question, as there are three interpretations circulating between MGM, episode guides and the fans. MGM refers to the race by both "Reetou" and "Reetouh" in their story bible and other directly generated sources. Many fans and online sources have accepted a third spelling that is abbreviated to "Re'tu" as an authentic Tok'ra spelling for the name. None of the three references are identified as being wrong, leaving would-be creators to decipher for themselves which is the most widely accepted, to maintain the standard of accuracy in their works. In the case of *Bug Hunt*, we chose the "Reetou" spelling, as it seemed to be the most prevalent among MGM sanctioned literature. A similar instance can be found with the spelling of Major Neumann's name from the episode "Shades of Grey." Several sources cite the spelling as "Neumann" and simultaneously "Newman." Both of these examples are somewhat minor, but nevertheless impact the accuracy with which die-hard consumers view products. The problem is multiplied several times over when actual actions are misquoted or there is ambiguity about what may or may not have transpired in an implied scene within the television continuity.

There is another factor to consider in the creation of the best-licensed comics. There are several experts who participate in the creation of the comics. Though a given project has a multitude of people who are well-versed in the licensed property—writers, artists, editors and license reviewers—there is one more highly educated party in the creation process. No matter how much your contributing creators know about the license, there is an entire demographic that eats, sleeps and lives the property. I am talking, of course, about the fan base.

Continuity errors devalue a product in the eyes of the fans If the source program quotes a particular event or action, they demand that it be represented accurately in the product they are purchasing. Fans tend to know the characters inside and out, like good friends you see often but don't get to visit with enough. They know each tale front to back and are rightfully discontented when something is left out or misrepresented. It simply takes away from their enjoyment of the product. It is incumbent upon creators in the licensed field to use every available resource to provide the most accurate depiction of the characters possible.

Fans are in the know on deep in-jokes and episode continuity that the writers of the series have worked into the program over the past eight years. Anyone who dismisses the power of the fan base when trying to create a viable licensed comic book is making a major mistake. The fans have a great ability to demand the best in the products they chose to purchase, and with those consumer dollars they influence the creation of licensed products. The Internet has become a universal communication tool for these fans who now band together in fan clubs and on sci-fi boards to discuss the ins and outs of their favorite program. By posting along with them, creators and publishers can increase the excitement for upcoming releases and open a direct line to the pulse of those who are the biggest proponents of the work—and also the biggest critics.

In the end, continuity for any licensed product presents a challenge and it takes a necessary love for the source show to accurately depict it. With programs that build consistent timelines and linear character development, it is an essential component to embrace. Without it, the product is an empty shell and the sales will reflect it through all selling channels. With strong adherence and attention to it, the fan is provided with a product they enjoy and will continue to support with their entertainment dollars.

The author wishes to thank Scott Braden for his contributions to this article.

James Anthony Kuhoric is known for his work writing licensed science fiction and horror comic books. He's crafted tales for many fan-favorite series including Battlestar Galactica, First Wave, Lexx, Army of Darkness *and* Stargate SG-1. *To this day he maintains that next to his family, quality science fiction is his greatest love. People who know him best sometimes call him "Starbuck."*

Julia Blackshear Kosatka

JACK'S BRAIN: WHAT WERE THE ASGARD THINKING?

I N THE SECOND SEASON EPISODE, "The Fifth Race," Col. Jack O'Neill has knowledge of the Ancients downloaded into his brain by an alien artifact. Subconsciously, he uses that knowledge to figure out where to go for help and builds the means to get there. Upon arriving on an Asgard world, they remove the unwanted knowledge and tell O'Neill that humans have "taken the first steps toward becoming the fifth race."

Now, let's see a show of hands. How many of you find it absolutely *terrifying* to think that the inside of Jack's head proves that humanity has what it takes to join the likes of the Asgard, the Nox and the Ancients? Don't get me wrong, Jack is a great character. Much smarter than he lets on; able to make the hard decisions when necessary; even willing to listen to and act on opinions he really doesn't want to hear. Well, from time to time. On a good day. Okay, when his team's winning. (Hockey, that is.)

Still and all, Thor thinks Jack's pretty special and Thor isn't a complete idiot. That goes for the rest of the Asgard as well. Of course, they did have that little problem with the Replicators. As Jack himself pointed out in "Nemesis," when Thor explained how bringing Replicators onboard an Asgard ship to study them started the whole thing. "We do that all the time. We kind of expected more from you guys." Gotta love the Asgard. Best poker faces in the known universe. I wonder how many fishing trips Jack's going to miss out on for that remark. I figure even though Thor didn't bat an eye over the comment (he blinked, he didn't bat), there's gonna be payback. Then again, being captured and having his brain sucked out by Anubis wasn't the brightest thing Thor's done in his life. There is precedent for Asgard mistakes and when they make 'em, they're doozies. (It would probably be rude to get into the whole reproduction by cloning debacle at this point.)

So, the nifty gray guys with all the cool toys and pretty impressive timing think that humanity is slated for the big time. Eventually. When we grow up. Based on what Jack was able to accidentally lodge in his head because he just *had* to see the pretty lights in the thing in the wall. Color *me* convinced.

Of course, Thor met Daniel and Carter first in his Hall of Might on Cimmeria, so, maybe, at least part of the Asgard assumption of humanity's future was based on them. On the other hand, they did have to 'fess up to blowing up his Hammer and leaving a previously protected world vulnerable to Goa'uld attack. Not to mention exposing one of the locals to the truth about Thor and the Asgard much sooner than the Asgard wanted. In short, Daniel and Carter pretty much trashed all the plans the Asgard had in mind for Cimmeria and left them to pick up the pieces. Um . . . bad example.

Of course, this might have something to do with Thor so readily agreeing to have Carter come with him to help defeat the Replicators in "Small Victories." O'Neill wasn't sure Carter would be "dumb enough." I noticed that Thor didn't think twice when she volunteered. He'd seen her work. He knew she could live down to his expectations. If she tried. She did try and he was right. Carter had the stupid idea to sacrifice the brand spankin' new Asgard ship (I hope they spelled "O'Neill" with *two* 'l's) to destroy the attacking Replicators. Makes me wonder if the Asgard only keep us around for the entertainment value and the occasional retro tactical exercise. Sorta like the Tok'ra.

Tok'ra One: "Oh, no, that's too dangerous!"

Tok'ra Two: "I know! We'll get the Tau'ri! They'll do *anything* if we mention technology!"

Now, the Nox met up with Jack and company long before Thor did. Surely the Alliance races still meet from time to time. (At least the ones living in adjacent zip codes. The Furlings apparently left no forwarding address.) They, too, thought humans were very young. They also wear leaves in their hair. Style sense aside, the Nox are great. They're just so *nice*. Sorta like the Canadians of the galaxy. They won't let you give into your baser instincts, but they're very polite about it. They've also got a smugly superior attitude that you can't help but, well, not necessarily *like* but at least not hate. It should be infuriating. Like the Tollan. (*They* are so smug and annoying that few people were terribly upset when they got their butts whooped while trying to sell Earth down the river. Make that "they *were*." They aren't much of anything anymore. Now, if only the SGC would stop saving Kelowna's butt. Has no one noticed that we have the most trouble with other humans? Well, besides the snakes.) Maybe it's because the Nox aren't human. It's easier to take that from someone so obviously alien. Much tougher to take it from someone who might just as well be your second cousin. Nobody annoys like family.

The Nox always seem to be on the verge of letting us in on some cosmic joke. It's like they're just not sure we'd quite get the punch line. I'm actually wondering if maybe we *are* the punch line. (An Asgard, a Nox and an Ancient beam, appear, coalesce in a Tau'ri bar . . . .) But short of getting Lya soused on fermented star fruit, I don't think anyone's going to slip up and tell us. Still, she seems to like us well enough. As she said in "Enigma" when Daniel ignored Maybourne's order to stop the Tollans from leaving, "Your race has learned nothing. But *you* have." Hard to tell if she's seeing humanity's potential in Daniel, or if it's just the vacuum where Maybourne's soul used to be that makes Daniel's action shine so brightly. Or maybe she was flirting. Aliens. Who can tell?

The Ancients are really the big players here. Or at least they should be. After all, they built the Stargates. Which means they must have mastered interstellar travel first. I just want to know how they managed to do that when they can't even hold a straightforward conversation with anyone. (I'm still trying to figure out what the whole "candle is fire and the meal" thing is all about.) All this had to have happened at least several million years ago, if the Ancient woman (Aiyana) found in Antarctica in "Frozen" is anything to go by. Even longer ago, if Carter was right and the Antarctic gate is at least 50 million years old. Pretty impressive. Especially since Aiyana was essentially human.

What was that? The Ancients were human? Well, well, well. Now isn't *that* interesting? We suspected it first in "Frozen." Then, later on, in "Full Circle," ascended Daniel actually says that the Ancients were human. The ones that didn't ascend died of the plague that was first mentioned in "Window of Opportunity." Which makes Oma's comment to Daniel in "Meridian" even more interesting. She told him that escaping death was the wrong reason to ascend. Do as I say, not as I do. Sounds pretty darned human to me. (I'm thinkin' the Ancients are writing their own press.)

But it *does* answer so many questions. Like the inconsistent way they deal with their messes. They were quick enough to "clean up" after Orlin's little adventure in weapons R&D. Wiped out an entire civilization just to make sure his intervention wouldn't cause problems. But did they deal with Anubis? Oh, dearie me, no. Couldn't have that. Tossed him out, but when he got hung up on the doorstep they just left him hanging there with one foot in their plane and one in ours. I'm guessin' that the paperwork to correct a botched forced de-ascension must be *mammoth*. Especially if it has to be done in Zen koans. The initial investigation into who ordered what to happen when is probably still going on. Should it be handled by Internal Security or handed over to the Office of Corporeal Affairs? They probably won't even get to the stage where they actually start pointing, um, tentacles at each other for another millennium or two. So what if he's wreaking havoc on *this* plane of existence? These things happen, dontcha know?

Regardless, Orlin's case was *obviously* handled by one of the rank and file. They booted him out and locked him on a planet with no problem at all. Didn't even have to make him corporeal. Don't know *who* ordered the mass destruction of the population, though. But it said it right there on the "Order for Technology Containment" form. They could have gone for a more surgical approach. Destroy the honkin' big space gun, wipe a few selected memories, that sort of thing, but no. Had to make an example, I suppose. Doesn't pay to argue with management. Just do the job, do it right and move on to the next one.

Looks like Anubis, on the other hand, was given directly to middle management to deal with. It's alternately comforting and terrifying to think that even the Ancients have to deal with pointy-haired bosses. Doesn't it just figure that even when we leave our corporeal selves behind, we take bureaucracy with us.

Also just who *can* ascend? Besides humans, that is. Both the Ancient sort and the current sort. Ascended Daniel was pretty confident that Jack could have ascended if he'd decided to. (Oh, boy, and wouldn't *that* have gotten the Others' knickers in a twist? Daniel can at least *do* subtle when it comes to not following the rules. If he decides it's worth it. Jack doesn't do subtle very well.) The Jaffa know about it through their legends of Kheb. Jaffa were genetically engineered from humans, so that fits. What about the Nox? The Asgard? Hey! Maybe that's what the cloning thing was all about. (Oops, wasn't going to bring that whole thing up. Must be terribly embarrassing.) They're really trying to avoid facing the whole ascension question at all. If they *did* ascend, they'd have to put up with the Ancients for eternity. Given that the Ancients appear to be nothing more than jumped up humans with a rule fetish, I can't really blame the Asgard. Who'd want to spend eternity surrounded by a race of powerful, immortal kindergarten teachers? (Really, think about it, it fits. They did put Orlin in time-out. They tried to expel Anubis and got hung up in the paperwork. No wonder Daniel de-ascended. It wasn't, as is *generally* assumed, due to a year-long coffee craving, but to get away from the *rest* of the Ascended Ones. Shoot, if you're going to have to put up with major league control freaks, you should at least be able to do it with coffee. Okay, so coffee did play a part. Like anyone's surprised.)

So, what we've got here is this: The Asgard were just kinda shading the truth a bit when they told Jack and his ego that we were headed for the big time. See, we *are* the big time. Take a look around, this is it. Or, we're at least related to the big time. We're the corporeal descendants of the Ancients. Whether in a direct line or because they showed up and mucked around with Neanderthals doesn't really matter. Since the Oldsters—I mean, the Ancients—retired from the field to play non-corporeal shuffleboard and whine about how the kids never come to visit, they pretty much gave up their place to their descendents.

The four-race alliance isn't going to become a five-race alliance at all. See, the Ancients bossed around the other races for millennia. The Furlings eventually got fed up and moved on just to get *away*.

The Nox, well, they're the Nox. They just stay home and try to avoid all the neighbors. If the kids' ball pops over the fence, they'll give it back, pat the youngster on the head and send them home. Life is much simpler that way. The Asgard are doing what they have to do to avoid spending any more time than they have to with their former buds. At the same time, they're keeping a close eye on us and trying to make sure we don't turn out like our elder siblings, um, cousins, um, whatevers.

As for us, well, we're going to continue doing what we're doing. We're going to do it with a great deal more humor than the others, though. Notice that with very few exceptions, only the Tau'ri have much in the way of a sense of humor. I can see it now. One day there will be a great meeting of the Nox, the Asgard, the Furlings (if anyone can figure out how to send them an invitation) and the Humans (corporeal *and* glowy). There will be much in the way of genial patting of backs and generally non-annoying smugness and all the while someone in the corporeal human delegation is slipping a little something extra into the punch bowl.

I just hope whoopee cushions will have gone out of style.

Julia Blackshear Kosatka was in her thirties before she realized that everyone else didn't have "daydreams" that ran for months with plots and subplots and several generations of characters. The year 2000 really was the end of things as we know them because that was the year she sold her first story ("Bones of the Dead," Black Gate, Summer 2001). Her most recent fiction sale is "Ned and the Cookie Girls" (The Four Bubbas of the Apocalypse, Yard Dog Press). Julia works at the University of Houston, doing computerish things and counting down the months until her pension is ripe. She lives inside the Loop with her insanely bright ten-year-old daughter and two cats who hate each other with a passion. Life is never dull.

Gina McGuiness, Col. USAFR (ret.)

VACUUM TUBES AND INTERGALACTIC PORTALS

J ANUARY 1965. It was only two months earlier that I received a surprise phone call from a Lieutenant Howard. I was in the last month of Officer Training School at Medina Base, an annex of Lackland AFB. A lieutenant calling me? I didn't know any officers except for those associated with my training. Was I in trouble? What could I have done to provoke a call from this Lieutenant Howard?

"This is OT Captain McGuiness, sir." OT Captain was my upper class training rank.

"Hi, this is Brenda Howard calling from Norton Air Force Base."

"Yes, Ma'am," I replied as I wondered where on earth Norton was and why was I getting this call.

In her deepest Kentucky drawl, Lieutenant Howard explained that her friend in personnel across base had just called to report that a new WAF officer was heading for Norton. She wanted to be the first to welcome me.

"Ma'am, where is Norton?" I sheepishly asked.

"It's in San Bernardino, California. I just wanted you to know that I have a small house and you are welcome to stay with me until you get settled. Here's my duty and home phone numbers. Let me know when and where you are arriving and we'll (she and Lt. Gerry Palmer) will come and pick you up," she added.

"Thank you, ma'am. I appreciate it very much."

How smug I was after that phone call. I knew where my first duty assignment was going to be before any of the other fourteen women officer trainees. We were the women of Air Force Officer Training School Class 65-D, Squadron Four. We started our training nineteen strong and would graduate fifteen. Not a bad percentage for young educated women who really didn't know what they were getting into. We all had believed the recruiter.

Squadron Four was unique at the school because it was the only squadron that included women. The other half of the squadron was made up of men who were to become weapons controllers. We all were college graduates whose motives for joining the Air Force and becoming line officers were as diverse as our backgrounds. The men had other avenues of commissioning to choose from, such as college Reserve Officer Training Corps or the Air Force Academy, but for us women, OTS was it.

In 1965, for the newly commissioned woman officer career fields were not the cornucopia of choices. There would be no future *Stargate SG-1* Maj. Samantha Carter emerging from Class 65-D. We went out into the real Air Force as administrative personnel, education and training, intelligence, supply, information, finance, manpower and other select desk jobs. Opportunities to explore the "wild blue yonder" were not an option for OTS Class 65-D. An Air Force woman would not wear aviator wings until 1977.

A few weeks after Lieutenant Howard's revealing phone call I received a welcome letter to the Air Defense Command from the WAF Staff Advisor, Lt. Col. Gladys M. Nelson. In addition to welcoming me to the command, Lieutenant Colonel Nelson said that, "we are happy to have you in the command, and I know that you will find life as a WAF officer most interesting and challenging." Her letter concluded, "best wishes for a successful future."

I arrived at Norton AFB to begin my Air Force career four years before *Stargate SG-1's* Maj. Samantha Carter was whisked back from the late 20th century to a top-secret facility ("1969"). That base may not have been too far from Norton—as the crow flies, that is.

Our facility was as far on the eastern end of the base as you could get and still be within the security parameters. We shared the isolated patch of property with World War II barracks that housed all of the single enlisted women on base, regardless of unit assignment. On the main base were huge, bustling organizations including the host Air Force Logistics Command with a mission to tear apart obsolete medium range missiles; the Ballistic Systems Division of the Air Force Systems Command, the developers of the heirs to AFLC's trash, and the major worldwide inspection team for the Air Force Inspector General. Units usually stopped concentrating on their primary mission in order to spit and polish and take paper clips out of files when they knew the dreaded inspectors were coming their way. Careers could be made or broken by that wrench left unaccounted for or that certain file folder found in the wrong place. The Air Force, with the IG looking on, certainly was, and probably still is, a much tighter operation than the Stargate Command organization, which seems to run on little paperwork and a penchant for defying orders from superiors.

So there it was: my first assignment headquarters, sitting on the very outskirts of Norton AFB—LAADS, the Los Angeles Air Defense Sector. On a clear day, which wasn't very often even in the mid-1960s, you could see the San Bernardino Mountains thrusting themselves proudly upward, dwarfing the headquarters for Southern California's Cold War first line of defense.

Our building was no ordinary structure. It looked like a four-story, four-sided concrete chessboard, windowless and surrounded by cyclone fencing and barbed wire. Once inside for the duty day, you had no idea until you stepped out at 4:30 P.M. whether the smog had rolled in from the Los Angeles and shrouded the air and mountains in a thick, smelly yellow haze.

This structural cinderblock, named the SAGE (Semiautomatic Ground Environment) Direction Center, housed a computerized system for tracing, tracking and intercepting enemy aircraft entering United States airspace. The entire first floor was occupied by dual IBM AN/FSQ-7 computers. One was operational and one was for training and backup. These vacuum tube monsters cost a whopping $16 million apiece and were the nerve center of SAGE. The AN/FSQ-7 was developed for the Air Force starting in the 1950s by MIT, more than five years after Stargate experiments were conducted by Professors Langford and Littlefield ("The Torment of Tantalus"). This computer was the first large-scale, real-time digital control computer supporting a major military mission and was only one of about thirty that were among the physically largest computers ever built.

Although the term bytes was not used then, a recent article on the Internet pointed out that its real time capacity would only be 256 bytes. To accomplish the same mission today the military could coordinate the entire U.S. air defense system from my iPod and have leftover capacity. But that was 1965, when Maj. Gen. George Hammond was still in college and not yet assigned to that top-secret base where Major Carter found herself transported back in time because of a solar flare.

With radar sites throughout southern and central California, the SAGE system could detect incoming Soviet long range bombers, the Bear and the Bison, while the threat was still far enough away to scramble our fighter interceptor F 102 "Delta Dagger" and F 106 "Delta Dart" aircrafts from their west coast bases.

Who knew that when I left OTS my first assignment would once again team me with some of the same Squadron Four mates, the weapons controllers. Like many career fields, weapons controllers had a nickname—scope dopes. It was a career field not open to women, I guess because it would have entailed combat from in front of a radar scope, directing fighter interceptor aircraft hundreds of miles away.

The hub of the mission was the Command and Control Center with Col. Joe Myers at the helm. With his World War II and Korea aviator experiences he was calm and decisive during our combat exercises. As the information flashed on his radar scope and on the big two-story status board, he was able to make tactical decisions immediately with accurate, up-to-date information.

My job as the information officer was to let the public know how their tax dollars were being spent and how our mission contributed to national security. Every once in a while I'd get a call from a reporter asking us to verify an excited citizen's UFO sighting. During my tenure, our system never detected a mysterious flying object crossing our airspace. Stargate transport surely would have been way under our radar anyway.

Once a year we were very good at picking up a strange object flying out of the North Pole. It was our parent command NORAD, the North American Air Defense Command, which was tasked with following Santa Claus from his frigid home to his U.S. destinations. I would give hourly reports of the famous reindeer driver's position to area radio and TV stations as Christmas Eve night approached.

One magical benefit of my job was being the Air Defense Command information officer that was the closest to nearby Edwards AFB. I was available to provide media assistance for our ongoing projects at the famous high desert base. During that time, the Air Force was testing both the joint venture XB-70 and the YF-12A, a stealth-like black beauty with fighter interceptor potential. In my mind, I could not have been much closer to the future than on those few opportunities I had to witness both aircraft flying. Eventually the YF-12A evolved into the now retired SR-71, which was the supersonic, edge-of-space spy plane.

My second assignment after the Air Defense Command's downsizing, as they'd say today, was to the newly named 27th Air Division at Luke AFB, Arizona. LAADS was gone, and 27th took over scanning the skies from the southwest. My new commander, Col. Leon Gray, was famous throughout the Air Force, having earned fighter pilot notches during World War II and later by setting jet aircraft speed records. He marched to his own drummer and, like the Stargate Command SG teams, Leon never seemed to get called on the carpet by the higher ups. His favorite place to go was Colorado Springs and when the mood hit him (at least it seemed to this first lieutenant) he'd jump into the unit's two-seater T-33, with his golf clubs in the place of a second pilot, and head to Colorado.

He'd exasperate the base operations folks because he'd never file a flight plan. Few like him were left in the Air Force. SG-1's cocky and independent-minded leader, Col. Jack O'Neill, would have made Leon smile.

Setting up community relations orientations to Colorado Springs was one of my responsibilities. We invited influential Arizona area business and community leaders and flew them to see how our Air Defense and North American Air Defense systems (with the Canadians) were working. This meant the ever-intriguing trip into Cheyenne Mountain.

Cheyenne Mountain represented the big picture. Take all the radar sites throughout the continental U.S. and Canada, and then add in BMEWS (Ballistic Missile Early Warning System) and we had the current state of our readiness if attacked by bomber or missile. BMEWS was our eyes over the north, which gave us early warning of a Soviet nuclear missile attack. The system was made up of three huge radar stations stretching from Clear, Alaska, through Thule, Greenland, and ending at Fylingdales Moor in Yorkshire, England. In the mountain our civilian guests were always impressed by all the dais, the radar scopes, the gigantic global status board and the generals and colonels running the show and the infrastructure, but most of all, they were thrilled at having access to such a unique and secret facility as Cheyenne Mountain. Today the chiseled opening to the hollowed out underground city still looks much the same as it did in the 1960s.

Stargate's headquarters location meshes well with the mission of today's three commands that occupy the innards of the mountain.

The North American Aerospace Defense Command, the U.S. Space Command and the Air Force Space Command—all contained within Cheyenne Mountain—monitor foreign aircraft, missiles and space systems that could threaten North America. Specifically, the Air Force Space Command has four primary missions: space force enhancement, space application, space support and space control.

Within the complex there are six centers (seven counting the SGC) that operate twenty-four hours a day, 365 days a year. The Command Center is the heart of operations in Cheyenne Mountain. The director and crew serve as the NORAD and US Space Command's Commanders-in-Chief direct representative for monitoring, processing and interpreting missile, space or air events which could have operational impacts on our forces or capabilities, home or abroad. The Space Control Center performs the surveillance mission to detect, track, identify and catalog all man-made objects in space. As such, they would have been the first to track the Goa'uld warships heading toward earth ("The Serpent's Lair").

From the old Air Defense Command's vacuum tube-run computers forty years ago, the Air Force has fine-tuned the defense mission into the Air Force Space Command with goals enunciated more than two decades ago. In a January 2004 article in *Aerospace America*, a publication of the American Institute of Aeronautics and Astronautics, author James W. Canan states that the Air Force first identified space control, or space superiority, as one of its prime missions and requirements at least twenty years ago. Air Force space officials, he writes, know that the nation has come to count on air superiority in war, and now must be able to count on space superiority as well. Canan's article quotes Robert Dickman, Air Force deputy undersecretary for military space, declaring "if we're attacked in space, and it turns out that we don't have space superiority, the American public is going to have every right to be very upset." There is no mention of Stargate . . . which, we assume, is still top secret.

In 1999 Congress called for the establishment of a U.S. space control program, and two years later the U.S. Space Commission emphasized the need for space superiority, which became the basis of the Air Force Space Command's numerous space control programs.

To identify systems that will give us space superiority, who better to hire than men and women who are intimately familiar with and expert in the environment of space?

Air Force Col. Susan Helms is one of those experts who now work in and around Cheyenne Mountain and the Colorado Springs area. She is one of more than 19,000 active duty officer and enlisted personnel worldwide who control and exploit the high ground of space. Colonel Helms is the Division Chief for Space Control Requirements for the Air Force Space Command. Her qualifications to direct such a program are unparalleled. She has already logged thousands of hours in space. As the Air Force's first woman astronaut, Colonel Helms flew on five Space Shuttle flights and served aboard the International Space Station as a member of Expedition-2. Specifically, she logged 5,064 hours in space and holds the world record of eight hours fifty-six minutes for a space walk, as she performed the installation of hardware to the external body of the Space Station laboratory module.

In *Stargate* we learned that Maj. Samantha Carter spent two years in the Pentagon trying to make the Stargate program a reality ("Secrets"). Although she could not share her real work at the SGC with her father, Major Carter admits that she always had a lifetime dream of going into space. Not knowing she was already a seasoned space traveler, her father was pulling the strings necessary to have her accepted into NASA.

The Air Force's Col. Susan Helms and *Stargate*'s Maj. Samantha Carter embody highly successful careers and the fulfillment of goals as a result of opportunities available to Air Force women. Their stories are very similar. Both are space explorers and pioneers. Both have been or are equal and contributing members of a team. But their similarities don't end there.

As we know from following seven years of the *Stargate* saga, Samantha Carter is the daughter of an Air Force general, a graduate of the Air Force Academy and has her doctorate in astrophysics. She brings to her assignment both an extensive scientific background and military training.

Colonel Helms is also the daughter of an Air Force officer and a graduate of the Air Force Academy, where she received a bachelor of science degree in aeronautical engineering and later a master of science degree in aeronautics/astronautics from Stanford University. She first served in the Air Force as a weapons separation engineer before attending Air Force Test Pilot School, graduating as a flight test engineer. While a flight test engineer, she flew in thirty different U.S. and Canadian military aircraft.

In January 1990, Colonel Helms joined NASA, and earned her astronaut designation eighteen months later. She became a member of an elite group of women including Dr. Sally Ride, a civilian physicist, who entered the astronaut program in 1978 and was the first American woman in space in 1983. To date there have been five Air Force women astronauts. All but one has traveled to space at least twice.

Col. Eileen Collins, still an active astronaut, joined NASA and became an astronaut in the same class as Colonel Helms, but did not make it into space until 1995. With three flights behind her, she has built a distinguished NASA career as the first woman to pilot and then command a space shuttle, logging over 537 hours.

When comparing Colonel Helms' distinguished NASA service to Major Carter's *Stargate* tour of duty, it is hard to say who can claim to have occupied space longer or be considered more heroic. After all, a Stargate traveler gets from planet to planet in a matter of seconds and only stays for short periods.

On the other hand, Colonel Helms, for all of her brave deeds in space, has never been captured by aliens, nor has had her body invaded by Goa'uld.

Both no doubt are role models for the next generation of women who aim higher. Prior to entering test pilot school, Colonel Helms spent two years at her alma mater, the Air Force Academy, as an assistant professor of aeronautics. Major Carter also returned to her roots at the Academy to lecture, where she befriended a rebellious female cadet and attempted to influence her career path ("Prodigy").

To impress the brilliant cadet she even took her through the Stargate portal. (No proper top security clearance ever stops our SG-1 team.)

Whether it be on a shuttle or space station crew or entering the Stargate portal, teamwork has been an important element of success for our two military protagonists.

Colonel Helms lived and worked onboard the International Space Station as a member of the second crew to inhabit the station. She served for 163 days in tight quarters with one other American and a Russian cosmonaut, all the while performing internal and external maintenance and conducting medical and science experiments.

Each time SG-1 passes through the Stargate we see the four team members working together as equals, respecting each other's unique role and contributions to the mission. Major Carter is the quintessential problem-solver whether it be in the arena of microbiology, astrophysics, medicine or tinkering with a time dilator. She is a combat warrior, a quick thinker, a doer, a person who can analyze deep space radar telemetry ("Secrets") or provide motherly comfort and save a child ("Singularity").

Colonel O'Neill calls her the technological brain. She says, "I've been thinking." He says, "I'd be shocked if you ever stopped," and then mumbles to someone else, "I only understand about one percent of what she says" ("Red Sky").

Will she ever quit? Maybe, eventually. But the real question is, will she ever command? Major Carter is certainly savvy and smart enough to lead SG-1. We'll have to wait and see.

As for Colonel Helms, she hung up her space suit after a twelve-year career at NASA that included 211 days in space. What she didn't do was pack away her Air Force blues. After twenty-two years in the Air Force, she could have retired after her NASA career as most military astronauts do. For her, however, it was payback time. As she told Stacey Knott, a Space Command reporter, "The Air Force has always been so supportive of the things I wanted to do, and I guess I felt that the time had come to help with the military space program in other ways," she said.

I still watch Major Carter on *Stargate* and even though I've never met Colonel Helms I feel a sense of pride in having shared the same uniform with both of these extraordinary women. As a young lieutenant in the Air Defense Command during the days of the Cold War, with vacuum tube computers and green radar scopes, I can relate to the sense of purpose and commitment that these real and fictional heroines exude.

What might have been in the Air Force cards for the fifteen women of Officer Training Class 65-D had broader career opportunities been available?

In retrospect, I believe that we did okay. Five of us, all that I know of, finished long, proud Air Force careers. Our class final statistics include one brigadier general, two colonels and two majors, with two of us having served in Vietnam.

The bottom line: thirty-three percent of us made it to the finish line.

I believe Major Carter would be proud to be part of that heritage.

Gina McGuiness spent more than thirty-five years in the public affairs arena, handling highly sensitive and controversial subjects of international, national and California interest, community relations and public information management with the U.S. State and Defense Departments, numerous California government agencies and non-profit, healthcare and educational organizations. She is an award-winning military journalist and a Vietnam veteran. She holds a pilot's license, but hasn't flown in many years. She retired from the United States Air Force with the rank of Colonel. She serves as a member of the Board of Directors of Air Force Women Officers-Associated (AFWOA), an organization dedicated to maintaining ties between active and retired women officers and preserving the history and promoting recognition of the role of military women. The organization also lends support to women engaged in education and training programs and sponsors a permanent award at the Air Force Academy.

Tom McBeath

RUMINATIONS FROM A RAT BASTARD

Tom McBeath plays a true fan-favorite on Stargate SG-1, Col. *Harry Maybourne, a rascally fellow with a flexible morality who knows just exactly how to press Jack O'Neill's buttons. You gotta love a guy with that kind of talent!*

O'NEILL: You rat-bastard!
MAYBOURNE: Hey, hey, hey, hey! Take it easy!
O'NEILL: I am SO gonna kick your ass!
MAYBOURNE: There's people watching!
—"Forty-Eight Hours"

COLONEL MAYBOURNE ON *STARGATE SG-1* is my first and only continuing role in a series, though I've been an actor for over thirty years.

I've played small parts in big films and big parts in small films. I've guest-starred on most series shot here in Vancouver, and I've starred in many stage productions across Canada. I spend about half my time each year in the theatre and the other half waiting to get work in film and TV.

It's actually a dream of an actor's life.

> O'NEILL: Nervous?
> MAYBOURNE: Me? Nah. I'm just taking a moment.
> O'NEILL: Done?
> MAYBOURNE: Yeah.
>
> —"Paradise Lost"

I'm what you call a character actor, which I've come to understand is an actor who'll probably never be a star. The best advice I ever got was in theatre school from a design teacher who is still a friend and mentor. She said, "You've a small talent, Tom—look after it."

I consider myself one of the legions of actors out there who love what they do and do what they love with commitment, hard work and passion.

Stargate has been good to me. Over the past five or six years it's the one job I don't have to audition for—except for the first for Maybourne, of course. I could get into the whole science of auditioning, but it might sound like sour grapes. What matters is I landed *this* one, a hard-assed colonel with a hate on for the SGC. It was possibly going to be recurring, and for once that worked out.

> MAYBOURNE: Things happen in high places, Jack. People get reassigned, so does property. Artifacts get misplaced, orders change. Every day's a new day.
>
> —"Forty-Eight Hours"

Sometime in the summer of 2000, the third or fourth season, I got a request for an interview from Jaclyn.

She prefers Jac.

Until Jac and Rachael (they come together) I'd never thought of *Stargate* or any of my work in terms of fans, and if I had an opinion of the phenomenon it fell into the "weirdo—get a life" category.

> O'NEILL: General Hammond, request permission to beat the crap out of this man.
>
> —"Paradise Lost"

That's especially true in terms of Maybourne. Of the approximately 700 days of shooting the series over six seasons I've worked all of twenty-one of those days—a minor contribution at best.

O'NEILL: Yes, Harry, you've been a very bad boy.
—"Touchstone"

Jac and Rachael and I have met three times in the last three years and, excepting the interview, all were purely social. These gatherings have taken place on the occasion of the yearly *Stargate* convention in Vancouver. The Vancouver con is a must for all the fans, as *Stargate SG-1* is filmed here, giving it an advantage over any other gatherings held around the world: the possibility of a tour of the *Stargate* studios.

It also gives Jac the opportunity to interview many of the Vancouver-based actors and production personnel, writers, directors, designers, etc., involved in the series. And so "Colonel Maybourne" meets the fans, Jac and Rachael.

MAYBOURNE: You're out of your league here, gentlemen. You're
playing in my ballpark now.
—"Bane"

Jac appears to be the driving force of the team. First impressions are memorable and the one Jac gives is more than most.

She's tattooed. Not the polite little things on the back of the shoulder or calf. Not the Celtic rope around an arm or ankle or the satanic teaser below the navel or on the small of the back, just above the crack.

These are British soccer players, headshots bleeding down from her shoulders to her arms, overlapping, monochrome, almost photographic—six or eight to the arm. They include Beckham before we knew who he was in North America. She's at one and the same time proud and dismissive of them as necessary and natural. Her unkempt light brown hair tops a half-back's body, and she dresses with no concern for fashion except for the tough streets of London: cargo fatigues with a sleeveless T and a half-open shirt on top, boot-shoes and numerous clumsy rings on square, strong hands.

Jac shares a home with her friend Rachael outside Bath, a house that gives them a lot of space compared to their London flat a few years ago—space for their cats and electronics.

MAYBOURNE: We have to connect someone with significant influence to the online websites. The only way to do that is straight through one of the high profile associates.
—"Paradise Lost"

Rachael's nothing like Jac, short dark hair, a simple ring or two, "sensible clothes," her fashion sense leaning toward anonymity. You wouldn't pick her out of a crowd unless you caught a glimpse of her dark impish eyes. Both women are sharp, though Rachael has the better sense of humor. Exactly who is "host" in this symbiotic relationship is open to discussion, but there's no doubt they're a team in living, working and their love for anything *Stargate*.

O'NEILL: I never thought I'd agree with you about anything, Maybourne.
—"Enigma"

Jac does the Internet and *Stargate* is her show. She has a website of pages or whatever those things are, and she spends her waking hours at home on the machine. She's a *Stargate* encyclopedia—every episode, every actor and writer, director, date of production, editor, etc. She does interviews, writes articles, analysis and also episodes (fanfic she admits) of her own invention, maintaining the integrity of characters as rigorously as the *Stargate* pros themselves.

MAYBOURNE: Looks like a party.
—"Chain Reaction"

My interview with them took place in their hotel room at the convention site. Meeting in the lobby, we negotiated the trip to their room without being mobbed by a single fan—much to their relief, but hardly a surprise to me.

Once there we covered my background and *Stargate SG-1* stuff: my relationship with Richard Dean Anderson, my favorite episodes and scenes, who Maybourne really was, etc. The five or six episodes I'd done to that date were as fresh in their minds as if they'd been shot yesterday. It was quite to the contrary for me. I could (and still can) recall scenes, but not necessarily in the correct order, nor the episode they may have occurred in. For that matter, if my life depended on listing the names of the episodes I've appeared in, in any order, I'd be a dead man.

CARTER: Maybourne, you are an idiot every day of the week. Couldn't you have just taken a day off?
—"Shades of Gray"

In the hard copy of the interview Jac sent me, none of my seeming ambivalence to their expert coaching shows. Bless them.

This interview set the major theme for the lunch that followed and our subsequent meetings, and that is the difference *Stargate SG-1* plays in our respective universes. To their amazement it is not the center of mine. By now I shouldn't have to remind you it is close to the center of theirs.

MAYBOURNE: It's good to see you, Teal'c.
TEAL'C: In my culture I would be well within my rights to dismember you.
MAYBOURNE: Well, that's interesting.
—"Chain Reaction"

That difference has provided for lots of laughter and outrageousness over libations, but we've each made inroads into the other's universe. They have an understanding that Maybourne is a very small part of my life as an actor and for me what I'd considered a somewhat foolish and insignificant passion on their part is no more foolish or insignificant than another's passion for golf or antiques or collecting fine art.

I like them simply for having a passion and following it.

MAYBOURNE: You know the real reason I wanna do this? I've never actually been through this thing before.
—"Foothold"

Jac and Rachael have been the vanguards in my education regarding fans. That interview was the foundation for what followed. Lots of fan mail, several more interviews and an invitation to a London *Stargate* convention that had over 1,500 fans appreciating and indulging "The *Stargate* Experience."

MAYBOURNE: A long time ago, some people from an advanced alien society—well—they chucked it all and formed this small, isolated community. They sent out representatives to meet and evaluate people from all over the galaxy and offer them a chance to join them.
—"Paradise Lost"

Whatever originally attracted those folks to embrace the show, it is people like Jac and Rachael who keep the pot boiling, if not always stirring it up. *Stargate SG-1* is successful because it has such an audience, part of whom are there because of what the über-fans provide. The websites and conventions generate a force outside of the producers' control: a forum to participate in *Stargate* beyond simply viewing it.

I'm looking forward to their next visit; and next time I get to England they'll have houseguests.

> O'NEILL: What are you going to do now?
> MAYBOURNE: Well, short term, I think I'll have a few margaritas—after that, who knows?
> —"Chain Reaction"

Tom McBeath lives in Vancouver, Canada, with Karin Konoval. He's worked on stages across Canada, most recently as "The Caretaker" (Davies) and "Othello" (Iago). His television work includes the movies Off-Season, Prince of Mirrors, Nick Fury *and* In Cold Blood. *In addition to his long-running role as "Harry Maybourne" on* Stargate SG-1, *he has appeared in over twenty different series, including* The X-Files, Millenium, Outer Limits, The Sentinel, Dead Man's Gun, Highlander *and* The Chris Isaak Show. *Blink and you'll miss him in feature films such as* Along Came a Spider, Double Jeopardy, Firestorm, Cousins *and* The Accused.